MW01596856

CAUGHT BETWEEN AN OOPS AND A HARD BODY

SHEILA SEABROOK

BY THE BOOK SHOP

Caught Between an Oops and a Hard Body

Copyright © 2015 by Sheila Seabrook
ISBN #978-1-7750680-6-8
ISBN 978-0-9877069-7-3 (ebook)

By The Book Shop

Cover design by SMScreates

Made in the USA
Middletown, DE
16 April 2019

4264291 3R00051

STORY SNYOPSIS

Stephanie Goodwin has never met a prince who didn't turn out to be a frog, but she's never allowed her personal feelings about men and relationships to interfere with her job as a wedding planner. Instead, she focuses on giving her clients their dream wedding, a magical day to get them through the trials and tribulations of the years ahead—before everything turns to dust.

Hotshot divorce lawyer, Stone Kincaid, has an aversion to marriage. His experience has taught him that wedding vows only lead to a broken heart that never really heals and an empty bank account. But when he returns to his family's Serendipity Island estate to stop his irresponsible sister's wedding, he encounters the wedding planner straight out of his nightmares—the gorgeous, sexy woman he met and bedded a month ago.

Can a woman with a history of picking the wrong kind of guy find a forever kind of love with a man who fears commitment almost as much as she does?

This story includes a marriage-phobic wedding planner, a hunky divorce lawyer whose attitude toward wedded bliss—and family—is about to change, one really big OOPS, afternoon naughtiness, peanut butter cookies, messy family relationships, and a battle-of-the-sexes secondary romance.

This book is dedicated to all of you soon-to-be moms out there.

It's exciting and nerve-racking and all kinds of scary, and the journey from here on out is totally amazing.

DEAR READER

Welcome to the Caught Between series!

When I wrote The Valentine Grinch, I had no idea that Mandy Goodwin's sister would get her own book. And yet, Stephanie Goodwin walked into my life, demanded I tell her story, and Caught Between an Oops and a Hard Body was born.

At the time, I had absolutely no idea that "conception" was going to play such a big part in the hero and heroine's growing relationship. I thought the book was going to be all about weddings and brides and all things nuptial related.

But the characters are always in charge. I simply take dictation and therefore have no control over their story. I mean, what would be the fun in that? It's not like I aspire to appear sane or anything...

Neither Stephanie nor her hero, Stone Kincaid, are looking for love. I guess that means I've ended up with two OOPS in this book.

Now turn the page and start reading already!

CAUGHT BETWEEN AN OOPS AND A HARD BODY

Caught Between Contemporary Romance Series

1

On an early spring morning in Seattle, a month after his great-uncle's wedding, Stone Kincaid's inner office intercom buzzed, and the disembodied voice of his legal assistant, Wanda, came through the device.

"Your mother called. She said your dad is at it again. I suggested he might be bored, but Grace reminded me that golf season on Serendipity Island runs year round. What more could the man possibly want?"

"Peace and quiet?" Stone scrawled his name on the document in front of him, then leaned back on his chair as his assistant walked into his office. "How much trouble can he get into down there?"

"I asked her that precise question."

When she didn't continue, he raised one eyebrow and finally prompted, "And?"

"She said keeping your father in line is your job."

"Yeah, right. Nobody keeps my father in line," he snorted and returned his attention to the file in front of him, pretty certain that being a divorce lawyer—not a babysitter—was his primary occupation. Although occasionally, he conceded, the two were eerily similar. "What about Mariam or Liz?"

"Exactly my question. She said your baby sister is far too sensitive to shoulder that kind of responsibility. And Mariam? Well, Mariam has her own problems right now." Wanda laid a single sheet of paper down in front of him and indicated the line at the bottom of the page. With a brief look to confirm the contents of the letter, he scrawled his name across the bottom. "By the way, Bill Tremaine called. He wishes to retain your services. It seems he's met someone."

"Again?" he muttered with disgust. Despite Stone's aversion for the institution of marriage, even he knew where to draw the line. "How many is this?"

"Wife number five."

"Bill's an idiot."

"Mmmmmm," she hummed. "Would you like me to pass on your sentiments?"

"Just book him in for an appointment as soon as you can. Let's see if I can talk some sense into him this time. He's not getting any younger, you know."

"But his wives sure are. And with every new wife, his bank account diminishes, just like his hairline." Wanda scooped the documents off his desk, stuffed them into the file folder in the crook of her arm, and jotted a note on her steno pad. "Did you watch your mother's show today?"

He glanced up at the dark screen that sat in the corner of his office. "You're kidding, right?"

"I never kid about marriage." She gave him one of her steely-eyed looks. "The *Eternally Yours* show is an institution. If you watched it, you might actually learn something about what makes the female species tick."

"Maybe I don't want to know what makes them tick," he said as he slouched back in his chair.

She shook her head, a disgusted expression creasing lines on her forehead and at the sides of her mouth. "You're as bad as Bill. The only difference between the two of you is that at least you have the common sense to refrain from giving wedding rings to every woman you want to get into the sack."

Sarcasm. Coming from the queen of sarcasm. He ignored it and with a resigned sigh, prodded her. "Was there something else or are you hanging around to make my life miserable?"

Lifting her chin and thrusting her nose into the air, Wanda headed toward the door. "Reminding you about your family is one of the few joys in my life."

"And forgetting I have a family is one of the few joys in my life." Stone watched as Wanda clicked the device at her hip to answer the main phone line.

"It's your baby sister." She switched the call over to his phone, then returned to his desk and riffled through the stacks of paper in his inbox.

Stone snatched up the receiver. "Hey Liz, what's—"

"It's Mother," his twenty-three-year-old sister wailed into the phone. "I need you at home today or I swear, Stone, I'll kill her and bury her on the ninth green of Dad's golf course."

Home. Stone's grip on the receiver tightened. His parents were no doubt at it again. Although what his sister was doing home in the middle of the week was a puzzle. "Liz, settle down. Take a deep breath and tell me what's wrong."

"She wants me to cancel my wedding. *My wedding.* How can she even suggest this? Less than a week before the wedding, and she wants me to call the caterers and flower shops and cancel everything."

Lucky you, he thought, and then her words sunk in. He frowned up at his assistant. "What wedding?"

A breath of total frustration whooshed through the phone. "I'm getting married on Friday. Didn't you get my email?"

3

"What email?" He watched Wanda pull out a single piece of paper from his inbox and set it on the desk in front of him. A big red sticky note was attached to the page with the word URGENT scrawled in his assistant's handwriting.

You are cordially invited...

He tried to get his mind around the fact that it still wasn't too late for his sister to escape a destiny worse than death. "Maybe this is fate's way of saving you from a bad mistake."

Stone heard Liz's feral hiss through the phone line. "Screw fate. Fate was when Roger blew into my life."

"No," Stone said in what he hoped was a reasonable tone. "Fate was when your ninth grade english teacher told you to become a journalist. Fate was when you landed the news job at CNN." He shook his head. "Who's Roger?"

"Roger is my fiancee, the man I'm going to marry on Friday." Liz blew an angry breath through the phone. "Roger and I planned to elope to Vegas. No fuss. No hassle. No family. Just the camera crew."

"Camera crew?"

"Roger wants to put the wedding up on You Tube for publicity."

"Publicity?" Okay, now he was starting to sound like a parrot. "What does this guy do?"

"He's a musician. If you got your head out of that office once in a while, you'd know what was going on in the rest of the world." Another hiss sounded. "This is Mother's way of wielding control. First, she talked me into having the wedding at the estate. I thought, great. Beautiful setting, no fuss, nothing elaborate. I should've known she had a hidden agenda." She sucked in a breath of air and continued. "Now, suddenly she thinks it's wrong that we get married at all?"

Empathy kicked in and he frowned. "She's just thinking of what's best for you."

"Yeah, right. You don't believe that any more than I do. All mother cares about is herself and her stupid show and her stupid viewers. Roger embarrasses her, that's the bottom line." Lizzie let loose with a growl, then lowered her voice and continued. "What am I supposed to tell him? He's arriving tomorrow, expecting to get married at the end of the week. He'll be so upset to find out that everything he's done this past month has been for nothing."

Stone covered the mouthpiece with one hand and glared up at his assistant. "Why is this the first time I'm hearing about this?"

Wanda smirked back at him. "Because you ignore your family."

Liz's wail carried through the ear piece, making Stone hold the receiver away from his ear.

"Stone, please. I need you at my side to support me. Now that she's got this crazy idea in her head, you know she won't let go of it. I need a buffer between us or she'll win. By the end of the week, Roger and I will be going our separate ways."

Silence filtered through the line and Stone had the irresistible urge to tell his baby sister to run like the wind. Because wedding vows only lead to a broken heart that never healed and an empty bank account. His sister, whether or not she'd agree, would be far better off with his mother's new plan.

Her voice came through the phone again, soft and pleading. "Don't you want me to be happy?"

"Of course I do." He motioned for Wanda's attention. "Just for the record, I don't give family discounts."

"What?" Pause. "Oh, never mind. Forget I called you. I'll just tell Roger that my favorite brother has tossed us to the big bad wolf."

"I'm your only brother." He rubbed the back of his neck. Frustration leaked into his voice. "Okay, forget about how I feel about marriage. You know Mom makes me crazy, Liz."

"Stone, she makes everyone crazy." A sob sounded over the telephone line. "Please. I can't deal with her myself."

"Darn it, Liz, don't you cry."

5

"I'm not." She sniffled, blew her nose. "I just want to marry Roger and spend the rest of my life making him happy."

He heard a click, blinked at his assistant, then realized that Wanda was eavesdropping on their conversation. More fodder for the gossip mill. Who cared? It wasn't his life, just another major moment in the lives of his crazy family. He covered the mouth-piece. "Find out everything you can about some musician named Roger."

The screen in the corner of his office clicked on and his assistant connected to the internet.

On the other end of the phone, Liz was still talking. "Do you know what Mother told me? She said, screw Roger. Literally. Forget about marriage and babies. Have sex with him, then move on to the next man."

An image popped onto the screen and Stone sat forward to get a better look. Standing beside his sister was a familiar busty blond. "She has a point, Liz. No commitment. No headaches. Just fun for both sides."

Fun, like he'd had a month ago with an unforgettable sex goddess who right this very moment was staring back at him from the screen. What was she doing with his sister?

Liz hissed into the phone. "I should've known that the king of divorce would be on her side."

Stone stared at the image of the woman he'd met at his great uncle's wedding and recalled the way she'd looked naked on the hotel room bed, hair splayed on the pillow, reaching for him.

Stephanie.

All they'd exchanged were first names...and one night of great sex and companionship.

And when he woke the next morning, she was gone.

A part of him had been relieved there would be no awkward goodbyes.

Another part of him—the one that occasionally wondered if

there might be one special woman somewhere out in the mass of people he passed on his way into the office everyday—had stared at the indentation left on her pillow and wondered, what if she was the one?

He squashed the wave of desire that hit him square in the gut. Now wasn't the time to recall how she'd come apart in his arms or to remember her tight warmth as she took all of him inside of her. The woman might have been great in the sack, but she was looking for a ring around her finger and a permanent man in her life, just like every other woman he knew.

He dragged his gaze from the gorgeous blond on the screen and, as Wanda began to cycle through screen shots and images of his sister goofing off, being silly and irresponsible and young as she dated and discarded men like they were a commodity that grew on trees, he turned his back on the TV. "Liz, you're only twenty-three. What's the rush? If this Roger fellow loves you, he'll wait."

"I've seen the way women look at him. I want to be married, Stone. I want a baby. I want to make a life with Roger and have a real family. Don't you ever think about that?" Liz sighed into the phone. "Never mind, I know how you feel. But despite that, can I count on you to help me out?"

He raked a hand through his hair and knew what he had to do even before he made the conscious decision to return home and somehow make his sister see reason. "Yes, I'll be there. You know I'd never abandon you."

The shrillness and panic in her voice softened to gratitude. "Thank you. You are *the* best brother ever."

She thought that now, but as they said their goodbyes and Stone set the receiver back in its cradle, he knew he had only one avenue of action. Return to Serendipity Island and stop the wedding, even if Liz chose not to talk to him for the rest of his life.

He swiveled back to the TV and watched the images of his

7

baby sister. With an eleven year difference between them, and parents who chased their careers instead of chasing their toddler, he'd spent most of his teen years playing the father figure. And now when she needed him the most, he couldn't let her down.

An image popped up on the screen.

"Stop right there." Stone pushed to his feet and wandered closer, ignoring the gorgeous blonde beside his sister. The man in the photo wore a red tuxedo, a pink shirt, and a purple bow tie. His long black hair curled to his waist and he wore more makeup than Stone had ever seen on anyone. "Please don't tell me that's the groom."

"Roger Gordon, aka Jingles, lead singer of the rock band Crazy Heart." Wanda checked her notes. "It appears your sister met him at a charity auction last month and they were engaged a week later."

He frowned. "Is she knocked up?"

"Haven't a clue. Always a possibility, I suppose." Wanda checked her notes again, then turned her head so she could look up at him. "The other woman. If you have a type, she's it, but I'm warning you to stay away from her."

Stone attention returned to the blonde. "Dating advice? When was the last time you went on a date?"

"My personal life is my business."

"While mine is a wide open book?"

"Works for me." She clicked through to another photo of his sister and Stephanie. "Stephanie Goodwin. Wedding planner extraordinaire. Liz loves her, maybe even more than she loves Roger. So whatever you do, be nice to the wedding planner and when this is all over, your sister may still be talking to you."

Everything in Stone screeched to a halt.

The woman he hadn't been able to forget was gorgeous and sexy and a freaking wedding planner, a lethal combination that he instantly recognized as deadly to his bachelor status.

Gut instinct warned him it was time to disappear, maybe do

8

something safe like climb Mount Everest. Stephanie Goodwin was the woman who for an entire night had kept him a willing prisoner in his hotel room and entertained him with her body, her wit, and her zest for life.

Stone dragged his attention back to his assistant. "Order the helicopter."

"Already done, sir." She handed him airline tickets that would take him from Seattle to Florida to St. Croix where he could either take the ferry to the small Caribbean island where he'd grown up, or book a helicopter for the short flight to the island. "Five minutes ago, you sent an e-mail to your mother confirming your arrival at their island estate tomorrow afternoon."

He returned to his desk, grabbed his briefcase, and started chucking items into it, trying to be cool and nonchalant while he struggled against the image he'd attempted to block from his memory. Stephanie Goodwin, naked and flat on her back beneath him.

Could they continue their sexual relationship without any complications like love and marriage?

He huffed out a sigh. Wedding planner? No way.

And yet, as the memory of making love to Stephanie flooded his body, he thought, if the sex could be that hot every single night of his life, it might make up for a miserable marriage—

No, what was he thinking? Marriage was for fools.

"My luggage?"

"It'll be on board the helicopter when you leave."

He finally stopped and looked at her. This woman who ran his professional life without so much as a blip in her expression. She was a mystery to him while his life was an open book. "Pack your bags, Wanda. I need you to come with me."

She backed up a step and crossed her fingers in front of her chest. "Deal with your family yourself."

With a sour look in his direction, she pulled open the door, exited the room, and left Stone alone to contemplate his family. At this moment, he was sure of only three things.

That he'd rather book a trip anywhere but home.

That marriage was for never.

And that when he encountered the wedding planner, he was going to avoid her like the plague.

If he didn't screw up and kiss her first.

2

Stephanie Goodwin had never met a prince who didn't turn out to be a frog, but she never let her personal feelings about men and relationships interfere with her job as a wedding planner.

Instead, she focused on giving her clients their dream wedding and never looked back to see how many of those marriages turned to ruins. It wasn't her job to get personal and give advice. No, it was her job to create a fairytale day the bride could remember forever, a magical moment to get her through the trials and tribulations of the years ahead.

A priceless memory before everything turned to dust.

Which was why, on this sunny Tuesday morning as she drove the rental car along Tranquility Drive, the coastal highway that circled Serendipity Island, she felt more like a fairy godmother than a wedding planner.

Until she'd had to pull over to the side of the road to throw up.

Afterwards, she drove back onto the highway, one hand on the wheel, the other on her churning stomach, determined that the flu wouldn't stop her from fulfilling her sacred fairy godmother duty. She had three days to tie up the loose ends of Liz Kincaid's upcoming wedding...a wedding that would no doubt end in divorce like so many other marriages.

Maybe it wasn't her fault that all those marriages ended in a nasty court case, but it made her feel like a marriage jinx anyway.

Which was why she was never taking the marriage plunge herself.

With her sister's map beside her on the seat, she made her way to Mandy's newly purchased beach house where she climbed out of the car, and headed toward the front door.

From the outside, the beach house was gorgeous. With a six foot tall stone fence separating the property from the street, it was like a tiny piece of heaven on earth.

She knocked on the door, the oversize sweater she'd pulled on that morning heavy and sweltering. It wasn't her usual attire, but had seemed perfect because she was feeling frumpy and bloated and totally un-Stephanie-like.

Through the clear pane of glass, she saw her mom, Dora Goodwin, emerge and bustle toward the front door. Confused, Stephanie pulled open the door and stepped inside. "Mom, what are you doing here?"

Dora gave a fake cheerleader jump. "Surprised?"

"Very." Stephanie shut the heat outside and toed off her shoes. As the scent of cinnamon drifted along with her mom, she resisted the urge to gag, and leaned in to give the older woman a hug. "What are you doing here?"

Dora pulled back, her attention fixed on the sweater. "Is that Tom's sweater? I thought I threw that old thing in the trash." Dora grabbed hold of the bottom edge of the sweater. "You must be roasting. Pull off that ugly thing before he sees it and wants it back."

"I'm fine." Stephanie pushed the other woman's hands away. "In fact, I'm a little bit chilly. And yes, it's Dad's sweater."

A frown of concern settled over her mom's features and she

set the back of her hand against Stephanie's forehead. "Are you coming down with something? I hate that you're in the city all alone with no one to care for you."

"You don't need to worry about me, Mom. I'm a big girl."

Dora's blue-on-blue eyes filled with affection. "Mothers are predestined to worry. You'll find that out one day when you have children of your own."

Stephanie decided it was time to change their conversation before her mom zeroed in on her favorite topic. Marriage and babies. Just because she was a wedding planner didn't mean she ever wanted to get married or have a family. Her sister could take care of those duties.

"You didn't answer my question, Mom. Why are you and Dad here? It's not like you're popping across the street for a quick visit." She eyed the guilty flush on her mom's cheeks and leaned forward. "Does Mandy even know you're here?"

"Of course she does." Dora waved one hand in the air, as though the hours of travel had happened in a blink of an eye. "Well, what am I supposed to do? Sit in a rocker on the front porch and wait for you girls to remember I'm alive? You're both so busy with your lives, I told your father it's time we started coming to you instead of always expecting you to come for a visit."

"How long are you staying for?"

Dora tsked, and the frown between her brows deepened. "You look exhausted, honey. What is that woman thinking? How does she expect you pull this wedding together in three days?"

The other woman may have smoothly changed the subject, but Stephanie was on to her. There was something going on. "It won't be the first time." Or no doubt the last.

"Well, I'll help, of course, if you want me there. And I know Mandy wants to talk to you about her wedding. Did she tell you I've already started baking cakes for her to try? And there's my birthday party on Saturday. That's why we're here. With both of you girls on the island at the same time, we decided to celebrate it

13

here." Dora's frown deepened and she brushed a gentle touch over Stephanie's cheek. "Maybe we should have spread things out. A little here. A little there..."

Stephanie was getting exhausted just listening to the non-stop chatter, but she couldn't let on for fear her mother would refuse to let her leave until she'd had a long nap and a belly full of food. "You worry too much. It'll all work out."

"Just don't try to do it all yourself. Call me when you have something for me to do. You know how I love planning." Dora gave another tug on the sweater. "I hope you're not planning to wear this ugly thing to the Kincaid estate."

Stephanie indicated the clothes hanging off her arm and gave another smile. "I came prepared, like you always taught me."

"Well, I wouldn't want the bride's mother to think your mother raised you to be a slob." Dora tugged at the belly of Stephanie's sweater. "Now, before you run off, come say hello to your dad." Her mom raised her voice. "Tom, Stephanie is here, and she's wearing your favorite sweater."

Stephanie let her mom drag her into the kitchen where Tom Goodwin stood at the counter, a bowl tucked under one arm, a whisk in his other hand. He wore an apron covered with tiny wedding gowns and groom's tuxedos and wedding cakes. No doubt Dora had slipped it on him the moment Mandy announced her engagement.

His warm gaze swept over her and settled on the sweater with love in his eyes. "I was wondering where that old thing went. Take it off, kiddo. I want it back."

Dora let out a big sigh. "No means no." She crossed the kitchen, and took the bowl and spoon out of his hands. "Go greet your oldest daughter."

Tom willingly gave up his possessions and crossed the room, arms outstretched, and pulled Stephanie into his arms. "Hello, stranger. We were beginning to wonder if we'd ever see you again."

She hugged him back and, inhaling the familiar scent of his Old Spice cologne, relished the warmth of his hug. As much as she enjoyed her independence in the city, there were times like these when she realized how much she missed family. "Sorry, Dad. I've been really busy at work."

He pulled away and frowned down at her stomach, and Stephanie followed his gaze. "Have you finally put on some weight? Is that why you're wearing my sweater?"

"Only a little." Before she could change the topic, Dora moved in for the kill—ah, the inspection—and the scent of whatever was in the bowl caused Stephanie's stomach to churn.

"Oh, honey, let's see how much. You know you have to fit into Mandy's bridesmaid dress. If you gain or lose weight before the wedding, the gown won't fit." Dora grabbed the bottom edge of the sweater. "And we have absolutely no idea how good the local seamstress is. I'd do the job myself, but I'm up to my elbows in baking."

With a smile and a laugh, Stephanie caught Dora's wrist, successfully preventing the other woman from lifting the sweater to see what was underneath. She eased back a step. "Don't worry, Mom. The dress will fit fine and in six months, I promise it'll fit even better. Does this mean Mandy decided on her colors?"

The front door banged open and footsteps raced toward the kitchen, giving her the opportunity to shift away from the inspection and the bowl that threatened the contents of her stomach.

Her sister popped through the door opening, spied Stephanie, and threw her arms around her. "You're here, finally. And just in time, because I'm one parent away from crazy mode."

Tom ruffled his youngest daughter's hair. "Welcome to my world, squirt." Then he headed back to the kitchen sink, ready to take his next order.

While her sister squeezed tight, Stephanie gave her a hug back and met Dora's gaze. "You need to remember that this is

Mandy's wedding, Mom. No forcing her to have your dream wedding."

Dora's back bristled and she handed the bowl back to her husband. "You're overreacting. I'm busy preparing for my birthday party right now. I don't have time to think about her wedding."

"She lies," Mandy whispered in her ear before she stepped back and faced her parents. "So tell Steph how many people you invited to your birthday party."

Beneath his breath, Tom grumbled, "The entire island."

Then to take the sting from his complaint, he gave his wife an affectionate pat on the butt.

Stephanie raised her eyebrows. "How can that be? Mandy and Dane just moved here? Isn't this your first time on the island?"

Dora blushed. "I can't help it if people adore me."

Mandy nudged her in the arm. "And if they don't, Mom harasses them till they cry uncle."

Dora fixed a determined gaze on Stephanie, and Stephanie thought, *Uh oh, here we go. This must be a record. Barely five minutes after the helloes.*

"I've heard the bride's brother is a hot shot lawyer from Seattle. Just think, honey, a lawyer. What a great catch." With barely a breath, she rattled on. "I wonder what his specialty is? We wouldn't want one of those smarmy lawyers in the family. A nice environmental lawyer would be perfect. He could help clean up the beaches."

"Forget it," she muttered.

The hope-filled look on her mom's face fell. "But honey, you're not getting any younger."

"And I'm not getting married either. One day of joy followed by a lifetime of prison." She repressed a shudder, then smiled at her dad and crossed her fingers behind her back. "If only I could find a guy like you, Dad, I'd be golden."

Dora huffed out a sigh. "You think your father is perfect? He has his frog moments, too, I'll let you know."

Tom raised his eyebrows. "And your mother has her broomstick moments."

And this is where it generally started, with the snide comments cloaked by an affectionate tone. Stephanie had seen it happen enough and it was always one step away from divorce court. How her mom and dad had managed to stay married was mind-boggling.

Before Dora could continue with her favorite subject, Mandy grabbed Stephanie's hand and tugged her toward the living room. "Come on, I want to talk to you about the wedding plans and Mom's birthday present."

Stephanie followed her out. "We'll have to talk while I get changed. I have to be at the Kincaid estate today and I don't want to be late."

As they disappeared around the corner, Dora raised her voice. "Really, you two don't have to get me anything for my birthday."

Tom's grumble followed. "Then why do I?"

"But if you really want to get me a nice gift, I'd love a grand baby. Not till after you're married, of course. A pregnant bride is so unseemly. What would the neighbors think? But just to know you girls are thinking about it would give me hope..."

With a patient sigh, Mandy led the way up the stairs and lowered her voice. "Dane and I want to wait a couple of years before we hear the pitter patter of tiny feet around the house. But once we're married, I'm afraid Mom will up the pressure. I mean, look. We move to the Caribbean to get some freedom from family, and before we even get settled, they're knocking at our door unannounced."

"I'm glad it's you, not me." Stephanie trudged up the stairs after her, tired, nauseous, and wanting nothing more than a bed and a nap. But this might be her only chance to have a private conversation with her sister. She went for the direct approach.

"You and Dane...you're kind of rushing the wedding, aren't you? Why not wait till next year or the year after? Or just live with him until—"

"Until what?"

Until the inevitable split.

Stephanie took one look at her sister's expression and pressed her lips together. "Never mind."

"Okay, I won't." At the end of the hallway, Mandy opened a door and gestured Stephanie inside. "Mom is right. You have a sick view of marriage."

Stephanie sighed and gave a tug on the sweater. "Lately, I've been working with a lot of unhappy couples. Everything seems to start out great. But then the groom sleeps with the bridesmaids—"

Amusement deepened the color of Mandy's eyes. "You're not planning to sleep with my guy, are you, sis?"

"No, of course not." She yanked the sweater up and over her head, and when she could see again, Mandy was staring at her chest with awe.

"Wow, where did those come from?"

Stephanie followed her sister's gaze down, and frowned. "Pre-period bloat."

"Wowzer, I wish I bloated like that."

"No you don't. It's really bad this time."

Mandy glanced down at her own chest, then back at Stephanie's, and with a shake of her head, refocused. "Well this changes things. I told the seamstress we were the same size, so she's basing the alterations of the bridesmaid's gown my bra size."

Stripping off her slacks, she yanked the skirt off the bed and bent to pull it on. "After the wedding, maybe I should stop in and see her before I head back to Seattle."

"Good idea. I'll give her a call and give her a heads up." Mandy watched her struggle with the skirt zipper, then headed around back to help out. "Suck in your stomach so I can do up the button."

With a frown down at her waistline, Stephanie did as instructed. The rasp of the zipper was loud in the silent room.

Mandy patted her waist. "There, you can let your breath out now."

The moment she did so, the waistband cut into her stomach. "Ouch, that's uncomfortable. Undo it, will you?"

"Huh, you really have put on a few pounds." Mandy undid the button, held out the shirt for Stephanie to slip on, then went to rifle through the dresser drawers. Within seconds, she produced a safety pin. But once again, her gaze zeroed in on Stephanie's chest. "I wish I had buttons that nearly popped once a month. It looks...sexy."

"It doesn't feel sexy," Stephanie grumbled. "My breasts are sore and tender, and my bra is too tight."

"Yeah, but Dane might really like the variety."

Stephanie grabbed her by the shoulders and gave her a shake. "See, that's what I'm talking about. You're stuck with him for the rest of your life. He's stuck with you. What happens when the pre-wedding glow wears off—and trust me, it always does—and you have the next sixty years to spend with the same man?"

"Comfort and companionship." Mandy headed around behind Stephanie and lifted the edge of the shirt. "I'm looking forward to settling in with the same guy. So what if the fireworks fade? As long as we love each other, we'll figure out the rest as we go along."

"You're not going to change your mind, are you?"

Mandy shook her head. "Nope."

Stephanie glanced at her watch. "I better get going or I'll be late."

As they came downstairs, Tom stood in the kitchen doorway. "Do you need your car filled up? How about the oil checked?"

"You don't have to worry about me, Dad. I'm not sixteen anymore."

He gave her a sheepish grin and a peck on the cheek. "You and Mandy will always be my little girls."

Dora elbowed him out of the way, her hands dripping soap and water on the floor, obviously on a mission. "A lawyer, honey. Think about it, will you? For me?"

Stephanie saw the earnest expression on her face and felt sorry for Mandy. There was no doubt about it, once Mandy and Dane were married, Dora would be after grandchildren.

"You're getting the floor wet." As she watched Dora dry her hands on her apron, she hooked a thumb toward the front door. "I need to get going or I'll be late."

Dora's frowning gaze swept over her. "I hope you'll tuck in that shirt before you meet your lawyer."

Mandy laughed.

Stephanie rolled her eyes at her sister. "He's not my lawyer."

With a huff, Dora set her hands on her hips. "Don't count him out before you meet him. A *single* lawyer." She threw her hands up in the air. "For goodness sakes, child, you're giving me grey hairs."

"Forget it, Mom."

"But a double wedding—my two girls—"

Tom held up his hands. "Whoa. I'm not made of money."

Dora sent an apologetic glance toward her younger daughter. "Sorry, dear. You know I love Dane like a son but..." She held out her hands in supplication and turned back to Stephanie. "A lawyer, honey, for goodness sake, you'll never do better than that unless you manage to snag a doctor."

Mandy crossed her arms over her chest. "I hope you don't talk like this in front of Dane, Mom."

Stephanie tuned out her family, and with a backward wave, headed out of the beach house.

Behind her, Dora called out, "Do you want me to come help

you with the wedding? I'd love to help. You know I'm a natural event planner."

"No, you have enough to do to get ready for your birthday party."

"You'll tuck in your shirt before you meet your lawyer, won't you, honey?" And her mom always had to get in one last—last-last-last—word. "I never should have let you go with *that woman*. She totally ruined any chance I might have had to get you married."

That woman may have saved her from a lifetime of heartbreak.

Without answering, Stephanie gave a final wave, and as she drove back onto Tranquility Drive, she swallowed back the nausea that seemed determined to make the next three days a challenge.

And it wasn't just the wedding that she was worried about.

Stone Kincaid, the man who starred in her nighttime fantasies.

The biggest mistake of her life.

The biggest frog, too.

She'd met him at her grandma's Valentine Day wedding, all five star fire alarm sexy, and slept with him, then snuck out before he woke. And even though she'd left a fake business card with a fake telephone number, she'd been annoyed because he hadn't internet stalked her and called.

Then unable to shake him from her thoughts, she'd internet stalked him and discovered he was a hotshot lawyer all right, the worst kind of all.

The kind that would send her mom into a bonafide tizzy.

3

Stephanie drove north along Tranquility Drive, taking in the beautiful shoreline and the white sandy beaches, enjoying her last opportunity for some peace and quiet.

Which turned out to be a good thing, because when she arrived at the Kincaid ocean front estate, chaos ruled everywhere. With only three days till the bride walked down the aisle, things were bound to get worse.

Outside, gardeners mowed and pruned and weeded and pinched. Inside, cleaning staff raced around the massive beach house, polishing windows and silverware and everything in-between.

And like frosting on a cake under the heat of the sun, the bride and her mother were in a state of meltdown, snipping and snapping and bickering over every little detail.

The bride, CNN up-and-coming newscaster, Liz Kincaid, was in the process of butting heads with her mother, Grace Kincaid, star of the popular TV talk show *Eternally Yours*. And the two women were arguing about everything.

From the type of cake—white or chocolate—to the color of

the icing—cream with pale rose tints or a kaleidoscope of blue and green and yellow and blood red.

From the location of the nuptials—outdoors on the Serendipity Island estate gorgeous gardens or in the middle of the Vegas strip—to the time of day—mid-afternoon or midnight.

From the style of bridal attire—a princess gown for the bride and a black tuxedo for the groom, or Zombie outfits for them both.

Stephanie kind of thought they were yanking her chain with the last one, but she couldn't quite be certain.

Somehow, someway, she had to pull this wedding together by Friday, all so it would coincide with the groom's schedule.

The bride's fiancee, Roger Gordon of the rock band Crazy Heart, wanted to release the band's fifth album and dedicate it to his bride to officially begin their life together. Sure, it was romantic and cute—and a really great publicity stunt for the band—but it had turned the young bride into a time bomb of nerves who at any given moment might detonate into tears.

Her gaze settled on the bride's sister.

Mariam sat on the corner of the couch, staring at the far wall, wearing the saddest expression Stephanie had ever seen on anybody. She appeared lost and lonely, which could only mean one thing...some schmuck had broken her heart.

Stephanie peered down at the little tyke hanging onto his mother's knee.

The kid was adorable, like most kids that age, but Stephanie didn't like children of any age anymore than they liked her.

He gurgled and blew spit bubbles, and entertained himself by pulling himself up to his feet, then plopping back down on the ground and landing softly on the padded diaper covering his tiny tush.

She didn't normally pay attention to the little ones in the room, but this little guy was so cute, she almost wanted to reach out and grab him into her arms. Occasionally he let go of the safety net of his mother's knee, happily content to wave his arms in the air like a drunken frat boy, until his mother put one hand against his back to steady him.

Even from this distance, Stephanie could smell the baby powder scent, and it made her insides squeeze tight with longing.

Mariam stroked a gentle hand down his back. "Would you like to hold him?"

"Goodness no," she breathed out before she could catch the words back. Clapping a hand across her mouth, meeting the other woman's curious gaze, she gave a self-conscious laugh. "Sorry, I didn't mean that the way it sounded. Kids and I...we don't get along. I much prefer them when they turn sixteen and you can reason with them."

The other woman slashed a glance toward her mother and sister. "You mean like those two?"

With a small smile, she shifted her focus toward the bride and mother-of-the-bride who were still arguing about the guest list and the flower arrangements and everything in-between.

As she watched their conversation volley back and forth, back and forth, and back and forth some more, her stomach began to heave from the dizziness of it all.

Pushing her hair out of her face, she attempted to ignore the queasiness in her stomach, and jumped back into the fray. "Ladies, the clock is ticking and we're getting nowhere."

Grace Kincaid sat in the armchair across from her, back stiff, hands folded primly on her lap, and sniffed. "Well, I'm attempting to be as cooperative as possible but I have my limits. Zombie outfits and a Vegas wedding are so beneath us."

"Mother," Liz growled from across the room where she paced and turned, paced and turned, and paced some more. "It's not your wedding."

Grace let out a breath of air. "Thank heavens."

Stephanie sorted through the binders of wedding bouquets and wedding cakes and wedding decorations. "So compromise.

Have a Zombie wedding at the estate or go to Vegas and get married in a traditional white gown."

Outside the large patio doors, the *whooop, whooop, whooop* of a helicopter sounded. And somewhere in the silence that suddenly filled the room, her heart went *thunk.*

Liz fisted her hands in the air and gave a triumphant jump. "My reinforcements have arrived."

A horrified expression marred the mother-of-the-bride's smooth complexion. "You didn't."

"Mother, you're not even supposed to be here till the weekend," Liz growled before she skipped out of the house and loped across the lush green lawn.

The mother-of-the-bride gave a disdainful and unladylike snort. "I don't know why she thinks he's going to support her decision to marry. Stone is a divorce lawyer. Shameful occupation. Every time his name is in the newspaper, my ratings drop."

Stephanie had to agree with her hostess. The world would be a far better place without divorce lawyers, especially when said divorce lawyer was one of the hunkiest specimens of the male species she'd ever met.

She tried to push away the memory of her night with Stone, but it slammed into her as it always did, with enough force it robbed the breath from her lungs and the stuffing from her legs.

The attraction between them had been so hot and intense, they'd barely had time to exchanged first names, make their excuses to get out of Grandma Elvira's wedding, before they were hotfooting it back to the city so they could get naked.

Through the bank of windows overlooking the park-like estate, Stephanie watched him leave the helicopter pad and head toward his sister.

Even from this distance, she recognized his broad shouldered build and loose limbed walk, and it turned her stomach in a decidedly more delicious fashion.

This was going to be awkward. Why oh why hadn't she found out more about him before she'd jumped into bed with him?

Because the moment she'd spotted Stone Kincaid and his ultra naughty grin across the dance floor, her hormones had started to do the Mambo Jumbo, and the loneliness she always experienced at weddings made her want to feel a man's arms around her, even if it was only for one night.

Even if the man she lusted after was all kinds of wrong.

Even if, after one amazing night, her traitorous body couldn't forget how terribly right he'd been.

Awkward and uncertain, she pushed back her hair, then did a quick check down her blouse and skirt, smoothing out wrinkles, checking buttons, and wondering why she even bothered.

Because they were never ever—*never ever*—hopping into the sack together again, at least not while she worked for his sister.

She smoothed another hand down her hip, reached around to check the pin holding the waistband of her skirt together, and caught a glimpse of herself in the enormous mirror over the fireplace.

Having the flu sucked. It especially sucked when the sexiest man alive walked back into her life and caught her looking like something already dead.

She smoothed out her expression and gave up on the idea of avoiding the man she'd had sex with, and instead focused on the sheer improbability of ever getting this wedding planned.

It was her job, her responsibility, to ensure that the idea of Prince Charming and happily-ever-after lived forever in the hearts and the lives of the women who hired her services.

Even if she no longer believed in happily-ever-after for herself.

"Mrs. Kincaid," she said as she refocused on the mother-of-the-bride. "Let me handle the details so you can relax and enjoy these special moments with your daughter."

Grace's mouth puckered. "But a zombie wedding theme?"

"I'll see if I can get her to tone it down a touch, but trust me, the more you object, the more determined your daughter will be to have her way." She recognized the disapproving lines around the other woman's mouth and felt her confidence falter.

"If it wasn't for that musician, Liz would want a normal wedding."

Stephanie channeled her own mother, and reached out to touch the *Eternally Yours* hostess on the arm. Beneath her fingers, the other woman's muscles tensed, and instead of relaxing, Grace only seemed to get...tighter.

She dropped her hand to her side and softened her approach even further. "I understand your concern for your daughter. I've been on my own for years and yet my parents still worry about every decision I make." She smiled a reassuring smile. "Liz is young, but she wouldn't be where she is today if she wasn't also smart. Marriage is hard, but you have to trust Liz and Roger to figure it out."

Before the older woman could reply, the swish of the screen doors whispered through the room and every thought but one vanished.

He was here.

Stephanie's attention swiveled to Stone.

As he walked out of the sunlight and into the room, his attention zeroed in on her. That something that had been there between them a month ago was still there. Heat flared in his gaze, instantly banked by...something cold and indifferent.

And then Mariam shoved the baby into her arms. "If you wouldn't mind..."

Stephanie forgot all about the man who rocked her world and the topsy-turvy condition of her stomach. She caught hold of the toddler under his arms and held him as far away as possible, the inkling to shove the kid back at his mother and say *no way* overwhelming.

She stared at the kid and he stared back at her. Breathless and near panic, she shoved the baby at his grandmother. "Mrs. Kincaid, if you wouldn't mind. I'm not very good with small children."

Grace sidestepped the child. "I don't want to get my dress covered with baby slobber."

And with one last look at the baby and his drool, the mother-of-the-bride abandoned her

"Don't judge me, kid," Stephanie muttered as she silently swore that if Mariam didn't get back soon and take the kid, she was going to drop him on the soft couch cushions behind her, and make a run for it. She might babysit brides and their grooms, but she drew the line at babysitting anything that resembled a kid.

Instead, she stood there frozen, holding the kid at arm's length. When his bottom lip began to tremble and his big blue eyes filled with crocodile tears, she felt another tug at her heart.

Then the kid opened his mouth and wailed for his mother.

Stephanie's panic doubled and as she looked toward the kid's mother for help, her gaze collided with Stone's. She watched him break away from the circle of women and close the distance between them, his long strides purposeful, his gaze oblique.

Between the panic of being responsible for something so tiny as the baby, and the fact that the man who starred in her nightly fantasies was approaching, she wanted to make a run for it.

Stone stopped in front of her. As he rescued the baby from her, his attention dropped to the kid.

"How's my favorite nephew?" he asked as he planted a kiss on the suddenly no longer crying toddler's cheek and tossed him into the air.

As he caught him safely, Mariam joined him, her sharp gaze accessing Stephanie. "Sorry, I assumed you were exaggerating about not being good with children."

Stephanie took a step back, her gaze fixed on Stone and the toddler safely nestled in his arms. "I wasn't."

28

"Jim Junior still plays strange sometimes." With another accessing glance in her direction, Mariam took the toddler from her brother and settled him on her hip. "Is it nap time, my big boy?"

Cooing gently to him, she walked away, only stopping to give Stone a kiss on the cheek. "I'm glad you're home to control the craziness."

As Stone turned to Stephanie, she felt the pull toward him, like the first time she'd seen him at her grandma's wedding, and resisted the urge to step into him.

But then she inhaled the scent of him—some light tangy scent of aftershave—and the discomfort in her stomach eased. As he captured her hand in his, heat rushed through her fingertips, up her arm, and infused the rest of her body with desire. She caught back the urge to step forward into him and press her nose against his neck.

"So a wedding planner, huh?"

She forced a smile and a saucy tone. "At least my clients get a happily-ever-after."

"Even if it's only temporary."

A woman in a bun and ugly glasses poked him in the ribs and nudged him aside, and the movement brought back the scent of baking. "Get a room, Boss."

Stephanie pulled her arm back and wiped her palm against her skirt, hoping to get rid of the feel of his skin against her own. Because it sizzled through her, all the way to her toes. And the last thing she needed in her life was a man to complicate things.

The woman elbowed her way in between them, shoved an armload of bride magazines into Stone's arms, and shook Stephanie's hand. "I'm Wanda, the hired help. Feel free to ignore me. That's what my boss does." Through the thick lens of her glasses, Wanda gazed at her as though she were a bug under a microscope. "If you need any assistance with the wedding plans, please give me a shout. I'd be more than happy to help."

Before Stephanie could thank her, Wanda took the magazines out of Stone's arms, and giving him a smirk, sat down and proceeded to look through the binders of photos on the coffee table.

In an attempt to control her hormones and the topsy turvy condition of her stomach, Stephanie turned and met Grace's inquisitive gaze. The narrow eyed woman looked from her son to Stephanie, then back again. A cold smile added to the brittleness of her personality. "Do you two know each other?"

Sending him a sideways glance, she shrugged and channelled innocence. "We met when my grandma Elvira married his great uncle Morty."

His mother raised one brow, then seemed to discard whatever she'd been about to say. Instead, she turned to face him directly. "Talk some sense into your sister. This zombie wedding is the most ridiculous idea she's ever had."

On the other side, Liz grabbed his jacket sleeve and stamped her foot. "Don't you dare. You *promised* to be on my side. You *promised* to get Mother off my back."

He glanced between his mother and sister, appearing calm and totally oblivious to their disagreement. The only giveaway was the tick in his jaw. "Where's the groom, sis?"

"I'm picking him up from the airport soon." Liz's annoyance turned to that sunny radiance that put a lump of dread in Stephanie's stomach. "You're going to love him, Stone. He's so sweet and funny, and he's written a song especially for me for the wedding. All of my girlfriends are so jealous."

Grace stepped forward. "I found the perfect gown at—"

Liz's mouth turned down at the corners. "Already arranged, Mother. The seamstress will be here tomorrow for the fitting."

The room turned scary quiet, and Stephanie wanted to grab Stone out of the line of fire, maybe escape someplace warm and cozy and private with him. Maybe pick up where they left off and—

Grace's mouth tightened, and through lips that barely moved, she said, "You picked out your gown without me?"

"Sorry." With a shrug and a grin, Liz held her arms out at her sides, threw back her head, and spun around the room, making it perfectly clear she wasn't sorry at all. "It's the most gorgeous gown in the whole wide world. My friends will be green with envy."

Her friends.

Not the groom or her mother. Stephanie resisted the urge to frown.

Stone shifted out from between the two women. "I'll pick up the groom. It'll give me a chance to get to know my future brother-in-law."

"Are you kidding? You'll give him the third degree and frighten him off." With a laugh and a shake of her head, Liz plucked the keys out of her pocket. "I'd rather you took Stephanie to the doctor. Maybe he can give her something to settle her stomach."

Stephanie took a step back. "No, that's really not necessary."

Stone indicated his assistant, who looked like she was attempting to disappear into the cushions on the couch. "Wanda can take the wedding planner to the doctor. I'll come to the airport with you."

"Liz doesn't want you acting like a third wheel," his mother stated, a smile blooming across her face. "You can stay here and help me personalize the wedding invitations."

Liz fisted her hands at her sides. "Mother, there are no invitations."

"Then I will order some. You can't have a proper wedding without formal invitations." Grace unclenched her teeth and turned her focus on Stone. "It will give us time to talk, catch up."

His gaze landed on Stephanie and she stilled the urge to take another step back. "Wanda's handwriting is far better than mine. She can help you. I'll take the wedding planner to the doctor."

31

His assistant shot to her feet, a feral expression on her sharp features. "I'll do the wedding planner."

Stephanie met his gaze head on.

He's already done me, but I wouldn't mind him doing me again.

It was almost as if he could read her mind. The edge of his mouth turned up in one corner.

A maid walked in with a tray of an assortment of baked goods and set it on the coffee table, and as the scent of yeast and sugar reached Stephanie's nose, the contents of her stomach rolled.

She swallowed hard and sat down on the couch.

Grace slid a small garbage can closer to her feet. "You look like you're going to be sick. What's wrong with you anyway?"

Stephanie shook her head and nudged the offensive tray back an inch. "Must be food poisoning. I promise it won't interfere with the wedding plans."

"I should say not. What kind of professional would you be if you allowed something so insignificant as an upset stomach to ruin the bride's beautiful..." Grace choked on the word. "...wedding?"

"You're right, of course."

Stone shoved his hands into his pockets and came to stand in the circle of people now eyeing Stephanie, a frown furrowing his forehead. "Maybe you should see a doctor."

"If it gets worse, I'll do that." She sat forward and hugged herself around the middle and rather than stare at the man who had rocked her world and her body, Stephanie pulled her cell out of her pocket and glanced at the list of items they still needed to accomplish. "Let's discuss the dinner menu—"

Grace turned her attention back to her youngest daughter. "I have seventy-five people to invite."

All the fake oomph Stephanie had mustered leaked out in a flash. She pressed one hand against her sweaty forehead and shook her head. "But Liz told me to plan for twenty people."

Liz stomped her foot. "Mother, Roger doesn't have any family."

Grace nudged the tray closer to Stephanie, and as the two women went at it again, Stephanie caught another whiff of the baked goods, clapped her hand against her mouth, and raced from the room.

If she didn't do something about this nausea, she'd never get the bride or her mother or the wedding under control.

Absolutely nothing could be worse...unless it involved the distraction of the hunky divorce lawyer.

4

The knock on the bathroom door was soft, the deep masculine voice laced with concern.

"Steph? Are you okay?"

Stone.

He'd followed her, and her heart went *so sweet*, while her brain rationalized *one night stand.*

Maybe being nice was a ploy to get her back in his bed. She could probably muster the energy...except business and pleasure rarely mixed well.

As the brother of the bride—and the son of the *Eternally Yours* hostess—he was off limits. No matter how her body responded to his, no matter that she craved his touch like a hound dog locked away from human companionship, she had to be strong...had to resist.

She folded her arms on the bathtub ledge and rested her forehead in the crook of her arms. With her insides still churning, she willed the contents of her stomach to stay down. "Go away."

The doorknob rattled and the door swished open.

Stephanie raised her head and looked up—way up—past the legs of his pants, the six pack hidden beneath his white shirt and charcoal gray jacket, and the matching tie that he'd loosened at the throat.

As Stone stepped into the small room, filling it with his size and his presence, she wanted to purr at the memory of running her hands all over his delicious body.

The door clicked shut behind him, drawing her attention to his face. Concern pinched his brow and when he reached her, he hunkered down to her level and tucked a strand of hair behind her ear.

"I have orders to take you to the doctor."

She shook her head and buried her face in the crook of her arms. "No time. As you can see, I have a wedding to plan. With difficult, uncooperative, *crazy* people, I might add."

He touched her again, a gentle caress the length of her back with the warm palm of his hand. It sent a shiver up her spine. "You need to go to the doctor, babe. Spending your time with your head in the toilet bowl doesn't get the job done."

It was nice, sitting here on the floor with his hand rubbing her back, listening to his low, soothing voice. She raised her head from the crook of her arm, and shifted to sit on the edge of the tub so he was no longer touching her.

And that's when she inhaled the scent of him. It eased her stomach and turned the topsy-turvy roller coaster sensation of his presence from dizzyingly terrifying to dizzyingly pleasurable. "It's nothing. Food poisoning from something they served on the plane, or maybe the flu."

He straightened to his full height, his hands stuffed into the front pockets of his slacks as he looked down at her. A glint of calculation sparkled in his gaze. "Save me from my family. If you don't let me take you to town, I have to help my mother with the wedding invitations."

"Invitations?" Stephanie frowned. "Liz isn't doing invitations."

"You can try to talk my mother out of it, but once she gets something into her head, it's a done deal."

"Sounds like my mom," she grumbled as she grabbed her purse off the floor, and pulled out a small tube of toothpaste and a toothbrush. "If you'll excuse me, I'll freshen up and get back to work. I'm on a tight deadline."

As she pushed to her feet, he leaned one broad shoulder against the wall, crossed his arms over his chest, and silently watched her.

He wasn't leaving.

Stephanie narrowed her eyes at him. "I can manage this on my own."

"Probably."

When he still made no move to leave, she shrugged one shoulder and turned toward the sink. Self-conscious, her cheeks heating, she scrubbed her teeth, rinsed out her mouth, than dabbed on some lipstick.

Turning from the mirror, she watched him push away from the wall to block the exit. He stood there, his gaze steady on her face.

"What?" she finally asked.

What was it about this man that made her stomach flutter, her bones turn to liquid, her knees weak. She felt his knuckles against the underside of her chin as he gently coaxed her head up until she stared directly into his eyes.

Eyes that were surprisingly serious.

"Ease my curiosity, Stephanie Goodwin. Why didn't you stick around for breakfast the next morning?"

She shrugged and focused on his mouth. "Because it's uncomfortable, and I don't do long term."

His eyes crinkled at the corners, his assessing gaze liquid fire against cold stone, while his voice deepened to a husky drawl that sent a seductive shiver through her entire body. "Seriously? You mean I threw that phony business card away for nothing?"

His hands drifted down her sides to her hips, silencing her, making her catch her breath in anticipation of what might follow.

The man had dangerous hands. He must have women drooling all over him—just like she'd drooled that one night.

She felt her stomach roll again while the rest of her body was trying to resist the urge to climb onto his body and have her way with him. She inhaled deeply, and attempted to hide her reaction to his scent. "So we're good? Things won't be awkward between us? Because in all seriousness, I could use your help getting your mother and sister to agree on anything wedding related."

One masculine eyebrow zinged upward. "I'll have you know I have a black belt in deflecting marriage minded women."

She huffed out a laugh. "My mother would kill me if she knew I'd let a divorce lawyer touch me."

"We didn't just touch."

His low, seductive voice tripped her internal defense system, and as she caught the scent of him again, the tightness in her stomach eased, and her heart rate kicked up a notch. She eyed his throat and sucked in her bottom lip.

He crooked one finger under her chin and brought her gaze back to his face. "Don't look at me like that."

Amusement climbed up her throat. "Like what?"

"Like I'm your next meal."

The edges of his mouth turned up into a smile. That crazy, half-crooked smile that had warmed her from the inside out at her grandma's wedding.

Heat rushed to her middle.

Ever since he'd slid into her life—into her body and her soul —she'd been hyper-aware of him. But she didn't want to get any closer to him than strangers in the night. She'd use him for sex, and that was it.

And one other thing...

She stepped right into his body, buried her nose against his neck, and wrapped her arms around his waist. The tightness in her stomach immediately disappeared.

It was the best she'd felt in days—maybe weeks.

His chest rumbled with suppressed laughter, and his arms slowly came up to envelope her against his body. His hands did a foray up her back, then down to her buttocks, snugging her closer. "The first time I saw you, I knew you were trouble."

She could feel his body's reaction to her nearness, and her body answered in a rush of desire and pulsing need. "Sorry. I'll try not to be too troublesome."

The sound of his laughter warmed her from the inside out.

His cell rang, and when she tried to pull away, he kept her tucked close. "Kincaid here."

As he listened to whoever was on the other end, Stephanie allowed herself to relax against him and let her mind wander.

Maybe she could borrow his tie, something small to tuck into a pocket so the scent of him would always be readily available. As ideas went, it wasn't a bad one, but borrowing his body—and getting him naked—seemed like it would be a whole lot more fun.

His deep voice rumbled from his chest into hers. "Bill, did you receive the prenup my assistant faxed over to you?"

Prenup? Right. He was so nice and she was so infatuated that she'd almost forgotten he was a divorce lawyer. Yet, he was the perfect guy, a man who didn't want marriage any more than she did. And even though she knew better—business and pleasure never mixed—he was so yummy and delicious that her body did a hopscotch whenever he was nearby.

"Take a look at it and get back to me. You can't keep getting married and divorced without one or you'll go broke." He clicked off the phone, tucked it into his jacket pocket, and wrapped his arm back around her waist. "Now, where were we?"

She nuzzled closer. "You were about to take off your tie and let me keep it."

"Why would you want my tie?" When she didn't answer, a laugh escaped him. "If I take off my tie, what will you take off?"

She nearly said *everything*, but instead, leaned back and grinned up at him. "You're bad, but I kind of like it."

"Only when I'm with you." His hands made another foray down her back. "What cottage are you in?"

"The Hole-In-One." She frowned. "What's with those names, anyway?"

A grimace crossed his features. "My dad's idea. Drives my mom nuts. He probably knew that when he named them." His gaze dropped to her chest, then back to her face, his eyes crinkled at the corners. "I'll take Two-For-Birdie. That way, I won't be far away, you know, in case you decide you need some badness in the middle of the night."

Stephanie sighed. What was there about a male wolf that taunted her to step over the line and go howl at the moon? She stilled the shiver working up her spine at the warm feel of his palm against her bare skin. "Sadly, Liz is staying there."

"Then I'll take Three-For-Shot. A little bit further away, but still doable...like you." He dipped his head closer to her ear and whispered, "I've been thinking about you."

The words left Stephanie suddenly elated. She pulled back and looked up into his eyes, unable to help the smile that crept out at the edges of her mouth. She'd been so sure he'd forgotten about her. "It was the sex."

His mouth quirked up into a sexy grin. "Yeah, that wasn't too bad, was it?"

"Not too bad at all," she murmured. In fact, the sex had been so good that they'd both barely gotten any sleep that night.

And judging by the growing length of him against her belly, a repeat might be in the nearby future.

As she stared up at him and he stared back, she wondered if he was waiting for her to make the first move.

Stephanie grabbed the front of his shirt, and he found her mouth with unerring accuracy, kissing her until all thoughts of troublesome brides and their mothers flew right out of her head.

His large hands cupped her face, angling her head for a deeper fit of his mouth to hers. Then he shifted his hands down her shoulders and over her arms. Goosebumps broke out on her skin.

"I've been thinking about you non-stop," he said against her lips. His fingers found the buttons at the front of her shirt. "In fact, I've been living with a semi-permanent hard-on since I woke up and found you gone."

"You could've called. I would've talked you through the basic steps to relieve yourself."

"How could I? You left me a phony number."

"I should say sorry, but I'm really not." She nipped at his chin, then palmed his crotch where his semi-permanent problem had become a full blown bone of contention. "You could have opened your little black book and called someone else."

"I have a feeling the wait is going to be worth it."

A knock on the door sent her pushing out of his arms and the nausea she'd been fighting all morning returned full force. Stephanie slapped her hand over her mouth and dove for the toilet.

Liz's voice carried through the wooden door. "Is everything okay in there?"

Stone's voice rose above the gagging. "Just fine."

"I'm getting changed, then leaving for the airport. I hope everything goes well at the doctor's office."

As the bride's footsteps disappeared down the hallway, Stephanie heard the soft tread of feet come up behind her.

"Go away," she grumbled the first time she could grab a breath, totally embarrassed to have him witness this. "I'm supposed to be working, not fooling around with you."

Behind her, water ran and then she felt a cold cloth wipe away the sweat on the back of her neck. When her stomach calmed down, she flushed the toilet, then sank back onto the floor and sat there, weak, exhausted, embarrassed, but somehow glad that he'd chosen to hang around.

He crouched down in front of her, a frown on his face. "I'm taking you to the doctor and I won't take no for an answer."

She closed her eyes, and let him wipe the cloth across her face and around to the back of her neck. "I suppose I should. Otherwise I'll be doing that—" She hooked a thumb toward the toilet and sent him a weak grin. "—instead of doing you."

The frown disappeared. The edge of his hard mouth turned up as he grabbed her hand and started to tug her to her feet. "Come on, then."

She waved him off. "Give me a moment to let my stomach settle."

They stared at each other and Stephanie became conscious of the intimacy of sitting here in the bathroom, conscious of him absently rubbing the inside of her thigh, conscious of her body coming alive at his touch.

"You know, maybe before we head into town," she suggested with a waggle of her eyebrows, then a moment later, her stomach heaved and she hit the toilet again. When she was done, she sank back onto the floor and tried to give him an apologetic smile, but she couldn't muster the energy. "Sorry."

"No problem. You're worth the wait." He was looking at her with concern. He also looked like he'd settled in for the duration, which made her and her stomach feel much better. Simply because he cared about her as more than an object in his bed.

Now wasn't that a dangerous thought.

Determined to keep feelings out of their relationship—and relationship out of whatever was going on between the two of them—she laid her head against the wall behind her and closed her eyes. "So tell me about yourself, Stone Kincaid. What are you most afraid of in the world?"

41

5

He wanted to admit that he was afraid of her, of falling hard and fast, of getting his heart trampled and his hopes crushed.

Instead he shoved the hope down deep, and went for something safer. "What am I afraid of? My family. Well, specifically my parents. And if you want to narrow that down further, mostly my mom."

She wiggled her toes and her bare feet drew Stone's attention.

Small, delicate, with hot pink polish on her toenails. His gaze skittered from her toes up to her smooth bare legs, and the memory of her soft skin under his hands and the vivid image of her naked in bed nearly made him forget that she was sick.

Stephanie looked up from her feet then, innocence gleaming in her gaze, and reached out to rub a thumbpad across his upper lip. But behind the innocence, there was the look she'd gotten that night, the one that she'd had every time she'd looked his way. He was surprised they hadn't scorched a few people in the fire they'd created.

As the color began to return to her pale cheeks, she prodded him to continue. "You're afraid of your parents? Aren't you a little old for that?"

"Yeah." Stone rubbed the back of his neck and felt his face heat. "Let's just say there's a reason why they've lived most of their married life apart."

She sent him a saucy smile and walked her fingertips up his pant leg. "They don't get along?"

He squeezed her calf, his mind going soft at the memory. Yeah, this was how to keep his distance. Let her turn his mind to mush. "Brace yourself, babe. You're about to be introduced to the marriage that should never have taken place."

Her gaze held his. "My parents' marriage is perfect. Or at least, that's what they want everyone to think. But the truth of the matter is, my mom runs their life, and Dad runs to do her bidding. Doesn't sound much like a partnership to me."

"Yeah, partnership." He scratched his chin, noticed that he needed to shave before he left whisker burn marks on her delicate skin. "Being there for each other, through hard times and easy times, through sickness and health."

She blinked back at him, and as his brain clicked into gear, he realized exactly what he had said. Except that she smiled, that naughty smile that had first caught his attention. On closer inspection, it wasn't so naughty as crooked and self-depreciating.

"Stone Kincaid, are you a closet romantic? That sounds eerily like you were quoting from a marriage ceremony."

"Well, it is why people get married, isn't it? To support one another?" He felt his face flush again. "So how did you end up as a wedding planner?"

"Mmmmm, that's a story for another day." As though she'd realized what she said, she got all flustered. "Don't worry. I meant it when I said I'm not out to trap a man. While I love brides and all of the magic of a wedding, I actually have this aversion to marriage. It drives my mom nuts. She can't figure out where she went wrong with me."

Curious, he found himself asking, "And why would a wedding planner have an aversion to marriage?"

"Speaking of weddings..." She glanced at her watch, straightened her skirt, and pushed to her feet, suddenly all efficient and closed in. "Well, I guess if we're going to go, we should go. Sitting next to the commode chatting with you is fascinating, but it doesn't get a wedding planned, does it?"

As Stone scrambled to help her up, he made a mental note to dig into this oddity further.

Out of the depths of her purse, she once again produced toothpaste and a toothbrush. "I'll—um—freshen up before we head into town."

"I'll grab the truck keys and meet you out front."

But as he watched her slather the toothpaste on the brush, squeezing right in the middle where he hated it the most, he got an image of waking up to this scenario every morning for the rest of his life.

It made him want to squirm.

He resisted the urge to lean down to kiss the spot right below her very sexy ear. Something in him warned him that he could get used to having her around all the time. Grabbing her, touching her, whispering sweet assurances in her ear. Then later...

Down boy.

Stone turned his back on her, opened the bathroom door, and came face to face with his mom.

For the barest of moments they stared at each other, him flushing red as though he were still thirteen and caught making out in the closet, his mom with her hand raised to knock on the door, startled by his presence.

He was the type of guy who never brought women home for the parents to meet. And as he'd explained inside, there was a good reason he kept his personal life personal.

As his brain started working again, and he found the sense to step out of the bathroom and close the door behind him, he grabbed his mom's elbow and steered her toward the kitchen.

Grace took a breath, her voice tight. "You have lipstick on your mouth."

Stone resisted the urge to wipe the back of his hand across his mouth and decided he needed to be more careful.

"For goodness sakes, Stone, she's the hired help. Keep your zipper closed and—"

"She's sick, Mom. I'm taking her to town to see the doctor. That's it." And then maybe, if his luck held, he'd get laid. He forced that thought out of his head and as they reached the key rack, he rifled throughout the keys.

"I've got your room all ready for you at the house."

He grabbed one off the rack for himself, then grabbed a second one for his assistant. "I'll be staying in the Three-For-Shot cottage."

"Hole-In-One. Two-For-Birdie. Three-For-Shot," Grace complained as she tapped one foot on the floor. "They were your father's idea. Those stupid names and that even stupider golf course."

Stone kept his silence and searched for the truck key.

"It's because of that wedding planner that you're staying at the guest cottages instead of the house, isn't it?"

"No," he said and kept his tone reasonable. "Wanda will be in the cottage next to me. We have work to do, and with all of the activity up at the house this week, I need the privacy."

"You know my rules."

"Yes, I do, and despite the fact that your rules are outdated and unnecessary, I have full intentions of keeping my distance. Weddings always make single women think about catching their own husband."

And despite Stephanie's assurances, he couldn't help but believe he should keep up his guard.

But the scent of Stephanie swirled through his head, and the

45

memory of her fingers walking up his trouser leg encouraged his body to stand up and take notice.

And as he drove around to the front of the house where Stephanie stood waiting for him, scarily he discovered that he felt good taking care of her.

She climbed into the cab with a wan smile on her lips, took one look at his face, and let out a heavy sigh. "It's just sex, Stone. I'm not looking for a ring on my finger or for a guy to take care of me. In fact—" And when she hesitated, and kept hesitating, he finally looked over at her and saw her waggle her eyebrows. "In fact, I can take care of most things all on my own, if you know what I mean."

Stone felt his body tense up in an entirely different way.

With any luck, and despite his mom's rules, there'd be a week of very hot sex in his immediate future.

6

J im Kincaid snugged the tie of his housecoat, rocked back on the heels of his golf shoes, and eyeballed the mid-afternoon sun.

This was the life, he thought as he lifted the coffee mug to his mouth and took a drink of the dark rich brew. Yes sireee, the good life, the only life, the rest of his life-life.

Overhead, a small flock of Bananaquit birds zipped past in search of sweet nectar, their yellow breasts brilliant against the lush green vegetation surrounding the course, their musical chirp a pleasant sound compared to the shrill trill of an unhappy wife who—thank you, God—spent more time on the Mainland than she did on the island.

Yep, he thought to himself as the warm ocean breeze rustled the leaves behind him, and he tried to ignore that something inside of him which shriveled and congealed and settled in the vicinity of his heart. This was a heck of a way to spend his retirement. The good life indeed.

His longtime friend, Harry Strom, standing on the tee off area of Jim's brand new nine hole golf course, swung his club back, then forward. The momentum of the swing and the weight of the club combined into a powerhouse of energy. As the head of the club connected with the ball, Jim heard the ping of the perfect shot, and his heart stuttered in his chest.

"Go, baby, go," he muttered as he instinctively clutched his chest, and watched the white ball arch through the air and gently curve over the fairway toward the green where it landed decisively at the top edge of the plush lawn. "Heck of a shot, Harry. Have you been practicing?"

"All week. Sandy's been reading me the riot act. Wants me to till the garden and help her dig up the flowerbeds instead."

Jim stepped up to the tee area, bent at the waist, and shoved his tee into the ground. "She should get a job, like my Grace. It'll keep her so busy, she won't have time to nag you."

Andy Johnson, standing to Jim's right, shielded his eyes against the sun, and chortled. "Who'd iron his underwear then, Jim?"

Ned Strom, Harry's twin brother, pulled his golf ball out of the wash and dried it on a towel. "You're a fine one to talk, Andy. Your wife greets you every night at the door with a drink in her hand, supper on the table—"

Andy's chest puffed out. "Wearing nothing more than an apron and her birthday suit."

Jim, along with the other two men, stopped to stare at Andy. "You're kidding, right?"

"Been doing it since the last of the kids moved out." Andy shrugged, a ghost of a smile flirting with his mouth as he eyed the tree line. "It's a nice treat, but nothing beats being on the golf course. Wish I could afford to retire and spend the day out here with you, Jim."

No you don't. Jim shut down his emotions and focused.

"Wind's pulling to the east today, Jim. Might want to adjust your aim."

"Thanks." With a frown of concentration, he bent and set his ball on the tee, eyeballed the sightline to the green and the flag in the distance, then straightened. He worked his shoes into the grass—proper stance, just right grip—and took a practice swing. His club whistled through the air and a shiver worked up his spine.

Perfect stance.

Perfect swing.

Perfect golf course.

Perfect life.

And maybe if he said those last two words often enough, he'd start to actually believe them.

He stepped up to the tee, positioned his feet the right distance apart, loosened his too tight grip, swung the club back and up, and let the weight carry it back down again—

Harry's voice broke his concentration. "Did anyone catch Grace's show today?"

The club head sliced into the soft turf, the force of the connection shuddering up the club, through the handle, into his hands and arms. The only thing that went flying through the air was a huge clump of dirt.

"Look what you made me do, Harry," Jim grumbled as he stomped off to retrieve the ragged piece of turf.

One of these days, he thought as he jammed the grass back into the spot it had come from, then just for good measure, gave it a stomp, he was going to quit inviting his friends over to play golf with him. His course. His rules. Yeah, and if Grace were here and could read his thoughts right now, she'd accuse him of being no more mature than a five year old.

"Well, did you?" his soon-to-be-ex best friend demanded.

"No." Jim reset the ball on top of the tee and ground his teeth together. "I haven't watched the show ever. Why would I start now?"

"Well, with you being newly retired and all, I just thought—"

"Don't think, Harry. Just shut up so I can hit this blasted ball."

The three men on the course exchanged a look, then backed up a step.

Okay, so maybe he was being a whiny-assed butthole, but he'd worked his tail off for the last thirty-some years, with plans of doing exactly what he was doing right now. Play golf on his own course. His retirement gift to himself last year.

Except his bad heart had forced him out the door of the New York Stock Exchange earlier than planned, and now he'd been relegated to the ranks of old age long before he was ready.

A sharp pang in his chest caught his attention and he went perfectly still. He sucked up a deep breath of air through his nose and exhaled through his mouth.

Stay calm. Focus. Remember to breathe and stay loose. No excitement.

He was invincible, a rock, and he refused to see himself as anything less. It was why he'd kept his heart condition from everyone, including his family.

What had the specialist said?

Learn to relax and you'll have a lot of good years left.

If he didn't keel over and die from the boredom of it all first.

He pushed away the ever present threat of depression and focused on the sport he loved.

He shook out his arms, rotated his shoulders, planted his feet apart, weighed the club in his hands, then braced himself for another practice swing. Yeah, he could get used to this life of leisure, which is why he wore his bathrobe and little else to his afternoon games.

The sensation of eyes drilling a hole into the back of his skull brought him around, and he peered through the trees toward the house.

No, it couldn't be...she couldn't be. According to his calendar, Grace wouldn't be back on the island until Friday, mere hours before Liz's wedding.

Jim decided he was being paranoid, and as the mid-afternoon

shadows moved in, he gripped the handle of his club. "Gentlemen, this conversation is over. Let's golf."

He ground his shoes into the turf for what he hoped was the last time, pulled the club back and—

Briiinnng.

Off-kilter, the head of the club connected with its mark and the ball lobbed fifteen feet down the fairway. Gripping the club in his hand, he jerked around.

Ned Strom, the best insurance agent on the island, grabbed his cell phone off his belt, leaned on his three-iron, and grimaced down at the display. "Sorry. I gotta take this. It's the old ball-and-chain."

Jim yanked another ball out of his pocket and tossed it onto the ground. "Rule number two, Ned. No cell phones on the course."

"I like rule number one the best," Andy stated.

Jim nodded in agreement and lined up his shot. "No women allowed."

7

Grace Kincaid watched Liz's wedding planner climb into the truck with Stone, and made a mental note to stop whatever was going on between the two of them.

She wasn't so ancient that she didn't recognize lust when she saw it and her son had been full of it when he'd opened the bathroom door. And while Stephanie Goodwin might be dynamite as a wedding planner, she was not the type of woman Grace wanted for a daughter-in-law. The moment Liz had informed her of her choice, Grace had done her homework and had her checked out thoroughly.

For Liz's sake, she'd kept her mouth shut, but once the wedding was over, the girl was gone. In the meantime, she had to make sure that her son didn't get carried away with lust and start believing that it was something else entirely.

Because marriage was not always forever and if she could prevent her own children from marrying the wrong person, then at least she'd have done something worthwhile in her life.

There'd been no mistake the flash of affection on Stone's face. Or the genuine concern he'd shown for her illness. Maybe it was just sex. After all, her son was a healthy male. Still, she frowned and made a mental note to nip whatever was going on between the two of them into the bud before it got out of hand.

As the truck and its occupants disappeared down the driveway, she turned her attention to the eyesore out her home office window where she saw Harry, Ned, and Andy clustered together like a small pack of beer cans.

Thank heavens she'd never married any of them. They'd have had her chained to the house, with no thought of her own but what they wanted her to think. Like the empty-headed housewives they'd married.

Then the breeze shifted the leaves on the trees and she saw Jim.

In the scheme of her professional life, Jim's golf course made not an iota of difference, and yet, she hated it more than the insomnia and the hot flashes that had plagued her since the onset of menopause.

She'd arrived at the estate early this morning, in plenty of time to meet with Liz to finalize the wedding plans, thrilled to be back on Serendipity Island after a month in the studio. She'd even planned for a short nap to get her through the day.

But she'd taken one look at the man sprawled out all over the bed like he owned it, listened to his chainsaw *snore-snort-snore*, and felt her temper spike.

This is what a long term relationship turned into, and it wasn't anywhere close to the fantasy she promoted on her show.

Life—and living—had robbed Jim and her of the first flush of love, and they'd ended up pursuing their careers instead of each other. And as busy as her life was, she hadn't given the growing distance between them a single thought.

Until he'd announced his retirement last year and turned into the schmuck who never climbed out of his housecoat unless he planned to hog the bed.

Grace turned her back on the annoying view, brewed a cup of herbal tea, and sat down at the desk to deal with the unopened fan mail. She grabbed an envelope, sliced it open, and scanned the contents.

Dear Dr. Grace,

I've watched your show my entire life and believed that there was one perfect man out there for me. When I found him, I married him without a second's thought. Yesterday, I came home from work and found him in bed with another woman. He says he'll never do it again. Should I believe him and give him another chance? I still love him and can't imagine life without him at my side...

"Poor darling," Grace tsked. A movement near the door caught her attention. She pushed to her feet and raised her voice. "Elizabeth Kincaid. I saw you. You get in here right now, young lady."

A moment later, her youngest daughter slunk into the room. "I refuse to let your bad mood spoil my good mood."

Grace glanced at the letter crushed in her hand. "Marriage is hard—"

"I know, Mother."

She quirked one eyebrow at her daughter's saucy tone. "It takes two mature people to work at making the right fit—"

"You mean like you and Dad?"

Grace caught herself short, then decided to ignore the comment. "Don't use that sarcastic tone on me, young lady."

Liz snorted. "If you want an example of two mismatched people, take a look at dad and yourself."

And didn't that just raise her hackles. "Elizabeth Kincaid, you take that back."

"No, Mother, I won't. It's the truth. You go on national TV and spout marriage wisdom like you're drowning in the perfect marriage. But when was the last time you and Dad spent time alone together?" Liz rolled her eyes. "When you conceived me?"

"Young lady, there is nothing wrong with your father's and my relationship. We are quite happy. Extremely happy. Ecstatically happy." Grace sighed at the lie, firmly keeping her game face in place. "Besides, this isn't about your father and me."

"Then what is this about?"

"It's about not making a mistake that's going to make you miserable for the rest of your life."

"Well, I guess you should know about that," Liz responded grudgingly.

Grace decided to ignore that. "I'm only thinking of what's best for you. You're so young. You have your entire future ahead of you."

"*My* future. Did you hear that? I get to decide what's best for me."

Grace snorted. "What do you know about this man?"

"Everything I need to know."

"What about his work?"

"What about it?"

"It starts there, Liz." Her voice broke and she glanced down at the letter in her hand.

What had she been thinking? Going along with Liz's choice of men because she was too busy with her show to see to her youngest daughter's needs first?

Roger Gordon was all wrong for her daughter—rough, earthy, raw. Totally incapable of making a good showing at all the right parties. Why, the man would ruin Liz's budding career as a prime time newscaster.

Grace decided that there was only one way for her to tell her daughter the problem and it was straight out. "What are you going to do when one of Roger's groupies ends up in his bed?"

"*Mother.*"

"I've seen the man, Liz. Watched how other women respond to him. He's a walking, talking advertisement for sex. If you want to sleep with him, then fine, have all the sex you want." There, that was it in a nutshell. She firmed her jaw. "In fact, that's what I'm recommending to all of my viewers from now on. Forget marriage. Just have sex. If you know what's good for you, Liz, when you pick him up at the airport, you'll tell him that the wedding is off and send him back the way he came."

"Mother, you're insufferable."

"Then it's a good thing I gave birth to you and you have to love me despite my shortcomings."

"Oooooh, I'm done talking to you until you've had some coffee." She glanced at her watch. "And now I'm going to be late for Roger's flight."

She stomped out, leaving Grace alone to contemplate the sickly green liquid in her teacup. She sighed. What she wouldn't give for a cup of caffeine right this very second. Or chocolate. Or coffee with a spoonful or three of chocolate added.

Maybe this was all her fault. Maybe if she hadn't been so focused on her career, she'd have done her job proper and nipped their budding romance in the bud before things got totally out of hand.

Now Liz thought she was in love with the man. What did the child know about love, anyway? She was twenty-three years old, still wet behind the ears, still running home to mama with her petty little problems.

With a depressed sigh, Grace randomly selected another letter from deep in the pile and sliced it open.

Dear Grace,

Yesterday was my tenth wedding anniversary and I spent it alone with the kids...

Been there, done that. Grace tossed the note into the trash can beside her desk and selected another letter.

Dear Dr. Grace,

I'm a stay-at-home mom. My husband spends all his time with the boys from work...

This letter followed the first two into the trash.

An hour later, she decided that all of the women who had written to her—all faithful viewers of her show who had once

56

believed in the Cinderella fantasy—were unhappy. They all sounded as miserable as she felt.

Grace swept the remainder of the unopened letters into the trash, sat back in her chair, and wanted to cry.

She was not allowing Liz to waste her life and heart on some man who took her for granted. Who didn't care whether she ever walked through his door again, as long as someone was there to do his laundry, cook his meals, and share the occasional romantic cuddle in the middle of the night.

No she would not.

She retrieved the letters from the trash and started writing her replies.

Dear cuckolded in L.A.,

Kick the cheating bastard out, then focus on your career. It's the one thing no one can ever take away from you...

Grace grabbed the next letter.

Dear depressed in Dallas,

What do we need men for anyway? To fix the washer and dryer? To move the piano from one room to another? I say that you hire a man to do these things for you and get rid of the cruel bastard who leaves you to sit home alone on your wedding anniversary. Evil scum...

She was on a roll now.

Dear lonely in Toledo,

Why are you waiting for him to come home when you know he's not giving you a second thought when he's out there with his guy friends? Kick back and kick loose and call all your old girlfriends—who are probably in the same boat as you are—and get out and have some fun. I suggest you start at the nearest Chippendales...

Deciding to take her own advice, she reached for the telephone.

She was woman. Let her roar.

8

By the time Stone drove into town, he couldn't wait to get his hands back on Stephanie.

She was staring out the window, and he let his gaze travel downward to where her skirt hugged her hips, her legs long and sleek. Into his thoughts crept the memory of those long legs wrapped around his waist and hips, pulling him deeper inside of her.

Man, he was in serious Stephanie-mode. Seriously serious Stephanie-mode. What did that mean? A full blown erection every time she came near? And why couldn't he get her out of his thoughts?

She'd been soft and welcoming and so warm, he'd never wanted to pull out. And she'd been funny too.

Then in the morning, she'd been gone. *She'd* left him, and now that he knew she was a wedding planner, he realized how lucky he was to escape the matrimonial shackles.

Even if she denied being interested in anything long term.

Even if he was currently in the middle of throwing himself back into the line of fire.

He pulled to a stop in front of the doctor's office, shoved the gear shift into park, and shifted on the seat so that he partially faced her. "Want me to come in with you?"

She smiled one of her extremely naughty smiles, and shook her head. "No need. What will you do while I'm in there?"

He looked around and spotted a coffee shop across the street. "I'll be in there when you're done." He couldn't stop himself from reaching out and nudging a stray strand of hair off her cheek. "Are you sure?"

Heat flared in her gaze and his body reacted. "About what?"

He grinned at her. "I can come in and hold your hand and, you know, distract you from your stomach while you're waiting for the doctor."

She laughed and swatted his hand away. "Are you kidding? If we're in there alone more than five minutes, you'll have all my clothes off by the time the doctor arrives."

"Five minutes? Hey, we were alone the whole trip into town and you're still clothed."

"Only because I'm sitting way over here and you've had your hands busy with the steering wheel the entire time."

He leaned forward, cupped his hand behind her neck, and gently eased her toward him. "Like this?"

She giggled, laid one hand flat on his chest to keep some much needed distance between them, while the other hand clutched the front of his shirt and urged him closer. Against his mouth, she said, "You're going to get me into trouble."

"We'll be careful," he murmured as he nipped at her bottom lip.

Stone slanted his mouth against hers and proceeded to devour her. Right there in broad sunlight, where anyone could see them.

She made him feel like a teenager again...wild and hot and desperate to explore where this thing between them was going.

Except he had to remember it wasn't anything but a quick affair because they were in close proximity. As his hand slid under her shirt and cupped her breast, she gave a breathy little moan and he groaned in response.

Her breasts were bigger, fuller, softer, and he suddenly wished he'd taken her to bed before making the trip into town.

When she finally pulled back and tugged his hand out from beneath her top, she was grinning with wicked delight and they were both breathing heavy. "Keep that thought in your head," she whispered. "As soon as we get back to the estate, I'm getting naked and you better join me."

"Definitely."

But as she slid from the truck and turned back, she froze. "Mom? Dad? How long have you been standing there?"

Stone craned his head around so he could peer out the driver's side window.

Sure enough, there stood a middle aged couple.

Her mom was grinning from ear to ear as though her daughter had just won a major prize, while her dad looked as though he wished he was holding a shotgun instead a woman's purse.

He took a deep breath, reminded himself that both Stephanie and him were of legal age, then climbed out of the truck, and held out his hand. "Mr. and Mrs. Goodwin. It's a pleasure to meet you."

Her mom jumped right in and pumped his arm. "You must be the bride's brother. The *lawyer*."

He shot Stephanie a look. Had she been talking to her mom about him? Was this a ploy to get him down the aisle, after all? "Yes, Ma'am."

Stephanie came to his side. "Mom, Dad, I'd like you to meet Stone Kincaid. He's a d—"

Her mom cut her off and yanked him toward the older

gentleman who was now clutching that purse like it was Stone's neck.

"Tom, say hello to your daughter's boyfriend."

The noose around Stone's neck tightened.

"Mom, Stone's not my boyfriend. He's actually a d—"

Tom growled low in his throat, interrupting his daughter. "Then why did he have his tongue down your throat?"

Beside him, Stephanie sighed, pulled his hand free from her mom's grip, and gave him a push toward the opposite side of the street. "If you know what's good for you, you'll leave town before she starts measuring you for a tux."

Stone restrained the urge to sprint, nodded in the general direction of her parents, then casually strolled across the street toward the coffee shop. As he reached for the handle, the front door swung open, and a couple stepped out into the sunshine.

The man glanced Stone's way, then immediately stopped.

"Stone," he said as he held out one hand. "When did you get back on the island?"

Stone grabbed the other man's hand and smiled. "Just this morning. How are you doing, Brody?"

"Great. Better than great." He released Stone's hand and turned to the woman at his side. Pure adoration shone from his gaze. "This is my wife, Paige Calhoun-Jackson. Honey, I'd like you to meet Stone Kincaid. We played football together in high school."

She held out her hand, a warm smile on her full lips. "It's a pleasure to meet you, Stone."

"It's a pleasure to meet you too." As she released his hand, he glanced over his shoulder and saw Stephanie's parents follow her into the doctor's office. Gesturing toward the coffee shop, he asked, "Do you have time to join me? We could catch up."

Brody glanced at his watch, then put one arm around his wife's waist. "We have an appointment across the street. Maybe you could come over for supper one night."

"I'd like that." Stone pulled a card from deep in his pocket and handed it to the other man. "I'll be on the island all week. Give me a call when you have time and we'll set something up."

"Will do."

With a wave, the couple left. Stone watched them go into the doctor's office. Then he headed into the coffee shop where he took a stool at the front counter.

His thoughts returned to Stephanie.

There was definitely something wrong with him.

A dozen times a day, the urge to call her came over him, and if it wasn't for the fact that she'd given him a phony phone number, he might not have been able to resist. All that time, he'd believed the urge would go away.

It hadn't and now here he was, under her spell again. So caught up in the feel of her lips against his, her full breasts in his hands, he'd forgotten they were in plain sight of the entire town.

Of all people, he should know better. The stormy relationship between his mom and dad was a perfect example of everything he wanted to avoid. Add in the dozens and dozens of divorces he handled each year, and how every time he saw how miserable those people were, he swore never to fall into the marriage trap.

Stephanie was dangerous with a capital D. He liked her— liked her more than was healthy for his single status. And yet, she'd sworn she wanted exactly what he wanted.

A no strings attached fling.

What he needed was time away from her to put this whole thing between them into perspective. Too bad he'd had weeks away from her and failed to do just that.

If he was smart, he'd steer clear of her this week, let this thing between them cool off, but he had a funny feeling she might be the one person he could turn to to keep him sane.

He straightened his back and something inside of him hardened.

After this week, he'd cut her out of his life. Cold, impersonal, without a hitch to his lifestyle. She'd return to wherever she lived and he'd return home alone.

And there'd be no marriage-minded mothers or purse-toting fathers in his life.

9

Stephanie had turned her back on her parents, fully expecting them to follow Stone to the coffee shop.

Maybe she was being selfish, but she had the inclination to let Stone deal with them himself. She had enough on her plate this week. She didn't need to play middleman between her lover and her parents.

Unfortunately for her, when she entered the doctor's office, she heard the distinctive click of her mom's heels as the older woman followed her in.

"Oh honey, a lawyer. I knew you could do it."

If Stone knew what was good for him, he'd hightail it back to the estate, grab his things, and make a break for the Mainland. If she had the choice, she'd run from her parents, too. "He's not my boyfriend, Mom. In fact, he's nothing to me."

Her dad followed them in, a concerned frown creasing his forehead. "Is that how you kiss a boy who means nothing? Then you're giving him the wrong message."

Stephanie looked around at the other occupants in the doctor's office and felt her face heat. "Will you two please keep your voices down?"

64

Dora grabbed her hand and tugged her onto a chair. "Spill. Tell us all about him. Has he popped the question yet? When is the wedding?" She clapped her hands together and gazed up at her husband. "A double wedding, Tom. It's a dream come true."

The frown on her dad's face deepened. He ignored his wife and focused on his oldest daughter. "Boys are trouble. Stay away from them and you'll never go wrong."

She lowered her voice. "What about Dane?"

"Dane's different." His furrowed brow deepened. "He's like a son to me. The son I never had." He speared his wife with a playful leer, the pained expression on his face momentarily gone. "Not for lack of trying, if I might add."

Stephanie wrinkled her nose and felt her stomach roll. "No sex talk. It grosses me out, okay."

"This has to be the one," her mom muttered. "Every day gets you one day closer to spinsterhood."

"Mom, forget it."

While her mom mulled over her failure to get Stephanie married, her dad fixed her with a fatherly look. "This Stone...he looks like a player to me."

She quirked one brow at him. "A player? How can you tell?"

"Because two-point-five seconds after he had you alone, he had his tongue down your throat and his hands...you know where."

A blush crept into her cheeks. If her dad only knew about what had happened the night of Grandma Elvira's wedding.

Leaning forward, she patted his knee and gave him her sweetest smile. "There was no tongue involved, Daddy."

"If you hadn't been uptown and in plain sight of everyone, I'm sure there would have been."

Her mom tsked and her concerned expression deepened. "I saw the way he kissed you, honey. A man like that can get a woman's panties off in no time at all. Just remember not to give away the cow before—" Her brow furrowed as she angled her body so she could see her husband. "What's that old saying?"

Tom growled, "Dora, don't give her ideas."

Her dad, bless his kind soul, still thought Mandy and her were as innocent as the day they arrived on his doorstep.

The office door jingled, momentarily capturing her parents' attention. A good looking couple walked in and sat down, and the young receptionist addressed them as Mayor and Mrs. Jackson.

Stephanie watched the man rest his hand protectively over the woman's abdomen before she dragged her attention back to her parents. "Don't you have enough to do without hassling me? Pestering Mandy for a grandchild? Preparing for your birthday party? Making the cake?"

"Oh honey, I'm an excellent multi-tasker. In fact, that's where you get your wedding planning skills from. It certainly wasn't from your dad." She glanced at her husband and gave a snort. "Or from that *other woman.*"

Stephanie raised one eyebrow. "You mean Diana."

Thankfully, the receptionist called out her name, and as Stephanie headed across the room, she noticed her mom slide onto the chair next to the couple and ask, "I couldn't help but notice. Are you pregnant?"

Sometimes the older woman had no boundaries.

Stephanie followed the nurse down the hallway and into one of the tiny rooms. She stifled a yawn, feeling much like she could use an afternoon nap, but knowing full well that she wouldn't get one. Not with the wedding only three days away.

It was going to be a very long week.

Except for the nights.

She thought of the toe curling kiss she'd shared with Stone. The way he'd tunneled beneath her shirt and cupped her breasts.

As the door swung open and the doctor walked in, she prayed he could give her something for the flu.

He was reading her chart through glasses that were perched on the end of his nose. He wore a cotton short sleeved shirt, a pair of tan linen slacks, and golf shoes. All that was missing were the golf clubs.

He glanced up at her and smiled. "Hello, Stephanie. I'm Dr. Strom. What can I do for you today?"

"I think I might have the flu. Maybe you could give me something to alleviate this nauseous feeling."

"How often and what time of the day are you sick?"

"Throughout the day. Cold food seems to stay down, but hot food comes right back up before it even gets down. And the smells...well, let's just say I've grown to immensely dislike certain scents."

He frowned as he felt her forehead with the back of his hand. "How long has this been going on?"

She shifted on the table so she could peer at the calendar on the opposite wall. Instead, she caught sight of the side profile of a very pregnant woman.

The sick feeling in her stomach got worse. "Maybe a couple of weeks. I'm not exactly sure. I've been busy, you know, getting brides married."

"Have you been around anyone with flu like symptoms?"

"I'm always meeting with people. Who knows if any of them have been sick."

He nodded, make a mark on her chart. "Period?"

She caught her breath and coughed. "What?"

He looked up and met her gaze head on. "Menstrual period? When was the last time you had one?"

Startled she shook her head and scrunched her forehead. "I've never missed one...I mean, I don't keep track...if I did, I probably wouldn't..."

"Are you on the Pill? Or another birth control? Have you had any sexual encounters lately?"

That sick feeling in her stomach got worse and she glanced at the picture of the pregnant woman again. "Yes, a few weeks ago and of course we used proper birth control."

She blinked and moistened her lips.

Mostly they'd used proper birth control, but there had been that one instance when they'd gotten carried away and...

She gave an uncomfortable laugh and shifted on the table again. "I'm hoping I have the flu. I don't want it to be...you know, the other thing."

"We'll check all of the options." He shone a flashlight in one eye, then the other, felt her neck glands for swelling. "Any other symptoms? Tiredness? Swollen breasts? Lack of or heightened sex drive?"

In the middle of stifling a yawn, she got that sick feeling in her gut again, and she slumped back against the wall. "Yes, yes, and definitely yes."

Especially the last one. And it was all Stone's fault because he was irresistible.

The doctor stepped back, his eyes kind and concerned, his voice gentle and fatherly. "We'll run some tests today. The results will be back within a couple of days. I suggest you make another appointment and we'll take it from there."

Her voice came out small and needy. "You won't tell anyone, will you? My dad..." She covered her face with her hands. "He'd be so mad and disappointed in me. And my career...I'm in the middle of planning the Kincaid wedding. I wouldn't want news to get out."

As she stood up, he set one hand on her shoulder. "This is just between you and me. If the test turns out positive, it'll be up to you when and how you break the news to anyone you care to tell."

As she headed down the hallway for the blood and urine samples, she struggled against the shock of it all.

Stone Kincaid, hotshot divorce lawyer, the man who starred in her nighttime fantasies.

It was his fault she was in trouble now.

His fault her ever expanding waistline might be...*expanding*.

No wonder she felt fat and frumpy.

If he hadn't been temptation with a twinkle in his eyes, a ready smile on his mouth, and the best looking shoulders she'd ever seen, she might have been able to resist him.

But one look had led to a zillion intimate touches later, and now...

A baby?

As she left the doctor's office, she resisted the urge to cover her midriff with her hands, and when a space between vehicles opened up, she hurried across the street.

What would she do if the test results were positive? Move back in with her parents? Work at the local grocery store just so she could put food on the table for her growing youngster?

No way could she be pregnant. They'd been so very careful... mostly. It had to be the flu.

She spied the Serendipity Island Pharmacy sign and stopped mid-step.

If she picked up a home pregnancy test, she wouldn't have to wait to find out the results.

Because if the results were positive, Stone Kincaid would never look at her like a goddess again.

10

Stone had been certain the Goodwins would stay with their daughter during her checkup—in hindsight, he now realized he'd been hoping on a prayer and a song—so when her parents followed him into the coffee shop and slid onto the stools beside him, he immediately shifted into defensive mode.

He never ever met the parents of the women he dated. Not only did it give marriage minded mothers and their daughters false hope, but he had enough problems with his own parents. He definitely didn't need another set of parents, although one look at Tom Goodwin's glare—his bushy brows pinched, his round jaw jutting out, his upper lip curled into a protective snarl —and Stone knew Stephanie's parents were the opposite of his own.

They were the involved sort. For the first time ever, Stone was glad for his own parents' hands-off attitude. He never had to worry about their interference.

Beside him, Dora Goodwin regaled him with tales from Stephanie's youth, from her baking skills to her seamstress abilities, and everything in-between. And all he could do was keep one eye on the doctor's front door, and pray for a quick escape.

The moment he saw the door across the street swing open and Stephanie walked out into the sunshine, his escape route finally at hand, he leapt to his feet and reached into his pocket to pay for his barely touched coffee.

Dora Goodwin's hand wrapped around his wrist like a convict's shackles, and dodging the parental bullet suddenly went out the window. "Stephanie probably needs to fill a prescription, so you have lots of time yet. Sit. Sit. We'll have another cup of coffee."

She didn't relax her hold which gave him no choice but to sit back down. Or arm wrestle her to escape her surprisingly strong grip. At which time she raised her coffee cup and waved to the waitress for a refill.

He met Tom Goodwin's suspicious gaze and his stomach caved.

The older man had obviously seen everything. The kiss, the way he'd tunneled up under Stephanie's shirt until he had her breast in his hand. He shifted, uncomfortable, and pushed away the vision of Stephanie naked in his arms and focused on his single status.

Because if ever he'd seen a marriage minded couple, these people were it.

He could feel Tom's glower right down to his toes, and as he dragged his attention back to whatever Dora was rambling on about, Stone couldn't help a guilty flush from working up his neck and into his face.

"Isn't that wonderful, Tom," Dora said, her smile widening until she looked over at her husband. She nudged his arm and repeated her question. "Isn't that wonderful, Tom?"

Tom grunted and kept his glare fixed on Stone.

Ignoring the surliness of her husband, Dora sat back and beamed. "Your mother was once a Weatherby, isn't that correct?"

She frowned. "I made a point of meeting everyone at Elvira and Morty's wedding. How did I miss you?"

He shrugged, and tried to maintain eye contact while images rushed through his mind.

The first moment he'd seen Stephanie across the dance floor, dressed in a sexy number that hugged her curves, and made his hands itch to touch her.

That second when she glanced his way and their eyes met. The floor beneath him had seemed to shift and tilt. He should have hightailed it out the exit right then and there.

"Why, Tom," she exclaimed and again turned to her husband. "Once Mandy and Dane get married, Stone will be *family*."

Tom regarded him from below bushy brows and if possible, his glower deepened. "Why does my daughter need to see the doctor?"

"Food poisoning." At the concerned look on her parents' faces, Stone backpedaled. "Or the flu."

Dora leaned forward and placed one hand on his arm. "Has she been throwing up?"

He looked deep into those eyes that reminded him so much of Stephanie, saw a look of hope, then suddenly straightened up and pulled away. *No way.* "It's food poisoning or the flu, that's all."

The older couple exchanged a look and dread filtered through Stone. He thought of the way Stephanie's body molded against his own, of the kisses that filled his head with thoughts of only her, of the smile that somehow managed to turn him on and turn him inside out too.

"I'm sure everything will be okay, Tom." Dora patted her husband's arm and tactfully changed the topic. "So how are your sister's wedding plans going?"

Thankful for the change in topics, Stone grimaced. "Liz and Mom can't seem to agree on anything."

"Stephanie is the best. She'll get it all sorted out."

"I hope so." He met Tom's gaze and thought oh-oh.

Tom's glower deepened. "Are you a player, boy?"

"No, sir." Or at least, not lately. For the last month, he'd been living like a monk.

He grabbed his coffee cup, lifted it to his lips, and looked for a place to hide.

There was only one front door, and unless he planned to escape through the kitchen or out the bathroom window, he was pretty sure he was stuck right here, waiting for Stephanie to rescue him. By the looks of things, Dora had him—and the entrance—covered and blocked.

As he searched for an escape route, he noticed a group of seniors huddled around one of the tables. Money exchanged hands several times and he wondered what they were up to.

"Now, Tom," Dora said, interrupting his thoughts. She patted her husband's arm. "I'm sure Dane's cousin is a fine upstanding young man with only honorable intentions toward our daughter."

Taking a sip of coffee, Stone nearly choked. As Stone looked out the window, Dora followed his gaze. "She's very pretty, isn't she. And those legs...she has my legs. Tom always says they go on forever."

"Dora," Stephanie's dad said, a warning in his voice.

She patted her husband's hand again, then turned back to Stone. "Stephanie never talks about her personal life. So tell us the truth. Are you her boyfriend?"

Tom stood up, grabbed hold of his wife by her upper arms, and urged her to stand up. "Go to the bathroom and fix your lipstick."

Dismay scrunched her forehead. "Is it crooked?"

"All over your face."

And with a tsk of dismay, she scurried away.

Stone was sorry to see her go, especially when Tom slid onto the stool beside him and faced him direct. There was fatherly concern etched into the lines on his forehead, which was totally different from Stone's own dad, who tended to avoid family situations.

If Stone was ever a dad, he wanted to be involved in his kid's life.

"Some things can't be hid, boy. Like lust and love. Which is it?"

Although he couldn't ever see himself being this direct and nosy. Stone forced himself to relax and hoped he didn't look guilty. "We're just friends."

The older man regarded him sternly. "The best life partner is someone who is also your best friend."

Okay, this wasn't going well. Every time he opened his mouth, someone said something that didn't bode well for his single status. "I'm not ready to settle down."

Beside him, Tom grunted. "Then if you know what's good for you, boy, you'll stay away from my daughter. Her mother wants grandchildren something fierce, and she's not above playing a little matchmaking."

He glanced out the window, where Stephanie had made her way across the street, and headed to the pharmacy next door, just like her mom had said.

"Stay on the straight and narrow, Stone, and you'll have nothing to worry about," Tom added, like Stone wasn't already thinking exactly just that. "My daughter is a wedding planner. She's had her wedding dress picked out since she was five."

Nervous now, he glanced over his shoulder, looking for a way to escape, and felt as though his tie was tightening around his neck. "Friends. Just friends. I promise."

"How old are you, boy?"

"Thirty-five."

"I'd run if I were you."

Behind him, laughter erupted—the group of old men—and he couldn't help but wonder if maybe they were catching an earful of his dilemma for their daily entertainment.

Stone pushed to his feet, determined to escape, and suppressed a shudder. Marriage and babies, the last two things on his bucket list. He reached into his pocket for some money to pay for the coffee, and get out of there.

He peeled off a twenty, dropped it on the counter, and indicated to the waitress that he was paying for the Goodwin's too.

With a glance over his shoulder, Tom lowered his voice and fixed him with a fatherly glare. "Don't make me tell my wife what you do for a living."

In the act of stepping away, he froze. "Excuse me?"

"She hates divorce lawyers more than she loves a good wedding."

"How do you—"

Dora pushed her way between them, her cheeks flushed, her smile beaming. "So what are my two men discussing now?"

Tom quirked one brow in Stone's direction, then went back to stirring sugar into his coffee. "We were discussing golf."

Dora grabbed Stone's forearm and stopped him from leaving. "We heard your dad has a private golf course. You should ask him if Tom could join him sometime. Now that our youngest daughter is living on the island, we'll be spending plenty of time here."

"Yes, ma'am, I'll do that."

He took a step away, but her grip tightened.

"Do you think your sister and her groom will start a family right away? I hope Mandy and Dane do. I want lots and lots and lots of grandchildren."

Over her shoulder, Stone met Tom's *what did I tell you* gaze.

And then he realized that once kids were involved, divorces got messier. "I have to go."

She gave her husband a dirty look. "Did Tom say something to upset you?"

"No, Ma'am. Stephanie's out, so I'll just take her back to the estate so she can get some rest."

Dora patted his cheek. "I wish she'd find a nice boy like you and settle down. With your handsome looks, you could give me some beautiful grandbabies."

"Dora," Tom warned.

A cold shiver went up his spine and straight to his brain. He muttered, "Never going to happen."

As he turned toward the doorway, he froze.

Stephanie walked into view, but instead of coming into the coffee shop, she sort of drifted toward the middle of the sidewalk and stalled, a pinched look between her brows, her bottom teeth gnawing on her top lip.

She held a bag in her hand—the prescription, he assumed—and had the other hand pressed protectively over her abdomen.

Panic started at the base of his spine and worked its way up his back, tensing his shoulders and neck, pinching the space between his eyes. As he headed out to collect her, two thoughts kept ramming into his brain.

Marriage and babies.

It had been a heck of a conversation to have right before he was going to make love to the sexiest woman on the planet. It was enough to bring down the mast forever and make a man swear off women.

When he reached her, he pressed his hand against the small of her back and guided her across the street. Neither of them said a word, which made Stone worry even more. As he opened the truck door, Dora came up from behind, startling him, and slipped around him and climbed into the back seat.

A look of dismay marred Stephanie's features. "Mom, what are you doing?"

The older woman beamed up at them both. "You're sick. You need my assistance. I'm coming out to the estate to help you with the wedding."

Hands in his pockets, Tom growled, "Dora, get out of there."

She smiled at her husband, then bent her head and clipped

76

closed her seatbelt. "Awww, that's so sweet. You'll miss me. Don't worry, I'll be back at Mandy's in a few days. While I'm gone, you can bake the squares for my birthday party."

"Who's going to cook my supper?"

The older woman's shoulders stiffened. "Tom Goodwin, I'll have you know I'm not just a meal ticket."

And with that, she turned her back on him.

Stone had the sudden vision of what life with an interfering mother-in-law would be like, and pure terror shuddered through his body.

And yet, at this very moment, he had only two choices.

Manhandle her out of the car or let her have her way.

Stone went with option number two and headed around to the driver's side of the truck.

Because, let's face it, there were things worse than a marriage minded mother.

And the woman in the passenger seat holding tight to the bag on her lap was it.

11

Stephanie clutched the bag on her lap and tried to come up with a reasonable excuse to escape so she could take the pregnancy test without anyone being the wiser.

She couldn't tell a soul, not her sister, not her parents. They'd fuss and worry, and bombard her with questions. She'd never get a moment's peace.

And before the day was over, Grace Kincaid would hear the news and personally escort her off the estate.

In the backseat, Dora chatted away, and it required minimal participation from the other occupants of the truck.

She snuck a look at Stone. His hands were gripping the steering wheel, his knuckles white, his patience clearly wearing thin. But other than an occasional grunt, he kept his mouth shut the entire way.

As they neared the estate, Dora tapped him on the shoulder. "If you could drop me off at the main house, I'd like to introduce myself to your mother."

Stephanie took this opportunity to make a quick escape. "Me too."

Stone arched one masculine brow at her. "My mother has already met you."

She quickly backpedalled. "Not to meet your mom, of course. But I need to check on the cake, the decorations, and..."

She snapped shut her mouth and gnawed on her bottom lip. *Find some alone time.*

Muttering something under his breath, Stone parked the truck at the back of the house, grabbed the keys from the ignition, and followed them out.

Oh oh. Something had happened to ruin his playful mood. Probably her mom's doing. All the older woman had to do was open her mouth and the inquisition began.

He stomped toward the kitchen entrance, and already committed, Stephane followed him in. The moment she stepped into the house, Stone yanked her to the side. A plate sailed past her head and shattered against the wall.

Stephanie spotted Grace on the opposite side of the room. She already had another plate in her hand, raised and ready to throw.

Stone slapped the truck keys on the counter and dragging her along behind him, stalked across the room past his parents, anger in every jerky movement of his body. "Get a divorce already, will you?"

He pushed open the door into the hallway, then turned back to wait for her mom.

But Dora stood looking down at the shattered plate.

"Oh my, don't you just hate when that happens?" She raised her gaze to Jim first, and as a smile spread across her face, she headed toward him, hand outstretched. "Why, I'll bet you're Jim Kincaid. Now I know where Stone gets his good looks. We're practically family, you know." She took his hand and pumped it profusely. "I'm Dora Goodwin, Stephanie's mom."

Stephanie couldn't help but admire her mom's determination, because despite Jim's lack of response, the smile never dimmed.

79

Dora turned her attention to Grace, and as she approached, said, "I apologize for intruding without prior notification. My daughter is feeling a tad under the weather, so I decided to come help her with the wedding plans. I hope you don't mind. Here, let me take that." She reached out and tried to pry the second plate out of Grace's hand, and finally succeeded. "It's such a pretty pattern, it would be a shame if it ended up broken like the other one."

Stephanie held her breath and waited for the fireworks.

Dora set the plate down on the countertop out of reach, closed the dishwasher door, and as she grabbed hold of Grace's hand, smiled again. "It's a pleasure to meet you, Mrs. Kincaid. I watch your show every day. I hope while I'm here, we can get to know each other better." She leaned forward and lowered her voice to a stage whisper, loud enough for everyone in the room to hear. "Men. Can't live with them, can't live without them. Right?"

Then with an overly cheery *tohdaloo*, she followed Stone and Stephanie out of the room.

And as the door closed behind them, the sound of crystal shattering followed them out. She tsked. "I wonder if your parents might like to come to my birthday party? It would be good for them to get away from the stress of the wedding."

"Wouldn't make any difference," Stone said, and she could tell that it was painful for him...a long time pain that had never healed. "I'm sorry you had to see that."

At that moment, his dad stalked past, and the pinch between Stone's brows grew into a full fledged frown.

Stephanie didn't know what to do, but her mom was good at dealing with bad situations. Maybe while her mom consoled Stone, she could escape and find the privacy to take the test.

She looked down at the way he'd manacled her wrist in his hand and thought, *maybe not*.

Dora touched his arm, her tone quiet and soothing. "Every marriage has its ups and downs. I'm sure they'll work it out."

A wry grin shaped his mouth. "I've been waiting my whole life for the ups."

Her mom placed one hand over her heart and gave him a heartfelt look. Then she backed away toward the kitchen door. "Well, I'll just leave you two alone to do whatever young people do. Maybe your mother has an extra bed for me to sleep in while I'm here. I wouldn't want to get in the way of you two lovebirds."

And then she turned on her heel and returned to the kitchen.

Stone gave a strained laugh and raked the fingers of his free hand through his hair. "Your mom is pretty cool. She's also a little nutty."

Stephanie tried to pull her wrist free, but he held on tight. "She's like the Energizer bunny, sticking her nose here, interfering there, and never running out of steam." She raised her gaze to his face, and that's when she noticed the deep well of hurt in his eyes, a hurt that definitely hadn't been there before they walked into the middle of his parents' argument. She lowered her voice. "I'm sorry."

As he dropped her hand, a shield went up over his expression, and his eyes narrowed. "What's in the bag?"

Fine. If he didn't want to talk about his parents' relationship, then she wouldn't waste her time. She clutched the bag a little tighter and backed up a step. "Just a prescription. Well, thanks for the ride into town. I'm going to—"

The pain filled little boy disappeared, replaced in a flash by the determined lawyer. He closed the distance between them, forcing her to take several steps back, his gaze never leaving her face. "What's in the bag, Steph?"

She frowned back at him. "The prescription. And if you must know, tampons."

With smug relief, she thought, *yeah, that oughta quell his male curiosity.*

Except it didn't. He made a grab for the bag and she tucked it behind her back, and darted around to the other side of the couch.

He followed her, advancing like a lion contemplating his next meal. Or a lawyer with an axe to grind. "What kind of prescription?"

She tucked the bag behind her back and hoped he didn't hear the strain in her voice. "Something to settle my stomach."

"Can I see it?"

She backed up another step and angled toward the exit. "What for?"

He followed her, determination in every step. "I want to see what the doc gave you, make sure it's okay."

Annoyance infiltrated her concern. "So you're a doctor now?"

His gaze lit on her briefly, his eyes sharp and hard. His court-room look, she surmised. She didn't much like it. "Do you have something to hide?"

An ugly feeling twisted in her gut. She spun around on her heels and stalked toward the front door. "I'm heading back to my cottage to take my medicine and rest. I'd appreciate it if you didn't follow me."

As she headed outside and across the patio, he dogged her footsteps. "If you have nothing to hide, why won't you show me what's in the bag?"

Over her shoulder, she glared at him. "What is wrong with you? What happened to the guy with his hand up my top?"

The sound of his laughter was harsh. "I had coffee with your parents. There were insinuations."

She snorted. The man was entirely too suspicious. "Go away."

"Insinuations which, given the fact that you can't keep anything down, suggests the possibility of a pregnancy."

Okay, that nearly stopped her, but somehow, her feet kept moving beneath her. "Unbelievable. If either of them thought I might be pregnant, my dad would have his shotgun out, and my mom would have you in front of a minister already." She quickened her footsteps, although all that did was tire her out. The man's strides could outpace her easily. She gritted her teeth. "Go away."

"Maybe you haven't told them yet."

Stephanie reached her cabin and stepped onto the first step leading toward the porch. She turned and eyed him, the bag tucked behind her and out of his reach. "Look, you have nothing to worry about. If I knew I was pregnant, if I was certain you were the father, I promise I would tell you."

His gaze narrowed on her face and the muscle in his jaw ticked. "How many other guys have you slept with since that night?"

She smile sweetly, but what she really wanted to do was club him over the head. "Would you like me to type you up a list with names and dates?"

"No. Just tell me what's in the darn bag." He grabbed again, this time capturing her against him and hanging on. And when he looked down at her, all brawny irritated male, something inside of her sizzled to life. "If you have nothing to hide, why are you afraid to show me the contents?"

"It's private."

He had her squashed up against him, and she saw sudden heat banish the darkness from his gaze. The feel of his taut body against hers sent desire swirling through her. And as his gaze dropped to her breasts, she held her breath, certain that the desire that was always so ready between them would distract him.

He'd throw her over his shoulder, take her to bed, and make love to her. By the time they were done, he'd forget about the contents of the bag and leave her alone.

She moistened her lips with her tongue and in anticipation of his kiss, dropped her gaze to his mouth.

But the kiss never came, and a moment later, he pulled back, one hand holding her arm to balance her so she didn't topple backwards without his support.

"Got it."

And then she noticed the bag in his hand. "Hey."

She grabbed for it but he held it out of reach.

"So what's in here?"

She lurched and jumped and tried to grab it out of the air, but he was so much taller than her, and the reach of his arm dwarfed her.

All of a sudden, she stumbled over her own feet. Stone reached out and caught her around the waist before she tumbled to the ground. She wrapped her arms around his neck and hung on, her chest pressed hard against his, feeling the sizzle all the way down to her toes.

Oh yeah, she had it bad. What had the doctor said? Heightened sexual drive?

She gazed up into his eyes, a heartbeat away from kissing his very kissable mouth, a word away from inviting him inside to scratch the itch he ignited without even trying.

Except that he was glowering down at her, his arm still tight around her waist. "What is the matter with you? You're going to hurt yourself."

She gritted her teeth against the desire and pushed against his chest, but he wasn't letting go. "Then give me back the bag. It's just a prescription for the flu. And some tampons. You don't want to see those. And maybe even something more unpleasant."

His eyes narrowed. "Like what?"

She thought fast. "Suppositories."

Ha, that ought to stop him.

Only it didn't.

With his face inches from hers, he sneered. "Why do women always have to be so stubborn?"

"It's an inherent gene. Otherwise you men would run amok over us." For a few moments, they glared at one another—as though that would solve all of their problems, *ha!*—and that sizzle she got in her stomach whenever he was around started again, and worked its way down into her lady parts. With the sudden realization that she was ready to wrap her legs around his waist and give him full access to her body, she pushed out of his arms and backed up a safe distance. "Fine, go ahead, open it. But take my word for it, you'll be much happier if you don't."

He bent his head, opened the bag, and short of tackling him to stop him—which might be fun if only she had less at stake—he peeked into the bag, then reached in. "So what is this?"

Stephanie sank down on the porch steps and covered her face with her hands. "You have to believe me, I was going to tell you, as soon as I took the test."

She heard the rustle of his clothes as he sat down beside her, followed by an extremely long beat of silence. Finally she opened two fingers a crack so she could look at him.

He had the box in his hands and his jaw worked with some emotion that she couldn't quite identify. All in all, he looked as dumbfounded as she felt...maybe more.

"How did this happen?"

She sighed and ticked off the moments she remembered—of which there were many. "Let me see. It could have happened in the car on the trip back to Seattle. Or in the elevator." She speared him with a sideways glance. "That was so fast, I can't remember if we took time for protection or not." As he sat there in stony silence, she blabbered on. "There was up against the hotel room door. On the bed. On the bed again. In the tub. On the bed yet again—"

"Okay, okay, I get the picture." He handed the box to her, speared his fingers into his hair, and sat there, elbows braced on his knees, his face turned down toward the ground. "Please don't take this the wrong way, but are you sure it's mine? You offered me a list of names, remember?"

Horrified, she gaped at him. "Out of all the lies I've told you today, that's the one you believe?"

She glared at him and he glared back, until with a shrug, he continued. "I had to ask."

"Fine, whatever." She twisted her fingers together like strands of spaghetti and whispered, "I'm never late. Never, ever even once."

It felt strange to be talking about such a personal topic with a man who was virtually a stranger. They'd spent one incredible night together. Then bam. "My breasts are swollen and tender. There's the throwing up thing." She slid a look his way but he seemed to be caught up in his own thoughts, staring at the ground, probably hoping a gigantic hole would appear and swallow him up, like a lifeline out of this potential mess. She pushed to her feet and held out her hand. "Well, if you'll give me the box, I'll let you know how the test turns out."

He came to his feet like a panther, swift and unexpected, his big body towering over her. "You're not getting rid of me that easy, honey."

"Stone, there's nothing you can do. I'll go pee on the stick and pray that it's negative. It would be nice if you did the same." A wave of heat washed through her face again, and she hastened to explain. "Praying, that is, not the other thing."

In unison, their cell phones buzzed, and they both jumped.

Stephanie pulled her phone out of her pocket, conscious of Stone doing the same. She stared down at the screen, blinking back unwanted tears. "The seamstress is here for your sister's dress fitting."

"She can wait." His head was bowed as he studied his screen, then he clicked off his phone, tucked it back into his pocket, and met her gaze, his lower jaw working as though he were grinding his teeth. "Everyone and everything can wait. But this...this is important."

She shook her head. "It's not going to make a difference whether it's now or later. If I'm pregnant—" There, she'd said the word out loud, and the thought sent fear rushing through her body. "—then I'm pregnant and it can't be undone."

He slipped her phone from her hands and thumbed the screen. "We're doing this together. When you're done with the fitting, I'll come to your cottage and hold your hand."

For some reason, the image caught at her funny bone, and she raised an eyebrow. "While I hold the pee stick with the other one?"

His head snapped up and he took a step back, all cute and flustered, like an alpha male totally out of his element. "What I mean is, I'll wait till you're done that part, then we'll watch the stick together."

As her phone vibrated again, reality set back in. Her grin faded and she held out her hand. "Fine. Give my phone back."

He bent his head again and continued to thumb the screen. "I'm adding my number to your contacts so you can get hold of me day or night."

As he finished typing and handed her the phone, his serious gaze stayed steady on her face. "If the test turns out positive, I want you to know that I'll stay by your side through the whole thing. Through the pregnancy, raising our kid...you won't be alone. But whatever happens between you and me, I don't want to turn out like my parents."

Pity morphed in her chest. "We won't," she said softly. She started up the steps, then turned back around. "Whatever you do, please don't tell anyone. If my mom even suspects I might be pregnant...well, you talked to her. You know what she's like."

"Right. Text me when you're done."

In a small voice, she asked, "Where will you be?"

"An old buddy of mine just arrived. Once I make sure he's

settled, I intend to track Liz down so I can meet my future brother-in-law."

With a wave, he loped down the steps and walked away.

No banging, no shouting. No blame. It eased some of the pressure in her chest.

Bag in hand, hand over her mouth, she bolted into the guest cottage.

12

Rattled by Grace's unexpected presence on the island, Jim hovered in the morning shadows at the end of the hallway and watched the seconds tick past on his wristwatch.

He needed his new putter. If he had any chance of improving his game, he had to sneak back into the bedroom and retrieve it.

What was she doing here today? Her schedule—the one that was planned nearly a year in advance, the one that her nice young assistant always made sure he had a copy of so that he could plan his schedule around it—had clearly shown that she wasn't supposed to fly home until the morning of Liz's wedding, then head right back to the Mainland that same night.

Thirty minutes later, he finally got up the nerve to open the bedroom door, and peek through the crack in the doorway.

She was sleeping on her stomach, her face buried in the pillow, the soft womanly snore cute and sexy. There was safety in the fact that she was dead to the world. Once asleep, Grace had the uncanny ability to sleep through anything.

He slipped into the room and headed toward the corner of the room where he'd stuck the putter.

Gone.

Jim frowned. He couldn't remember putting it away, but in case his mind had vacated, he went to search through his closet.

Still nothing.

He stood up, hands on hips, and swept the room with his gaze. And when he found himself engrossed in the sexy curve of Grace's neck, he turned his back on her and headed toward the walk-in closet that was hers.

Inside, he pushed aside the boxes that lined the top shelf, searching, then when he couldn't find it there, he started on the bottom of the closet, hoping against hope that she'd simply thought to outsmart him by sticking the thing in a corner, then forgetting about it.

Although Grace didn't forget about much. And she didn't let him forget either.

He could feel his blood pressure rise and his heart begin to pound. As he pushed aside a silky nightgown that he hadn't seen Grace in for more years than he could count, he inhaled a deep calming breath.

With his nose buried in the soft material and his hand blindly searching the back of the closet, he inhaled the unique scent of his often absent wife. His erection returned in full force.

He was getting turned on. And with her in residence, too. That would never do.

He stopped breathing, although by now the scent had filled his brain, and burrowed further into the closet until his fingers wrapped around the handle of a golf club. Bingo.

Holding his breath, Jim backed out of the closet, ignoring the scent that tickled body parts that hadn't been tickled in years.

Putter gripped in his hand, Jim schlepped out of the closet, tiptoed through the bedroom, and headed outside where he climbed on his golf cart and sped toward the course. He didn't stop until he reached the first green where he was enveloped by the peace and quiet all around him.

Jim set up the ball, lined up his shot, and caressed the ball with the putter. It zinged to the left and ended up in the shrubs surrounding the course. He tossed another ball on the green, lined up for another shot, and—

"Here you are."

His body jerked. His shot went wild. The ball flew toward the nearest water trap. "Geez, Harry."

"Sorry, old man."

Jim rounded on the other men. "Couldn't you wait until I finished swinging?"

"We've got a surprise for you," Ned said.

"A belated birthday gift," Andy added.

Grumbling under his breath, he said, "All I want is a little peace and quiet, and some time to practice my swing."

Harry interrupted his tirade. "We've got something that'll help with that."

With the head of his putter, Jim nudged another half dozen balls into a line. "What could possibly be better?"

"Our surprise."

He lifted his head, glanced at his friends, saw Ned poke Andy in the ribs as in unison, all three mens' attention turned toward the path coming out of the trees. Jim followed their gaze.

A young woman with long tawny hair appeared. She picked her way over the gravel along the path, stepped onto the first hole green, and headed toward him, the spikes of her high heeled shoes leaving an indent in the grass.

"You're ruining the green," he ground out.

She peered over her shoulder, then bent down and pulled off one shoe, then the other. Her tank top pulled away from her chest, giving him an excellent view down the front of her top. Her short shorts rode up her thighs and he felt something in him uniquely male stir.

Twice in one day.

His heart did a flip flop.

If he didn't get his frustration—and these sexual urges—under control, he was going to be a dead man before the end of the day.

She straightened, holding the shoes by the heels in one hand. "Better?"

He gritted his teeth. "Much."

She turned a wide smile on the other men. "Hi, boys."

"Gisele," they all said at the same time and when Jim looked over at them, he could've sworn he saw them preening.

He turned his attention back to her, gave her a narrow eyed, suspicious look. This woman was breaking his number one rule. "Is there something I can do for you?"

"Harry and the boys didn't tell you?"

Harry and the boys. He turned back to them and they were all ogling her like a bunch of junior high, sex-starved boys. "No."

She stuck one hand on her hip and sashayed toward him. "I'm your birthday present, Jim."

For a second, his thoughts hit the gutter and he envisioned an act so naughty, he was certain his heart would give out before the dirty deed was even done. Then he cleared away the images, eyed the ball on the ground, and gave it a tap with his putter. "My birthday was last month."

"I know." Her ultra sultry voice sent a shiver up his spine. "Forgive me. This was the earliest I could pull myself away from the circuit."

Despite her close proximity, he held his ground, refusing to be cowed by this young woman. "The circuit?"

She stopped inches from him and dropped her shoes on the green where one of the heels dug into the soft ground. "The pro circuit, Jim. Happy birthday. I'm your new golf instructor."

Something in his chest squeezed tight, forcing the air from his lungs, and for a split second, he figured he'd died and gone to heaven. But then he heard the sound of his wife's voice in the distance, and he took a deep breath and exhaled.

Life on the stock market floor had certainly been a lot less stressful.

13

Grace wasn't certain what she needed to do to get Jim's attention off the golf course. But she did know that she needed help if she was going to succeed...even if she didn't necessarily relish the help she'd enlisted.

Which was why the three women approaching her were both welcome and unwelcome.

But this was better than losing her temper as she so often did these days. Imbalanced hormones. Lack of sleep. Lack of sex. Any one of those could be responsible for the fact that she could go from a cool-headed business woman to insane in under three-point-five seconds.

"Good morning, Grace," Leta Johnson sang out as she crossed the pool area to the patio where Grace was enjoying a tall glass of iced lemon water. "We heard you were back on the island."

She pasted a polite smile on her face. "News travels fast."

Nancy Strom pulled a cigarette out of her pocket and stuck it between her lips. "We're also surprised you called us. What do you want?"

Sandy Strom stopped beside her sister-in-law, yanked the cigarette from her mouth, dropped it onto the patio tiles, and squashed it below the heel of her flip flop. "Never mind her," she explained as she turned a sunny smile on Grace. "She's annoyed because her receptionist quit, and now Ned expects her to answer—"

"—every frigging call at the office while he spends his time on the golf course." Nancy gave her sister-in-law a dirty look, bent to pick up the ruined cigarette, and shoved it in her pocket. "Yeah, well, unlike some people I know, I don't sit around the house eating bonbons while their husband is off playing golf. I have to work hard for my money."

"Stop it, you two." Leta shouldered her way between them. "I heard Jim was late for his game yesterday morning. Cost him a pile of cash, too."

Grace turned her gaze toward the golf course. In the distance, she could see the four men gathered around the first tee, wallets out, money exchanging hands. "It did?"

"Uh huh." Curiosity flitted through Nancy's gaze. "You have heard of his fifth rule, haven't you?"

Grace attempted to clear the frown that tugged at her brows, but by the look on the other three faces, she could tell it was too late to pretend. With a sigh, she asked, "What rule?"

The three women exchanged a look, which probably meant that they wondered why the perfect married couple didn't share details about the thing that was most important in the other person's life. Gosh, she had to work harder at that.

Sandy piped up. "Rule number five. No being late to the game or it costs a thousand big ones."

Nancy glanced over her shoulder toward the course and smirked. "Right now, Jim is paying them each a thousand bucks. I see a shopping spree in my near future."

As silence swelled around them, Leta dropped onto the chair beside her and grasped her hand.

"Is everything all right, Grace?"

For a moment, Grace just stared down at their joined hands.

The physical contact caught her off guard. In fact, it felt so good, she wanted to reach out with her other hand and make contact with it too.

A tiny sob worked its way up her throat, and as she swallowed it back, she extracted her hand from Leta's. "Of course it is. Why do you ask?"

Sandy moved to her side and bent down to envelop Grace in a hug. It was everything that Grace could do to stop herself from wrenching out of the other woman's arms before she hugged her back. "Honey, we're here for you."

"Thank you," she said quietly because what else could she say? *Please, be my friends?* She forced a smile. "Are you coming to Liz's engagement party?"

"Wouldn't miss it for the world," Nancy said as she reached in her pocket, produced another cigarette, and sent her sister-in-law a dirty look before she refocused on her hostess. "So why did you call us?"

"I—uh—" Out of the corner of her eyes, she saw Jim leave the course and drive toward the house on his golf cart. Grace pushed to her feet and started to back toward the house. "I wanted to say hello, that's all. Well, gotta go. There's a wedding calling my name."

And as the three women stared after her, Grace turned on her heel and fled into the house.

Was she that obvious? That lonely that she was even considering spilling her guts to the three women who were virtually strangers?

She leaned against the wall and peered out the patio doors until they'd disappeared from sight.

In a weak moment she'd called them and invited them over for a visit. Big mistake. Huge mistake. One she vowed never to make again.

By the time that she walked into the master bedroom, Jim was hunched over the keyboard, tapping at the keyboard. He didn't even bother to acknowledge her presence.

"I ran into Leta, Nancy, and Sandy," she said in an effort to open up some kind of communication between them.

"Nice women," he muttered.

She stared at his back, hating the deafening silence that always seemed to hover around them, except when they were in public and had to put on a happy show. "I think Stone is attracted to Liz's wedding planner."

"Pretty girl." He tapped on a couple of keys and the screen filled with letters and numbers and code that she couldn't even pretend to comprehend.

He was lost in his own little world again. It was as though she hadn't been gone for the last month.

From the depths of her bra, her phone beeped, and she pulled it out to check the message.

It was from Liz. *Seamstress here for dress fitting.*

Grace silenced the phone and headed for the bathroom where she pulled off the summer dress she'd put on that morning, the one with damp patches under her arms, tossed it into the laundry basket, and padded over to the mirror where she studied her body.

Not too bad for fifty-seven. A little plump, but then she'd always been on the plump side, even when she was young. The extra padding had once served her image as homemaker and wife and mother extremely well.

But most important of all, the number one reason that she'd never really bothered to lose those extra twenty pounds was because Jim had once told her that he liked his women with a little extra weight.

Grace leaned back slightly, till she was able to look past the doorframe at her husband's back.

He was a good looking man—tall, firm, a fifty-five-year-old hunk who still caught the eye of women half his age. If there'd been one thing she could always count on throughout their thirty years together, it was the sex. He'd always desired her, always been faithful to her. But this last year, it seemed he'd lost all interest in her and sex combined in the same thought pattern.

Was it the thickening of her waistline or something else entirely?

Dressed only in her bra and panties, she padded silently out of the bathroom to stand behind him and look over his shoulder. "What are you doing?" she asked, simply because she hated the deathly silence that always seemed to hover around them.

He glanced over his shoulder and met her eyes before his gaze swept over her barely covered body. Then without even a hint of emotion, he turned back to the screen and tapped more keys, and more code spread across the screen. "Nothing that would interest you."

This wasn't how she wanted to spend the next three days, alone in bed, alone in the house. She laid one hand on his shoulder, gave it a squeeze, and leaned into his back. "Jim, I'm going to lay down and have a—ummm—nap."

His body tensed beneath her touch. "Fine. I'll wrap this up and get out of your way."

Grace removed her hand and stared down at the top of his head, sorrow welling up from deep inside her. They had nothing in common anymore. It was like he didn't care about anything but golf and computers.

She turned and climbed into their big bed. Alone and lonely.

Grace stared at his back, willing him to come to her and make love to her with all the passion that they'd shared in the early days of their relationship. But the only movement was his fingers flying across the keyboard.

He should have been jumping her bones by now, because she'd been away from home for an unusually long time. Or maybe they'd never had anything between them but the sex.

Maybe that wasn't enough for him anymore. Maybe it wasn't enough for her either.

She closed her eyes and listened to the click of the keyboard, the whir of the computer. And then there was only silence.

Grace didn't have to open her eyes to know that he was gone. She felt it in the hollow pit of her stomach, in the ache behind her eyelids, in the pounding of her heart.

She pushed out of bed and headed to the closet to find something comfortable to wear for Liz's dress fitting. Halfway there, she felt a tear escape the corner of one eye, and she sat down on the edge of the bed to have a good cry.

Just once, she wanted Jim's attention.

Just once, she wanted to know that she was more important than that stupid game of golf.

Just once, she wanted reassurance that the life they'd built together hadn't been for naught.

14

Stone headed down the pathway toward the cottages on the east end of the estate. All he wanted to do was shut off all thoughts of babies and marriage and sexy wedding planners. In fact, he'd been so self-involved that he'd barely given Liz—and the reason he was here—the attention she deserved.

When he reached the Eight-For-Mulligan cottage, he bounded up the steps and knocked on the door. Kevin Donahue, his best friend from way back, answered the door. "Hey, Kev, great to see you."

The other man stepped onto the deck, wrapped him in a bear hug, then gestured toward the chairs. "Thanks for letting me crash here."

"No problem." Stone sat down. "How long are you staying?"

"A few days. Then I ship out again."

The crunch of footsteps on the pebble path alerted him to someone's approach. Stone saw Mariam and Dora stroll along the path toward them. Dora held Mariam's toddler as though she might never let him go.

If Stephanie was pregnant, he had no doubt that the child

would be welcome into both families with open arms. He, on the other hand, would probably be put in front of a firing squad.

Stephanie's mom appeared to be doing most of the talking, which he'd discovered that she was very good at, while Mariam...

Mariam looked like she wasn't eating, wasn't taking care of herself, and it worried him. Her divorce had been the toughest case he'd ever handled, mainly because he'd hated to see her in a world of hurt.

And Liz wanted to marry some guy she'd barely known for more than a few weeks. Unlike their mother, *she* didn't have a career that depended on hiding an unhappy marriage. So if things didn't go well, he'd find himself with her in his office, asking him to represent her in a divorce.

It had nearly killed Stone to watch Mariam go through her painful divorce. He wanted to protect Liz from her own foolish jump into the matrimony pool.

As the women approached the cabin, Mariam glanced up. Her warm smile vanquished the sadness from her face. "Stone, what are you doing way out here?"

Kevin slowly pushed to his feet. "Hello, Mariam."

Mariam's gaze went to the other man and as she changed course toward the cottage, Dora at her side, she cocked her head. "I'm sorry. Do I know you?"

A small smile escaped Kevin. "Kevin Donahue."

"The pest?" she exclaimed and laughed. Her cheeks flushed, vanquishing the wanness from her complexion. "I'm sorry. That was mean. I was mean."

He shrugged and the smile changed to self-conscious and unsure. "Yeah, you kinda were."

Stone glanced between the two of them, and as the silence stretched, he came to his feet.

At the same moment, Dora came up the steps, the toddler in one arm, and grabbed Kevin's hand. "I'm Dora Goodwin."

Kevin shook her hand. "Hello, Ma'am."

She beamed at Stone. "I was just telling your sister about Morty and Elvira's wedding." She turned her attention to the other man. "It's where Stone met my Stephanie, you know."

Stone felt Kevin's gaze on him and he glanced toward the other man to explain. "Liz's wedding planner."

Jim Junior reached out his chubby arms and when the toddler screamed for his attention, Stone took him from Dora's arms. "How are you doing, little man?"

Dora reluctantly released him into Stone's arms. "Do you like babies, Stone? Stephanie loves children. Someday she'll be a great mother. All she needs to do is find the right man."

He recalled how terrified she'd been when he'd rescued her from Mariam's baby, and he bit back a smile. "I'm sure she will be."

"Why I remember when Stephanie was born. Tom and I were scared we'd break her." Dora turned her attention to Mariam. "I love babies. As I was telling Stone earlier, I want lots and lots of grand babies. Is Liz planning to start a family right away?"

Mariam shrugged. "I believe her and Roger have decided to wait a while."

"They are young. It's better to have time alone with your new spouse before the demands of little one's become priority." Dora slid her hand over Stone's and gave it a friendly squeeze. "Stephanie is at the prime age for having children."

Stone resisted the urge to squirm. "Yes, Ma'am."

If Stephanie was pregnant, he only hoped he turned out to be half the father Tom Goodwin appeared to be. He attempted to push the thought away, determined not to think of babies and all things related to the possibility of fatherhood. Although until Stephanie took the pregnancy test, he doubted he'd have much success.

Mariam's phone buzzed and she glanced down at the screen, then peered up at Dora. "Liz is having her dress fitting and wants me to rescue her from Mother's interference. Would you like to join us?"

"I would love to." The older woman reached for the toddler. "Here, let me take him off your hands."

Stone released the boy into her arms, then watched as she dabbed at the drool running down the toddler's chin, ignoring the drool marks that made their way onto the shoulder of her blouse.

Before Mariam turned away, she smiled up at Kevin. There was a light in her eyes that hadn't been there since before the divorce. "I guess I'll see you around."

Kevin shoved his hands into the front pockets of his jeans, his gaze never once leaving the woman on the path. "I'll be here till the end of the week."

And as they left, Stone eyed his best friend and noticed the way the other man's gaze followed Mariam's progress. "Is there something going on between you and my sister?"

Kevin blinked and as he turned to face him, his cheeks flushed with color. "No, of course not."

Stone didn't believe him. "Because if there is, I know I can't stop you. But she's been hurt before, really badly, and the last thing I want to see her do is jump into an affair while she's vulnerable and still hurting."

The other man's gaze turned opaque. "You have nothing to worry about, man. She doesn't see me that way."

Unwilling to correct the other man, Stone pulled out his cell. "I'll catch you later, bud. There's something I need to do."

Meeting Liz's fiancee would have to wait till later.

Right now, he felt the need to rescue the woman who might be the mother of his child.

15

Stephanie needed a nap.

But instead, as Liz stood behind the divider changing, the seamstress assisting her, she reviewed her To-Do list, of which there were far too many things to do in such a short time. She'd have to be a miracle worker to get everything done. Maybe it was a good thing that her mom had tagged along to help.

Liz came out from behind the divider, drawing her attention. "What do you think?"

Stephanie walked around the pedestal so she could see the gown from all sides. Despite the blood red color of the silky material, and the entrails sewn into the lace, the color suited Liz's black hair and matched the red stripe that wound through her hair. "The gown is beautiful and you look gorgeous."

"Thank you." Liz smoothed her hand over the delicate fabric. "I can't wait for my friends to see me in it."

Stephanie frowned.

There it was again. Not the groom, but her friends.

The bit of concern that had plagued Stephanie earlier

returned full force. She swallowed it back and maintained her smile.

Liz grimaced. "I'm sure Mother will find fault, though. Nothing is right unless she has complete control over the job."

Stephanie's phone buzzed. She glanced down at the screen and saw a message from Stone.

How is the dress fitting going?

"Excuse me. Another client." She turned her back on the bride. *Liz looks beautiful, well, except for the blood and guts on her gown, so no worries.*

Grace Kincaid will find fault.

Exactly what Liz said.

There was a tap of heels in the hallway outside the room. Glancing up, she saw Grace come through the open doorway. A moment later, Mariam and Dora followed her in.

Keeping one eye on the new arrivals, she typed, *Are you on your way to rescue your sister?*

I'm afraid of my mom, remember? Liz is on her own.

Stephanie snickered. *Chicken.*

But I'll man up and come rescue you.

She could almost hear the husky tone of his voice and she repressed a shiver. Wow, if a text could turn her knees to mush, she was in deep trouble.

Her fingers flew over the keypad. *Sweet, but I don't need to be rescued. Don't worry. If I can't handle your mom, my mom will help out. You can go hide under your bed.*

Dora stopped beside her and squinted at the small screen. "Who are you texting?"

"Nobody." Stephanie tucked away the phone before her mom could see the messages. "Where have you been?"

"Mariam gave me the grand tour. And Grace gave me my own guest cottage. Isn't that lovely?"

She angled a look at her mom. "So you're serious about abandoning Dad?"

Dora frowned. "I'm not abandoning your father. If he can't do without me for a day or two, then we've lived our married life wrong." With the back of her hand, she checked Stephanie's forehead. "You look like the walking dead." She lowered her voice and glanced toward the bride. "Although truth be told, your paleness fits in perfectly with the wedding theme."

"I'm okay, Mom. If there's a break in my schedule, I'll lie down and have a nap."

"Good. Well, since I'm here to help, tell me what you want me to do."

Stephanie checked the list on her phone. "There's a delivery of flowers today at two. The plan is on my tablet. If you could make sure all of the flowers are here and set up properly, I'd really appreciate it."

"Lovely. This is an excellent warm up for Mandy's wedding preparations."

Stephanie touched her mother's arm to regain her attention. "Mom, I'm worried—"

And just like that, Dora refocused on her. "I knew something was wrong. It's not just the flu, is it? What's going on with you?"

"Don't you think Mandy's wedding is too soon? She barely knows Dane."

Her mom blinked, clearly startled. "They grew up right across the street from each other."

"Yeah, but they were kids. They barely know each other now."

Her mom leaned closer. "Honey, what are you really worried about? Is it that nice lawyer?"

"No, Mom. This had nothing to do with Stone. I don't want Mandy to get hurt. I mean, I've seen so many disappointed brides. I give them the fairytale wedding, and in the morning instead of waking next to their prince, they realize they're sleeping with a frog."

"Your sister is very much like you—well, except for the fact that she can talk to Grandpa George. Mandy is smart and practical and independent. She's not going to let a man pull the wool over her eyes." Dora patted Stephanie's cheek. "I've always trusted her to make the right choice, just like I've trusted you."

"But Mom—"

Her mom put the tips of her fingers against Stephanie's mouth. "Do me a favor and keep your doubts to yourself. And if in five or ten years, your sister is miserable, you can say *I told you so*."

She pushed her mom's hand away. "Fine. I'll be quiet for now, but I swear, if Dane tries to sleep with any of the bridesmaids—"

Dora chortled. "Dane? Oh my, you know nothing about your future brother-in-law."

"I swear, I'll rat on him, Mom."

"If you catch him trying to sleep with a bridesmaid, you have my permission to spoil your sister's wedding." Dora got a calculated look in her eyes. "Now, about your lawyer."

"He's not my lawyer."

"But he could be." She reached out and pinched Stephanie's cheeks, then smoothed back a strand of hair. "All you have to do is put on a sexy dress and some makeup, and before you know it, he'll be popping the question."

"I don't want him to pop the question."

"But he likes you." Her mom eyed her. "And I can tell you like him too."

"Maybe a little," she hedged. She pressed her lips together before she revealed something her mom could really sink her teeth into, and gestured toward the bride. "The mother-of-the-bride doesn't appear to like Liz's dress."

Dora tsked, instantly distracted by the storm brewing between the bride and her mother. "You take it easy for a few minutes. I'll go play mediator."

And then she was gone, headed toward the circle around the bride.

Hearing another sound at the doorway, Stephanie looked

over her shoulder, and there stood Stone, his phone in his hands, an unreadable expression on his face as he met her gaze. He bent his head to the phone, and started typing.

The seamstress came to stand beside her. Her gaze slid to Stephanie's chest. "Your sister called about scheduling you in for a fitting, so I brought the bridesmaid dress for you to try on today."

"Wonderful. I'm looking forward to seeing it."

The seamstress's gaze slid to her chest again. "She told me you were the same size. It looks like we may need to do some unexpected alterations."

Stephanie resisted the urge to hunch her shoulders and make her chest smaller, and when her cell buzzed yet again, she backed away with an apologetic smile. "Excuse me, I need to reply to this."

Stephanie turned her back on the seamstress and glanced at the screen.

I think we should take the test sooner than later. The suspense is killing me. Isn't it killing you?

Of course it was killing her, but she didn't have the time to be distracted, not right now. She quickly put some distance between her and the seamstress, and plopped down on an armchair. As Stone took the chair next to her, she typed, *Forget the test. The seamstress wants to know why my breasts are bigger than my sister's, since Mandy told her we were the same size.*

She glanced up at the other women in the room, but they were all focused on Liz who stood in frozen anticipation. She snuck a glance toward Stone. He had his head down, staring at the screen, a ghost of a smile flirting with the edges of his mouth while he typed.

When he looked over at her, her phone buzzed and she checked his message.

I thought they looked bigger, but I didn't want to say anything for fear you might think I didn't like them before.

She snickered, then glanced up to see everyone watching her. She waved her phone at them. "This bride is a real jokester. Every time I'm around her, it's a laugh riot."

She returned her attention to the phone, holding it closer to her chest so no one could see, and typed, *No wonder I fell into bed with you. You're a smooth talker. Now go away. You're distracting me. Didn't you want to meet the groom?*

Right.

But he didn't move. She tucked the phone away, pushed to her feet, and as she headed toward the circle of women, she was conscious of his gaze drilling into her back.

The mother-of-the-bride's gaze darted from her son to Stephanie and back. As her eyes narrowed, Stephanie forced a warm smile. "So what do you think of Liz's gown? Isn't it fabulous?"

False sincerity dripped from each word. "Fabulous indeed. I love it."

Liz grabbed the full skirt, hiked it up to her knees, and stepped off the raised platform to face Grace directly. "Mom, what do you mean, you like my dress?"

"Why, it's lovely, dear. In fact, Stephanie is doing such a wonderful job, I want to offer her a job on my *Eternally Yours* show."

A heartbeat of silence filled the room. Beside her, Dora gasped and clapped her hands to her chest. "You want my Stephanie to work with you?"

Grace's smile reminded her of a shark approaching its prey. "Yes."

"Well, of course she will."

As both women turned to her, her phone buzzed and she glanced down to see a two word message from Stone. *Say no.*

"Please, call me Grace," the mother-of-the-bride said as she brushed a piece of lint off her sleeve. "I'll have my assistant draw up the contract right away. You can look it over, sign, and you'll be my employee within the hour."

Working on the *Eternally Yours* show would be a dream come true. Stephanie smiled at her hostess. "Thank you, Mrs. Kincaid... Grace. I don't know what to say, but I'll definitely consider your offer."

Liz stamped her feet, regaining everyone's attention. "Mother, what's wrong with my dress?"

Grace gave her a loving smile which didn't quite reach her eyes. "Absolutely nothing, dear. As Stephanie said, it's absolutely fabulous."

Liz looked down at the gown and mumbled, "If my mother likes it, something must be wrong with it."

Behind her, Stone's phone buzzed, and as Grace reached into one pocket, and handed a piece of paper to Stephanie, she could see him out the corner of her eye thumbing the screen.

"Since we didn't finish discussing the guest list, I took it upon myself to invite a few of my closest friends."

Stephanie glanced at the long list, then silently passed it to Liz.

As Stone turned to leave, Stephanie's phone buzzed and she glanced down at it.

Text me when you're done and we'll do the test together. And remember...before you sign any contract my mother gives you, we're going over it together, word by word and every nuance in-between.

She thumbed a message back. *I've changed my mind. I'm not doing the test.*

He paused in the open doorway, his steady gaze on her face before he refocused on his phone. *Not taking the test won't change the results.*

Stephanie heard the bride hiss, and sent one last message. *But sticking my head in the sand helps me stay focused on your sister's wedding. Now please go away.*

She tucked the phone into her pocket and turned her back on him.

Liz waved the note in her face. "We wanted this wedding to be a simple affair. Family, a few close friends, and that's it."

Grace folded her hands in front of her. "I'll pay for my share of the guests."

"That's not the point, Mother." Liz turned away in frustration and started to tug at the gown to get it off. The seamstress jumped up to help her.

"What's the big deal, Liz? It's not as if I'm asking you and Roger to foot the bill."

"It's not the cost."

Stephanie took the list back from Liz and intervened. "The guest list is going to be awfully one sided now."

Grace waved a hand. "Tell Roger to invite more of his family. Second, third, forth cousins. The more the merrier. I'll even pay."

Liz growled. "There are no cousins. No parents, no aunt and uncles. Nobody but a few of his closest musician buddies."

Grace raised one brow. "Well, it's too late. I've already invited them so you'll just have to make do."

Then she turned and walked out of the room.

In a small voice, Liz said, "Roger is going to be so upset."

Stephanie patted her client's arm. "He loves you. It will be okay."

Liz began to tug off the gown. "I can't do this right now. It will have to wait till later."

"But Liz, the wedding is only three days away."

"Screw the wedding. I should've agreed to elope, like Roger wanted to. Now I'm stuck with—" She ripped the list out of Stephanie's hand and crumpled it in her fist. "—this."

The moment the younger woman had the gown off, she dropped it into a pile on the floor and ran out of the room. The seamstress carefully gathered it up and said, "We weren't done the fitting."

Stephanie took a deep, calming breath. "I'll have her back here tomorrow at noon. Can we reschedule?"

The seamstress nodded. "Fine. I can fit you for your bridesmaid's gown now. Strip to your bra and panties, and we'll see how it all fits."

Dora frowned after Liz. "I should check to see how she's doing."

As her mom headed out of the room, Stephanie reached for the hem of her top and wondered how she could hide the growing bulge of her stomach.

Or maybe she wouldn't have to. Maybe it was just a false alarm.

She stripped down to her bra and panties. A moment later, the gown dropped and settled with a sweet swish over her body.

"Turn around and I'll button you up."

She sucked in her belly, but the buttons pulled everywhere. Her cheeks flared with heat. "I've recently put on a little weight."

With a tsk, the other woman bent her head and examined the waist and bust of the gown. "It's going to have to be let out here and here and here." Her dark gaze rose to meet Stephanie's and she lowered her voice. "I get it. You haven't told anyone yet. Our little secret then. I'll add some panels for expansion. But we'll have to get you in for a final fitting right before the wedding."

"Thank you."

"No problem." She directed Stephanie to the pedestal, then knelt at her feet. Around a mouthful of pins, she said, "It's what those of us in the wedding industry do, right? Nothing, absolutely nothing, should spoil the bride's wedding day."

Stephanie smiled down at the top of the other woman's head. "I'm sure it's a false alarm. Just pre-period bloat, but I don't want to say anything until I know for sure."

But she feared that in another few months, the situation would be even worse. The dress wouldn't fit in the waist or the chest. Probably not in the butt area either.

The seamstress stood up, examined her work, and rubbed her hands together. "There, done. Now be careful when you pull it off. You don't want to get stuck with a pin."

Stephanie gently removed the gown and redressed. The moment the seamstress had left the room, she sighed and placed her palm against her stomach.

Every time Stone came near, her body recognized him, and her insides began to hum. She feared she wasn't just in trouble with the possible pregnancy, but that her heart might be getting involved.

Sinking into the armchair, she blindly stared at the cell screen and the lists and lists of things still to do. More guests meant more seating, more food, more of everything.

The wedding had seemed so simple. Life had seemed so simple. Now she had to deal with a high-strung bride, a troublesome mother-of-the-bride, and the possibility of being pregnant.

She cleared her mind and set to work, texting, emailing, phoning. By the time she was finished arranging everything for the extra guests, the evening shadows had darkened the room, and there was only one thing left to do.

She texted Stone.

My cabin or yours?

16

After Stone left Stephanie and the dress fitting behind, he stuffed his phone into the front pocket of his trousers, and followed the steady throb of a bass guitar to the far end of the estate where the Nine-For-Loft cottage sat nestled among the trees.

He banged on the door, and when no one answered, peered through the front window.

Liz's fiancee stood in the middle of the room, headphones on, eyes closed, guitar slung over one shoulder, oblivious to everything but the noise he made.

With a disgusted shake of his head, Stone tromped down the steps, pulled out his phone to check for Stephanie's text, then stuffed the device away. He needed to ignore his phone until it buzzed so he could get some work done.

Hours later, with Wanda working quietly at his kitchen table, and Kevin sitting on his couch killing time, Stone found himself distracted for the umpteenth time.

If there was a baby on the way, he wanted to share in the responsibility of raising their child. But he also wanted to avoid the emotional complications of a relationship.

He'd seen other couples do it, some successfully, some not quite so successfully, but if Stephanie and him could come to some kind of agreement, then it would all work out.

It *had to* work out.

And yet, he couldn't help but wonder what it would be like to wake up every morning with her at his side, her body changing with the growth of their child.

He checked the phone for the umpteenth time, and when it vibrated in his hand, he saw Stephanie's message and jumped to his feet. "Sorry. I—uh—have something I need to take care of."

Kevin shifted on the armchair across from him, his face in shadows, his long frame slouched. "Go, man. It's not like I need you to stick around and hold my hand."

"Sorry, Kev. You know I wouldn't dump you unless it was really important."

The corner of Kevin's mouth crooked up. "Is she hot?"

A flush worked up his neck and into his face, and he rubbed the back of his neck. "Yeah."

Wanda stood up, her oval face dour. "Why are all men pigs?"

With a grin, Stone headed for the door. "Because if we weren't, we'd be irresistible all of the time."

"Right." She lowered her voice and hissed, "Do I have to entertain him?"

From behind, Kevin drawled, "I'm okay. I don't need a babysitter, just a place to chill for a few days."

A knock sounded on the door.

Maybe he'd taken too long and she'd brought the pregnancy test to his cabin. He hoped not. He didn't want to explain that to his assistant or best friend. Let them believe it was all about sex.

He opened the front door and there stood Liz, poised to knock again.

Her gaze darted past him and her eyes opened wide. "Oh, I'm sorry, I didn't realize you had company."

He peered around her. "Where's your fiancee?"

"He's working on a super cool idea for a new song." She gave him a huge smile and slid past him inside. "So I thought I'd come hang out with my favorite brother."

Stone eyed her with suspicion. "I was just on my way out."

She gave him another sunny smile, turned her back on him, and then did a fake *startled*. "Hi Kevin. I didn't see you standing there."

Kevin thrust his hands into the front pockets of his jeans, and eyes hooded, nodded. "Hi Squirt. Good to see you again."

She sidled closer in his direction. "Good to see you, too."

Stone suddenly had a bad feeling in his gut. "Liz, I was about to leave."

She waved one hand in the air, never taking her eyes off Kevin, and dropped onto the couch. "Don't let me hold you back. I'll keep Kevin company while you're gone."

"Oh good." Wanda headed for the door. "I was beginning to worry I'd have to make small talk."

And with that, she brushed past him and disappeared out the door, heading in the direction of her own cabin.

Stone's cell vibrated again.

Where are you?

He texted back *hold on*. "Liz, maybe you should come back later."

Without looking his way, she waved him off. "Go. I'll catch up with Kevin while you're gone. You don't mind, do you, Kevin?"

A corner of his mouth kicked up. "So what grade are you in now, Squirt?"

Stone's cell vibrated again. He angled his hand up so he could read the display.

It's not important you be here.

Yes it is. I'm coming. Just hold on till I get there. "Kev?"

"Yeah, man, go ahead. We're good here."

His phone vibrated.

116

Don't bother. Just like certain other things, I can take care of this without needing the assistance of a man.

Without another word, Stone rushed out and raced across the clearing to Stephanie's cabin. As he loped up the steps, he felt a noose tighten around his neck.

With his grandma's wedding ring in his pocket, he had to still the urge to run away like a coward.

A baby? It was the last thing either of them wanted.

He knocked on the door and listened for her footsteps.

If the test came out positive, they'd have to have a heart to heart talk. About what he wanted from her, what she could expect in return.

Despite the severity of his situation, his blood stirred with desire. They wouldn't have any problems in the bedroom. But he knew they couldn't spend their life in bed. At some point, they'd have to deal with each other out of the bedroom.

Stone knocked again. When he still didn't hear a sound, he started to get concerned. He tested the doorknob and found it unlocked

What if something had happened to her? What if something had happened to the baby? If she miscarried, all of their problems would be taken care of.

He shoved away the thought, twisted the knob, pushed open the door and saw Stephanie sitting on the couch, her arms crossed over her chest, her gaze fixed on the pharmacy bag sitting on the coffee table in front of her.

The scrunched up expression on her face got scrunchier. "What took you so long?"

She was feeling bitchy. He understood that and forced a smile as he took a single step over the threshold. "I had unexpected company."

Her gaze lifted slowly to his face. "In bed or the other thing?"

"The other thing?"

117

"Yeah, you know, the part where you rip apart a marriage and forever put the once loving couple forever at war?"

He moved further into the room. "You do realize people wanting a divorce come looking for me, not the other way around?"

"Right," she muttered, and as her gaze returned to the bag, she almost looked disappointed. "Go away. I've changed my mind."

Stone came all the way inside and shut the door behind him. "It's too late for that, sweetheart."

"No, it's not. I know my body." She lifted her gaze to his face and there was desperation in her eyes. "This definitely feels more like the flu than a pregnancy."

"Have you ever been pregnant before?"

Silence met his question, and he wondered what was going on in her head.

All he knew for certain was that she was scared, as scared as he was, and the realization eased something within him, helped to calm him down. He crossed to the coffee table, picked up the bag, and held out one hand for her to take. "Shall we get this over and done with? Find out whether we're going to be tied together for life?"

17

As a bubble of panic worked its way up her throat, Stephanie stilled the urge to run away like a coward.

A baby? She twisted the material of her dress in her hands and stared up him. "In case you didn't notice, I'm no good with kids."

"Oh, I noticed all right." He came closer. "In case *you* didn't notice, I'm very good with kids."

A sad pang deflated her heart.

This had never been in her life's plan.

Her gaze lifted slowly to his face.

He had never been in her life's plan.

Her gaze returned to the bag. If he slept with another woman, it would be easy to get rid of him. But when he was being so nice...

Stephanie pushed up from the couch to her feet, the urge to cower in a corner and run away almost overwhelming. But Stone stood there, the bag now in his hand, supportive and brave. She took a deep breath and held out her hand. "Just so we understand each other, there is no tied together for life."

"We'll discuss that after you take the test."

A knock sounded at the door. Stephanie grabbed the bag from him and shoved it behind a cushion just as the door swung open and her mom stepped inside.

"Oh, excuse me, I didn't realize you had company." With a twinkle in her eyes, she backed up a step. "I'll leave you two alone. Is two hours enough or should I stay away longer?"

Stephanie sighed. "Nothing is going on, Mom."

"Just don't let your father catch you two alone. You know how protective he is of you girls." With a wave, her mom left, locking and shutting the door behind herself.

Stephanie glared after her. "She's not going to give up, you know. And if it turns out I'm pregnant..."

He had the audacity to laugh. "According to your dad, she hates divorce lawyers. So if you want to stop her matchmaking attempts, just tell her I'm the king of divorce lawyers."

"You wouldn't mind?"

He crossed the room, placed one hand on her stomach, and softly said, "Not if it takes the pressure off you."

For just a moment, she let herself get lost in the feel of his hand, protective over her abdomen, the warmth of his body, urging her to move closer, the kindness in his gaze that always took her breath away and made her wish for the impossible.

Stephanie broke the physical contact, grabbed the bag and headed down the hallway to the bathroom, conscious of him following her. As she reached the doorway and stopped, he bumped into her and placed his hands on her shoulders.

"It'll be negative."

"Sure. Right." She turned to face him and had to raise her chin to look up at him. There was a breathless moment when she thought something passed between them, but then it was gone and he stepped back.

"I'll leave you alone to—uh—"

Right, the king of divorce didn't do relationships any more

than she did. And even though he looked calm, he must be freaking out inside. "Yeah, I've got it."

"I'll wait—uh—" He pointed to the floor right where he stood. "Right here."

"In the living room would be better." She stared at him and he stared back. Finally, she sighed. "I'm not going to disappear out the bathroom window."

"Promise?"

With a grumble, she turned her back on him. "It's kind of late for that, isn't it?"

Behind her, she heard the rustle of his clothes as he retraced his steps down the hallway, then the door clicked shut sealing her in with her fate. She put the bag on the counter and stared at it.

The bag sat there, teasing her, taunting her. It wasn't as though she'd slept around a lot. Stone had been her first indiscretion in too many years to count. Maybe it was a mistake, some godawful trick to make her aware of the risk she'd taken.

Warmth stole over her.

But what a night. Even now, every time they were in the same room, they connected. And she knew without a doubt that if she could go back to that night, she'd do it all over again.

Except for the getting pregnant part.

She glared at the bag.

Putting it off wouldn't make the test negative instead of positive. She grabbed the bag, pulled out the box and opened it up.

Skimmed the instructions.

Followed them to the letter.

Washed her hands, opened the bathroom door, and called out, "You can come in now."

As he came down the hallway, he looked kind of greenish—or maybe it was the light—but it somehow made her feel better. For right this very moment, she wasn't in it alone.

He stood shoulder to shoulder with her and grabbed hold of her hand while he kept his gaze fixed on the stick. "How long?"

"Five minutes." Pure terror for them both. Followed by, she hoped, pure, unadulterated relief and joy.

The feel of his palm against hers gave her a measure of comfort and now she was glad to have him here, sharing this with her, willing to take some of the load off her shoulders, if only temporarily.

He nudged her shoulder. "I googled health tips for expectant mothers."

Surprised, she glanced at his profile. "You did?"

He turned his head, met her gaze, and squeezed her hand. "Well, yeah. If you're pregnant, I want to make sure both you and our baby stay healthy."

She shook her head and turned back to watch the stick. "I'm not pregnant."

But the thin flat stick taunted her with uncertainty while she watched for the bands to appear.

One band, though. Not two.

Nervousness swamped her and huffing out a breath, she slid a glance his way. "Are you breathing?"

"No." His gaze connected with hers and he squeezed her hand. "We're in this together."

One band meant she was safe and Stone was off the hook without any guilt on his part.

Two bands meant—she stifled the urge to throw up—she'd be a mom, with this tiny defenseless person to take care of.

A hint of color appeared on the white strip. A single band that sent a wave of relief rolling through her. And by the sound of Stone's sigh, him too.

Stephanie looked at him and he looked at her, and the desire that always flared through her body whenever she was in his presence came to life in his eyes too. Without thinking, reacting on total instinct, she threw herself against him and wrapped her arms around his neck while he encircled her around the waist with his arms.

"Did we just dodge a bullet?" he whispered in her ear.

"I think so," she whispered back.

But then he spoiled it all by turning back to the strip and she saw the relief wash away from his face.

Stephanie reluctantly craned her neck and caught a glimpse of a second faint line. She felt Stone slowly release her, keeping one arm around her waist so they stood hip to hip, and watched in horror as the pregnancy test kit confirmed their worst fears.

Positive.

"I don't get it," she babbled. "Logistically, I should've been able to get laid ninety-nine times before this happened."

"You and me both," he mumbled.

He tugged her out of the bathroom and over to the couch where they both sat silent and edgy until she whispered, "What am I going to do?"

He squeezed her hand, drawing her attention to his face. "You're not in this alone."

"Stone, you don't have any obligation. I would never expect you to stick around if you don't want to. I won't keep our child away from you, but I won't expect you to stick around either."

"Maybe I want to." He let go of her hand, pushed himself off the couch, and paced across the floor.

She felt the sudden urge to be held, to have him rub his large hands up and down her back, to have his naked chest against hers, to have him join with her body one more time and help her forget this moment.

She raked her fingers through her hair.

What was she thinking? This is how they'd gotten into this mess in the first place.

Although, what was there to be afraid of now? It wasn't like she could get pregnant a second time.

She sighed and watched him pace.

Stone Kincaid was like her favorite flavor of ice cream. Simply irresistible.

And she couldn't help but wonder how he would react to a roll in the hay to ease the tension.

She bit her lip.

He'd probably scream and run at the suggestion.

She watched him reach into the pocket of his trousers and pull something out. He approached her and dropped to his knees in front of her, took her left hand, and slid something on to the third finger.

"Marry me."

Stephanie stared down at the diamond ring on her finger, then up at the man who was so totally wrong for her, even their careers clashed. Finally catching her wits, she scrambled away from him and somehow landed on the floor on her butt.

Panther like, he rose to tower above her, a frown on his face as he reached down and assisted her to her feet. "What's wrong?"

"This." She tugged the ring off her finger and shoved it into the pocket of his white shirt. The warmth of his skin through the material nearly distracted her, so she pulled away, hands on hips. "I don't want it."

"You're having my baby. Getting married is the right thing to do." He pulled a folded sheaf of papers out of his pocket. "I even drew up a prenup to protect you and the baby."

That silenced her for all of two-point-five seconds, and then her brain cells began to function again. "Do you love me?"

His gaze hooded over. "I'm sure that will come in time."

"And if it doesn't?" She could tell by the way he didn't answer that he hadn't thought that far...or more than likely was hiding his head in the sand like some delusional idiot. "I'm not marrying you, Stone. Never ever."

18

As she threw up her hands in exasperation, Stone caught a glimpse of her belly—the belly that he'd kissed all those weeks ago after his great-uncle's wedding, the belly that cradled his child.

She turned and walked to the front door, tugged it open, and glared at him...barefoot, sexy as sin, and pregnant with his child.

Was it any wonder he found himself infatuated?

He gave himself a mental shake.

Okay, no more being stupid over her. There were things they needed to discuss, things he needed to confirm. Since she was pissed with him anyway, he leapt in with both feet.

"How do I know it's my kid?" The glare turned to the frost level of a glacier. Stone raked his hand through his hair and mumbled, "Never mind."

His gaze moved down, past the fullness of her breasts, to where the button of her skirt was undone. And while he wondered if he should go over there and do it up for her—or maybe convince her that he should undress her totally and make love to her—it hit him.

She hadn't been able to do up the button because of his baby.

His groin tightened in reaction.

If she fascinated him before, now he felt bewitched.

She turned her head and met his gaze. "You know what, Stone. Just forget me. Forget I told you about this child. Forget we even exist. I don't need you in my life."

And then leaving the door open, she turned and walked away without a backward glance and disappeared down the hallway.

The bedroom door slammed, shutting him out.

Well, she was a whole lot better off than he was, he decided as he stormed out of the cottage. He had a family he didn't want...except...

His footsteps slowed as he spotted Liz standing on the front porch of his cabin talking to Kevin. When she walked her fingers up his chest, Stone frowned and wondered what she was doing, especially since she was getting married in three days.

As he headed across the clearing, Kevin shifted back, his gaze slashing to Stone. Then the other man sidestepped Liz, scaled the steps with one leap, and headed off down the path.

Stone frowned. "What are you doing, Liz?"

"Nothing." She toed one foot against the wooden panels and refused to meet his eyes. Then she raised her gaze, a frown pinching her brow, and whispered, "You won't tell Roger, will you?"

"If nothing was going on, then what do you have to hide from your fiancee?"

"I—maybe I'm just getting cold feet." She stepped forward, earnest. "Please don't tell Roger. The wedding is only three days away and I don't want to screw things up."

She'd grown up when he hadn't been looking. And while she still needed to grow up—a lot—he couldn't discount that she was old enough to make her own decisions.

Maybe not smart enough, but old enough.

And besides, who was he to judge her, especially since he'd managed to screw up his own life?

He nodded his head once, sharp, and she gave a squeal and launched herself against him, throwing her arms around his neck.

"Thank you. You won't be sorry, I promise."

And with a kiss on his cheek, she pushed away from him and skipped down the steps, thankfully headed in the opposite direction of his best friend.

His mom came down the path, a frown on her forehead. "Was that Kevin Donahue? What is he doing here?"

He shrugged. "Just visiting."

"Well, don't let him overstay his welcome." She handed him some papers. "I'm about to offer Stephanie the wedding planner position on my show, but I want you to go over the contract first to make sure I haven't missed anything. Then, if you could go over it with her, I'd appreciate it. I'd like to get it all wrapped up by Friday."

"Sure." And as she headed back to the house, Stone tucked the papers into the pocket of his jacket.

Now that Stephanie was pregnant, he didn't have to worry about her working for his mother. There were enough clauses in the contract to prevent such a thing from happening.

Stone's phone buzzed and he glanced down at the screen to see a message from his assistant.

I need to take a personal afternoon tomorrow.

Grumpiness settled deep in his chest.

Stone wished he could take a personal afternoon.

Somewhere far from his family.

And oddly enough, the only one he wanted to take with him would be the mother of his child.

19

Wednesday morning, Jim frowned down at his watch, then back at the computer screen. Grace had caught him—again—before he could escape. "What do you mean, nothing works."

"Just what I said. I push the ON button and nothing happens. I thought you said you fixed this?"

"I did. Here, let me try." He gently shouldered her aside, tried to ignore the scent of her body wash, pushed the button, then glanced at his watch again. No time for this now. He was late.

And getting more distracted with each breath he took.

She smelled good. Like vanilla and homemade apple pie and sex all wrapped up into one.

He gave himself a mental shake.

No time for that now.

The guys were waiting.

Gisele would be standing there ready to badger him into improving his golf game.

Jim pushed the button again, breathed deeply to calm himself, inhaled more of Grace's essence, and felt his pecker stand to full blown life.

"See?" she said, her breath tickling his ear, while nothing happened on the computer screen.

His phone buzzed. He straightened, glanced at Harry's message on the screen, and started backing from the room, desperation clawing at his guts. "I'm late."

She frowned at him, her beautiful blue eyes filled with something that reminded him of hurt. When was the last time Grace had been hurt by anyone but an angry fan? "Late for what?"

"The guys. My lesson." He grabbed his golf bag from beside the doorway and hefted it onto his shoulder. "I'll work on it tonight, Grace."

She glanced at the computer, gave it a closed fisted whack. "Tonight? But I need it now. Today."

"Grace, that's sensitive equipment. Be gentle with it."

"When will you be back?" she asked in a small voice that caught him by surprise.

Grace was never small. She was always larger than life, in charge of every situation, in control of everyone and everything around her.

"I'll take another look at it tonight. Sorry honey. You'll have to use a pad and paper today."

Before she could say anything else, Jim slipped out of the room and as he headed for the golf course, focused on clearing his mind.

There was no way that he'd allow a wife who was slowly driving him insane ruin his game. There were enough other things to ruin his game.

Like friends who didn't turn off the sound on their cell phones.

And an inability to master the intricacies of the game.

Once he reached the course, he set his golf bag aside and tried to focus on his stance and the way he clutched the five iron. But he knew he was off...everything was off.

Including the fact that he could have sworn Grace had come on to him.

Over the years, their careers had kept them apart. And during these past few months, while he'd struggled with his health and resisted the urge to get worked up—in bed and out—she'd seemed more than willing to accept the death of their love life.

Which left him both relieved that she didn't seem to notice their sex life had disappeared, and concerned that when he got past the worry of having a heart attack while in the saddle, she'd proclaim she wanted to continue with their no-sex relationship.

A low growl of frustration brought his attention back to the woman now in front of him.

Giselle stood there, hands on her model thin hips, a curl to her glossy lips. "Let me show you again, Jim, and pay attention this time."

She moved behind him, barefoot and silent, put her arms around his body, and covered his hands with hers. As she guided him through his swing, her technique got lost in the feel of her lithe body plastered against his back.

Imprinted, where before only Grace's imprint had been.

What had Harry and the boys been thinking? That he was too old for a woman like this? That he'd view Giselle in the same manner he saw his daughter? That he wouldn't get the urge to jump her bones and—

His body responded to the womanly touch and he willed himself to ignore it. Because if he didn't...it wouldn't be a heart attack that would kill him. Grace would do the deed herself.

"Are you paying attention, Jim?"

His breath rasped from his lungs. "With every fibre of my being."

"Come on, Jim," Gisele said in that pouty, honey-smooth tone that slid down his spine and made him think of hot oil and sex...and Grace. Everything always came back to the woman he'd been living with for the past thirty-five years.

"Forget everything else. Just focus on the ball and that little hole. You do remember how to aim for the hole, don't you, Jim?"

He gritted his teeth, clenched his hands around the top of the club, and eyed the path from the ball to the hole. "Of course, I do."

Gisele leaned in closer, the indent of her breasts pressed against his back. As she grabbed him by the buttocks and squeezed, she breathed into his ear, "Come on, Jim. Concentrate. There's nothing else that matters but you and the club and that little ball."

He squirmed and tried to shrug her away. "How am I supposed to concentrate when you're climbing all over me?"

Her throaty laugh filled the air and she placed a wet kiss on the side of his neck. "A real golf pro doesn't let anything interfere with his concentration. Not a negative crowd, a ballsy opponent, or a beautiful woman."

He stiffened and ignored other parts of his body that still hadn't lost their stiffness from the encounter with Grace. "Piss off, Gisele."

"Ooooh, such a dirty, dirty mouth you have, Jim." From the back, she reached between his legs, grabbed his balls, and squeezed, the sharpness of her nails digging through the thin material of his slacks.

What little concentration he had remaining scattered and Jim jumped away from her, covering his private parts with both hands. "You're insane, woman."

She advanced on him, her slim hips sashaying, her generous mouth curved up into a wicked smile. "No, Jim. I get the job done and I don't particularly care what I have to do to do it."

He threw his iron onto the ground. "You're crazy."

"Tsk tsk." She stopped, one hand on her hip, her gaze fixed on the golf club. "Maybe I need to teach you some respect for your equipment and the course." She took another step closer and grinned. "I am the master. You are the student. If I tell you to wear a g-string beneath your trousers, you will obey me."

He stepped back, out of her reach for fear of her hands and her nails. "Not likely. Grace would have me at a shrink."

"I doubt she'd even notice, Jim." One pencil thin eyebrow raised. "When was the last time you made love to her? To any woman?"

"Way too long," he admitted before he caught himself. "Get out of my head, Giselle."

Both eyebrows spiked. She bent and picked up his five iron and held it out to him. "Go screw your wife. Then maybe you'll get her out of your head, and your game will improve."

He snatched it out of her hand, then glared at her as turning, she slipped on her shoes and ground one spiked heel into the green. As she strolled away toward the cottages, she said, "And you've forgotten the most fundamental rule of golf. No swearing on the course. Next time, I'll make you pay."

Jim sucked in a deep breath of air and uncovered his balls.

The bitch really was crazy.

A movement through the trees caught his attention. He hunched down and peered through the leaves, seeing nothing. Squaring his shoulders with determination, he wrapped both hands around the handle of his club, pretended it was Giselle's neck, and gave up all pretenses of trying to control his dick.

There was no problem with getting it up. He was just scared spitless that if he dared do something about it, his family would be burying him six feet under.

20

G race scurried through the trees, heart pounding, breath coming fast, careful to stay out of sight.

If Jim could get away with it—*the dirty, rotten, cheating bastard*—she could too.

Who was that woman? And why had Jim allowed her on the golf course? If there was one rule Grace would never forget, it was his no women allowed on the course rule. It had hurt her deeper than anything else could.

The tall, slim, shapely young woman had been no older than Liz. With tawny blonde hair that floated down to the middle of her back and barely any clothes covering her tanned limbs, she'd been young and fresh and so sexy, even Grace had thought about humping her...except she didn't swing that way.

As she reached the pool, she saw her neighbors sitting around the patio table, and their laughter reached her ears.

What were they talking about? And why were they here when she'd made it so clear that she didn't need their company? Were they waiting for their husbands to join them? She'd seen the men all disappear the moment Jim's bimbo showed up on the course.

Did she care what Jim did—or *who* Jim did—in his spare

time? She'd known it was a risk leaving him alone so much of the time, but they'd both been busy with their careers.

And then the son-of-a-bitch had *retired*.

What was she supposed to do with that? Retire along with him? Die after a horribly long boring retirement?

Somehow she kept the panic at bay, determined to appear serene and in control when she reached the patio and the tiny trays of sweet snacks the staff had brought out for the women.

Without saying a word, she reached for the richest of them all and stuffed it into her mouth.

"A pound in the mouth, two on the hips," Nancy said as she nudged Sandy's hand away from the tray. She raised her gaze to Grace. "So are you going to stand there and hyperventilate? Or are you going to sit down and help us figure out how to get our men back?"

The emotions she'd tried so hard to hold at bay swelled up her throat and burned at the back of her eyes. No, she would not cry. Around the explosion of sugar in her mouth, she said, "I haven't a clue what you're talking about. Go away."

Sandy pushed her sister-in-law's hand away and reached for another square, this time successfully snagging one. "It's too late for that, Grace. We're here and we're not leaving until we get our men back."

A comforting hand on her shoulder caught Grace unaware. She turned and met Leta's gaze, kindness and understanding and friendship radiating from the other woman's eyes. "It's easier to deal with their indiscretions if you have someone to share your pain with."

They knew.

Nancy tapped the edge of her coffee cup. "So, marriage expert, what are we going to do about it?"

Grace dropped onto a chair and pressed her hands against her burning cheeks. "I'm a marriage fraud."

Sandy snatched another square, popped it into her mouth,

and around the mouthful said, "No you're not. You actually give really great advice. Why I've—"

She pressed her lips together and blushed.

Nancy elbowed her sister-in-law. "Tell us your dirty little secret, honey."

Sandy peered around the patio, which caused the other women to look over their shoulders too, and almost by instinct Grace did the same. Then Sandy leaned forward and grabbed Grace by the upper arm to bring her closer into the little circle.

Despite her reluctance to join them, she didn't want to be rude. But they weren't exactly her type of people. Housewives, all three. Well, not Nancy, who co-owned the local insurance office with her husband. Or Leta, who worked part-time in one of the local shops.

No, not her *people*...although truth be told, she really didn't have *people*.

Or friends.

Or a husband that wanted her more than his next breath.

She leaned in closer, suddenly desperate to be a part of this group of women.

Sandy smiled. "Remember the *Eternally Yours* episode on the top five ways to keep your husband's attention at home? Well, every night since then, I've greeted Harry at the door with a drink in my hand...naked except for the apron I wear while I make his supper."

Leta's eyebrows winged up.

Nancy sighed. "So that must make your sex life pretty hot?"

"Hot?" Sandy blinked and squinted up at the sky. "Yeah, sure."

But she didn't sound convincing.

Grace took hold of her hand. "I thought you and Harry...the apron and the nakedness."

"Sandy, is Harry not giving you any?" Nancy drawled.

Sandy glanced toward the golf course, her shoulders slumped, and shook her head. "It worked for the first couple of years after the kids moved out, but now—at first the sex was naughty and explosive and so like when we were first dating. Now, Harry comes through the front door, takes the drink out of my hand, gives me a peck on the cheek, then turns on the satellite to watch Golf TV."

Three sets of accusing eyes turned toward Grace. She barely stopped herself from squirming. "Why are you looking at me?"

"It's that course Jim built," Leta said.

Sandy nodded. "It's got all our men addicted to the great outdoors."

"We've let them take us for granted for far too long," Nancy said as she pushed to her feet and started toward the house. "This calls for more than coffee. Where's your wine, Grace?"

She sighed and gave in to the inevitable. They were here to stay until they got their husbands back. Although there was no need to serve them the good stuff. "Fridge. Glasses are in the cupboard next to it."

While Nancy toddled off, Sandy leaned forward. "So girls, what's the plan?"

Silence fell over them again and the downcast looks on her guests' faces squeezed Grace's heart.

What were they going to do? The golf course was like a beautiful woman to the men, teasing and taunting.

Nancy returned, popped the cork, filled the glasses, handed one to each woman, then plunked back down on her chair. "So where were we?"

Three expectant gazes fixed on Grace, and without a brilliant idea to wow them with, she went with her regular advice. "You should go home, talk to your husbands, tell them what's wrong. Work on a solution to solve the problem together. Work as a couple."

"Already tried and failed." Nancy made a *pfttt* noise, pulled out a cigarette and lit it, then drawled, "Honey, it's clear you're in the same boat as us. Why won't you admit it?"

The corners of Leta's mouth turned down. "Worse."

Sandy leaned forward and patted Grace's hand. "We saw her, Grace. That child was all over Jim. It's not right."

Embarrassment flooded Grace's cheeks.

Maybe they were right. It was time to take action.

Out the corner of her eye, she saw Jim on the putting green, sans his little golf slut. But she couldn't rid herself of the image of that young woman climbing all over him while she pretended to teach him how to golf.

Across from her, Leta fidgeted with the edge of her blouse.

Nancy stubbed the cigarette out in the flower pot next to her chair and pulled out another.

Sandy sighed, turned her attention to the squares, dragged the plate across the table to the spot in front of her, and dived in.

Grace sipped at her wine and realized the women were waiting for her to come up with a plan. All she really wanted to do was climb back into bed, pull the covers up over her head, and hide there for the rest of her life. But she couldn't disappoint these women any more than she could disappoint her viewers.

She took a huge sip from the wine glass and took the plunge. "Would you like to help me hire a male assistant?"

With a grin, Nancy grabbed the wine bottle and topped up the glasses. "Now you're talking."

Grace thought of Jim, eaten alive with jealousy. She'd laugh in his face while she walked into the sunset with her terribly attractive, terribly sexy hired help. Two could play at this game.

She tapped her fingers against the top of the table. "I'll call the agency and ask them to send over some candidates. The sooner the better."

Sandy leaned forward, elbows on the table. "Criteria?"

Grace frowned. She hadn't given this any more thought than getting even with Jim.

Leta jumped to her feet and paced. "He has to be young. Definitely under thirty."

Nancy's eyes brightened. "I like that. Very naughty."

Grace refused to squirm. "Maybe an ex-lifeguard, so he can watch over the people in the pool." She glanced at the empty pool, then looked back at her companions, refusing to roll her eyes. "He must agree to be on call twenty-four-seven. Since my computer whiz man can't take the time to fix my computer, I'll need someone else to do that job too."

The implication was there for everyone to read.

Sex would be the assistant's number one priority.

Deep in thought, Leta tapped one finger against her nose. "He has to be handsome. Otherwise what's the point?"

Nancy nodded. "Someone to make Jim sit up and take notice."

Sandy winked. "Someone who doesn't mind an older woman."

Leta amended, "Someone who finds older women attractive."

Nancy let out a wistful sigh. "Someone who can satisfy an older woman's sexual needs."

Sandy and Leta nodded and said in unison, "I'd like to find me one of those too."

Grace studied the three of them and realized that even though they'd all led different professional lives, their personal lives were scarily similar. They needed her as much as she needed them.

She reached into her pocket, pulled out her cell phone, and made the call. When the receptionist picked up, she said, "Hello, I'd like to hire a man."

The three faces beaming back at her brought her more joy than she'd experienced in...forever.

Two hours later, the first of the first of the first to interview walked onto the patio.

Nancy sat up straight and purred, "Hunka hunka hunka love."

The potential candidate swaggered onto the cement, all two hundred pounds of tanned hard male muscles and brawn. Around her, Grace heard a collective sigh of satisfaction.

Dressed in a pair of faded jeans that hugged lean hips and a t-shirt that showed off the breadth of his shoulders, the width of his chest, the tautness of his belly, Grace swallowed back her own sigh. Then she raised her gaze to look at his face.

And in a heartbeat, every sexual fantasy she'd had vanished.

He was nothing but a boy. Twenty-five at the most. Only a few years younger than Stone. Somehow the thought of doing him seemed a little bit...too naughty.

He walked onto the deck, his mouth hitched into a reckless grin. "Morning, Ma'am. I'm here to interview for the assistant job."

If there was one thing Grace hated more than the loss of her own youth, it was the word Ma'am.

Other than that, the boy was perfect for the job.

21

Mid-morning, Stephanie answered the door and saw the father of her baby looming in the open doorway. He stood there handsome and hunky and hot... three of her top favorite things in a man.

He shifted the weight of his body from one foot to the other, rubbed his palm against the back of his neck, and grimaced. "I'm not exactly sure what the morning after protocol is—"

She gritted her teeth and hissed, "Go away."

The self-conscious appearance faded and one masculine eyebrow quirked. "Somebody got up on the wrong side of the bed."

She glanced over her shoulder and lowered her voice. "My mother is here and she's driving me n—"

A swish on the floor behind her made her snap her mouth shut.

Stone's gaze went past her and he smiled that warm welcome smile that did funny things to her stomach. "Hello, Mrs. G."

"Stone? Come in, come in. You must have received my message," her mom exclaimed.

"Message?" Stephanie sent Stone a narrow-eyed look. "What message?"

He grinned down at her. "You mom said she made a batch of my favorite peanut butter cookies for me."

"And you're just in time," Dora said. "I'm about to pull them out of the oven, so they'll still be warm. I'll make coffee, then you two can sit down and discuss the plans for the day."

The stove timer buzzed, and as her mom scurried away, Stephanie reluctantly pulled the door wide open. "How does she know what your favorite cookies are?"

Stone stepped inside. "She doesn't. I was being polite."

As he passed by her, she tried to ignore how good he smelled. Why was that, especially when everything else seemed to turn her stomach?

She glared at him. "No still means no. No trying to butter me up with hopes I'll change my mind."

The corner of his mouth quirked up and he nudged her aside so he could close the door. "I'm just here to check on how you're doing this morning."

"She woke me up to make my bed. How do you think I'm doing? And the scent of those cookies makes me want to throw up all over them."

He leaned forward and tweaked her nose, pity in his gaze. "Poor baby. What can I do to help?"

Stephanie inhaled another breath of delicious male. She eyed his broad shoulders, then his neck. "Please don't judge me for doing this."

Then she stepped forward, wrapped her arms around his waist, and pressed her nose against his neck.

Against her chest, she felt the rumble of his laughter. "What are you doing, gorgeous lady?"

She closed her eyes, breathed deeply, and as the twisted nauseous feeling in her stomach eased, sighed a happy sigh. "You smell so good. And it settles my stomach. I'm not exactly positive, but I think your aftershave or cologne or deodorant is what's doing the trick."

Or maybe it's just you, she nearly added.

Another chuckle escaped him. He wrapped his arms around her and tucked her close to his body. "What about your mom?"

Some of her grumpiness returned. "She can go stick her nose in my dad's neck."

He tunneled his fingers into her hair. "So it looks like you might need me after all."

"Just till the gagging stage ends."

"I read it can last through the whole pregnancy."

"Is that supposed to cheer me up?"

"I'm just saying, you might need me around for more than the sperm donor."

A scrape on the kitchen floor sounded. Stephanie popped her eyes open and pushed out of Stone's arms just as her mom came around the corner. The Cheshire grin on the older woman's face warned her that she hadn't moved fast enough.

"Come," Dora said. "The coffee is poured. Let's sit down and get to know each other."

As Stephanie followed her mom into the kitchen, aware of Stone's large body bringing up the rear, she realized it seemed strange to talk about the pregnancy with him, almost like a real couple. It was...*nice.*

He was nice.

Maybe *too* nice.

Her heart hiccuped.

Dora passed by the table on the way to the stove. "Sit. I'll have these cookies on the table in a jiff."

Stephanie sank onto a chair, and now that she didn't have her nose buried against Stone's neck, her stomach began to flip-flop again.

Stone leaned over her and whispered in her ear. "Where do you want me to sit? Far away or close?"

In answer, she grabbed a chair, yanked it close, and pulled him down to sit next to her.

His cell phone buzzed. She grabbed him by the shirt sleeve and hissed into his ear, "Don't you dare leave me alone with those cookies."

He pulled the phone out of his pocket, glanced at the screen, and set the device on the table. "I won't."

Her mom turned from the stove, her cheeks flushed, her eyes sparkling as she approached the table with a plate of cookies which still steamed with heat from the oven.

Assured he wasn't going anywhere, Stephanie released her grip on him, leaned slightly closer, and inhaled. He didn't even so much as look at her, but she saw the crook at the corner of his mouth.

Yeah, the fact that she needed him might improve his mood, but it didn't do a darn thing for hers. She still felt like crap.

Dora sat across from them, held out the plate to Stone, and he took a cookie, then set it on the plate in front of him.

"These smell delicious, Mrs. G."

"They're one of my family's favorite." She held the plate out to Stephanie, who shook her head and pushed it away. Her mom tsked. "I know you've gained a little weight, honey, but you're not on a diet, are you?"

"No, of course not, Mom. I'm just not hungry this morning."

Her mom turned to Stone. "Do you think she needs to diet?"

His hooded gaze turned toward Stephanie, and he raked her body with a look that made her want to fan herself. "Nope, she's perfect as she is."

"She has my legs, you know."

His smile deepened. "I believe you already mentioned that."

Stephanie grabbed his arm and glared across the table. "Run before she starts measuring you for a tux."

Her mom frowned, and then her face cleared and she beamed a smile in Stone's direction. "A lawyer is such a reputable profession. I'm surprised some lucky woman hasn't snaffled you up already. You're not divorced, are you?"

She said *divorced* like it was a dirty word and Stephanie winced. Oh, if she only knew the truth...

"No, Ma'am." He picked up the cookie and took a bite.

"Still married?"

"Not that either."

"A man your age should think about settling down." Her brows lowered into a frown. "Why aren't you married yet? Is there something wrong with you?"

The grin on Stone's face widened. "No, Mrs. G. I guess I haven't found the right woman yet."

"Sometimes the perfect match is right under your nose." Dora sent a non-too-subtle sideways glance toward Stephanie. Then she brushed her hands over her apron and pushed to her feet. "Will you look at the time? I promised the bride that I'd join her for tea so we could discuss some ideas I had for the zombie wedding theme. I better get ready to go."

As she scurried from the room, Stone laughed and snagged another cookie before he stood up, grabbed the plate, and took it to the far end of the kitchen. "Your mom doesn't believe in being subtle, does she?"

"Now that Mandy is engaged, I'm next on her hit list." She tilted her head. "You realize, of course, that she has you at the top of the list."

He retraced his steps to the table, leaned down, and gave her a peck on the cheek. "Maybe I should show her the engagement ring you threw back in my face."

"Don't you dare." She gave him a sideways glance. "By the way, your mom mentioned a contract yesterday and I haven't heard anything since. Has she said anything to you?"

He straightened and studied the cookie. "No, nothing. Do you want me to ask her about it?"

"If you wouldn't mind. Working on the *Eternally Yours* show would be a once in a lifetime opportunity." She inhaled the scent of him and sighed. "I wish I could tuck you into my bra and keep you there so I could smell you all of the time instead of all the other stuff that makes me sick."

His gaze dropped to her chest. "I'd accommodate you if I could, believe me, sweetheart."

And then he took all of that delicious scent with him and headed out of the house.

Her mom walked back into the room, bringing with her the sickening scent of hairspray, looked around, and blinked. "Where's your nice young man?"

"He's not my man, Mom." Stephanie pushed to her feet, brushed her hands across the butt of her jeans, and tried to breathe through her mouth. She had a funny feeling it would be easy to keep Stone at her side. She was beginning to realize that he was one of those guys who took his responsibilities seriously.

But she didn't want to be just another responsibility. She wanted to be...

What did she want to be? She gave a shrug of her shoulders. "He had things to do."

Dora faced her square, her expression serious. "Honey, I can tell he likes you. *A lot*. If you're smart you'll snaffle him up. I mean, for goodness sakes, girl, he's a *lawyer*. If you're waiting for something better than that, you'll go to your grave unmarried and unhappy."

Something in Stephanie snapped and she remembered Stone's words. She gazed back at her mom and bit back a grin. "Stone is a divorce lawyer, Mom."

Dora paled and backed up a step. "Excuse me?"

She kept her expression neutral. "That's right. A *divorce* lawyer. One of *those*. So now you know why I could never marry him."

Dora set her hands on her hips and glared at her oldest daughter. "You mean all this time I've been schmoozing up to him, baking him cookies, treating him as though he were already part of the family. For nothing?"

She bit her cheek to keep from outright laughter. "It's really low of him to have tried to fool you like that."

"Really low...unless..." Dora tapped her index finger against her chin. "But a lawyer is such a good catch. Maybe you could convince him to change his specialty."

She gritted her teeth, but kept her cool. "I'm in the business of getting couples married, while Stone is in the busy of tearing married couples apart. We'd make a horrible match. We'd disagree on all wedding related issues and eventually end up in divorce court and go our separate ways."

"Divorce?" Dora began to fan herself again. "No, no, you're right. Once a divorce lawyer, always a divorce lawyer. If he so much as looks at you with that naughty gleam in his eyes again, I'll sic your father after him."

The click of the front door alerted them to another's presence and as Stone walked back into the kitchen, Dora's shoulders and back stiffened.

"Sorry to interrupt. I forgot my cell," Stone said, and as he passed Dora, he gave her the once over. "You look really nice, Mrs. G."

She swept her skirt out of the way, as though she couldn't bear the thought of him touching her, and lifted her chin into the air. "It was cute when Dane called me Mrs. G. It was even cute the first few times you did too. But now that I know the truth—"

Stone halted, a frown creasing his forehead. "Excuse me?"

"A divorce lawyer. For shame." Her mom swept past him, yanking the edge of her skirt aside as though she couldn't bear for him to touch her, or as though he'd suddenly developed the cooties. "I suppose you're against marriage too. You know Stephanie is a wedding planner. She's devoted to her career, and she's single because she never has time to date. And when she does, she has *horrible* taste in men."

146

Success. Finally, her mom would get off her back.

Stephanie wanted to pump her fist in the air, but as she lifted her gaze from her mom's departing figure, and focused on Stone, she noticed the stunned expression on his face.

He turned to her, hurt lingering in his gaze. "What was that all about?"

She swallowed a bubble of guilt and reminded herself that he didn't feel anything. He was a destroyer of relationships. What did it matter if Dora hated him? He wasn't in her life for the long term.

Except that he was the father of her baby and she was only beginning to understand that he wasn't one of those guys who would eventually fade out of their lives.

"I—uh—just told Mom that you were a divorce lawyer." As the front door closed with a bang and understanding lit Stone's gaze, the bubble of guilt grew larger. Now she felt awful. She closed her hands into fists and forced an apology between her stiff lips. "I'm sorry. I was tired of her poking me about marriage and you were the one who told me to do it. You said *just tell her I'm a divorce lawyer*."

He raised his eyebrows. "I did, didn't I."

She shuffled her feet and clutched her hands together over her heart where it ached. "I'm sorry. I snapped, okay? I told her the one thing that I knew would get her off my back."

The hurt vanished from his gaze and a smile lit his eyes. He closed the distance between them, splayed one hand across her abdomen, and peered deep into her eyes. "Never mind. She's not the first marriage minded mama who's been put off by my profession. And if it means the mother of my child is happier, then I can handle your mom disliking me. Hey, I'm already used to it from your dad."

At the gentleness of his touch, Stephanie's guilt doubled.

Because she suddenly realized that she liked this man.

A lot.

147

Now, all she had to do was figure out a way to make up for her bad judgement and selfishness.

And as she raised her gaze to his handsome face, and remembered how they connected in bed, she followed her instincts and wound her arms around his neck.

22

Stone recognized the wicked glint in Stephanie's eyes a split second before she slid her hands up his shirtfront and around to the back of his neck. Before she sidetracked him with sex—which unfortunately would be far too easy—he decided it was time to figure out what made the mother of his child so wary of marriage.

Because he wasn't done with popping the question. For as long as it took, he'd keep finding new ways to convince her to marry him, until she finally said yes.

All for their child, of course. It had absolutely nothing to do with the fact that he liked her so much. Or that he found himself obsessed with this woman who'd wormed her way into his heart and his future.

He caught her wrists, pulled her arms from around his neck, and pressed her hands against his chest. "Tell me your story."

Confusion tumbled through her liquid gaze, and as she slid her hands free of his hold, he sensed her withdrawal. "My story?"

"Yeah. I want to know why you're a wedding planner who's soured against marriage."

One delicate eyebrow quirked up, and an impish grin turned

up the corners of her delectable mouth. "If I show you mine, will you show me yours?"

He couldn't help himself, he laughed. "You're naughty."

Now she waggled both eyebrows at him, and as the heat of her palms pressing against his shirtfront filtered through the material to his chest, she made another attempt to slide her arms around his neck. "Maybe I need to be spanked."

With another laugh, he dragged her arms from around his neck and stepped back to put some space between them. "We'll get to your fantasies later. I promise."

She inched one foot closer. "How much later? Because my mom will be back. That's a one-hundred percent guarantee. And when she comes back—"

"When she comes back, she'll find you sitting over there." He pointed to the armchair near the front window. "And I'll be a respectable distance away."

Her bottom lip protruded and she swept a glance down his body. "I liked you better when you were bad. Respectable is so...boring."

"Had I been respectable in the first place, neither of us would be in this situation," he reminded her.

"Fine." She threw herself down on the armchair, her hands between her knees, her lower legs in a knock-kneed position. She looked so much like a sulking teenager, he wanted to laugh some more. "What do you want to know?"

"Let's start with why you don't want to get married."

"If you're hoping to find something that changes my mind, you're going to be disappointed."

Biting back a smile, he sat on the armchair across from her. "I'll take my chances."

With another baleful look in his direction, she slumped against the back of the chair. "I'm adopted. Mandy and I both are."

He stayed silent, giving her a chance to speak without interruption. But there was a well of hurt in her beautiful eyes, hurt that she'd covered well till now.

"Our mother—" Her gaze slid from his face to her fingernails and she started picking at a cuticle. "Do we have to talk about this now?"

He leaned back in the armchair and forced the tension from his shoulders. "I have nothing better to do."

"Well I do," she muttered. "There's still a hundred tiny details to sort out before tomorrow night's party and Liz's wedding."

Calmly, he said, "Start talking."

Her bottom lip curled into a cute pout. "I'd rather talk about your family."

"No you wouldn't."

"Yes, I would." She gave him a baleful look. "Fine. My mother is Diana Goodwin-Vaughan-Abercrombie-Style-Vail-Peterson-Miller-Voss." After a moment of silence, she said in the driest voice possible, "Need I go on?"

Stone blinked, confused and absolutely speechless.

She crossed her arms over her chest, pushing her full breasts up so they almost overflowed the rounded edge of her sweater, distracting him momentarily from their conversation. But when she slouched down on the armchair like a discarded rag doll, desire morphed into pity.

She sighed. "Diana is Tom's younger sister. She tried to take care of Mandy and me, but she was young, unmarried, and clueless about children. One day, she dropped us off for a visit with Tom and Dora, and she never came back. I suppose they eventually tracked her down, and since they couldn't have children of their own, they adopted us and made us theirs."

He stroked his chin and watched her. "That must have been rough."

"Not really." She stared back at him. "Tom and Dora made the transition easy. They both have so much love in their hearts, and

Mandy and I were very young. It didn't take long for us to forget that they weren't our biological parents."

"So what happened to sour you against marriage?"

"When I was thirteen, Diana reappeared." Her gaze shifted to the wall behind him, a faraway look in her eyes. "I'm not sure how many times she'd been married and divorced by then, but this time she needed children to convince the man she wanted to marry that she was maternal."

There was a heartbeat of silence before the distant light in her eyes grew hard and she met his gaze. "Thirteen is such an impressionable age. I was fascinated by her. She was beautiful and elegant, and full of light and life. I stayed with her that summer. Poor Dora was beside herself with worry. When Diana asked me to help her plan her wedding, I said yes."

"That's how you became a wedding planner?"

"Dora always tells people that I inherited my organizational skills from her, but since we don't share the same blood, I'm afraid she's delusional." She released a heavy sigh. "I'd grown up watching the *Eternally Yours* show with Mom—I mean, Dora. Every day after school, we'd sit on the couch and ooh and ah over the gorgeous princess gowns." She shrugged. "It turns out I was so good at planning Diana's wedding, I got the joy of planning each one after that. And then, because she treated me like a best friend instead of her impressionable daughter, I got to listen to her cry every time one of her marriages crumbled."

He had this vivid image of the young girl she must have been, trying so hard to be the grownup, while the woman who should have cared for her fell apart in front of her. "I'm sorry."

She shrugged and forced a smile. "Well, enough of that already. In a nutshell, my experience with Diana taught me that I'm more in love with the wedding preparations than I am with the thought of being tied to one guy forever. Which of course pisses Dora off. Now I give the bride a day she can cherish forever, or at least till the honeymoon is over."

As she pushed to her feet, he followed her up. "Not every marriage ends in divorce."

"No, it doesn't, but why take the chance of all that disappointment and heartbreak?" Her smile faded. "Tom, of course, always says there are a thousand-and-one men out there who are right for me, and I need to keep looking until I find *the one.*"

He chuckled. "No wonder he doesn't like me. He's still looking for the perfect man to give his daughter to...which of course we both know there will never be a perfect man. Continue."

She stared at him, her gaze thoughtful. "See, that's the part I could never figure out. How do you know when someone is *the one*?"

He shrugged. "I don't know. I've seen enough heartbreak to last me a lifetime, and yet there are couples out there who have found the right fit. Like your mom and dad, Mandy and Dane."

She crossed her arms over her chest, which pushed up her breasts and momentarily distracted him from her expressive features. Then he felt a tap on his chin.

"Eyes up here, buster."

"Sorry. You have some irresistible qualities."

She got this far away look in her eyes and he wondered who she was thinking of. "I almost got married once. I was twenty-two, old enough to know better, but still too stupid to care. I was in love with the wedding preparations and ceremony, and the Cinderella promise of happily ever after. And so I fell in lust, head over heels in passion, and mistook it for love." She sighed and met his gaze. "Kind of like with you. By the time the glow had worn off and I realized I couldn't spend the rest of my life with him, it was too late. The wedding guests were gathering in the church, and my dad was waiting to walk me up the aisle."

"What did you do?"

"Run."

He smiled down at her and took her hands in his. "Maybe he wasn't the right guy."

She raised her gaze to his face. "And you think you might be?"

"Maybe." He shrugged his shoulders. "How long have your mom and dad been married?"

"Almost forty years. I think they've stayed together out of sheer stubbornness. Although it appears the stubbornness might be wearing thin."

"I noticed they've been a little snippy with each other, but I'm sure they'll work it out."

Her voice softened and as she sighed, the sound went straight to the core of him. "The bottom line is that I'm too selfish for a couple."

He'd watched her sacrifice everything for her family. "I don't think that's true. I think you're one of the least selfish people I know."

She stared at him for a moment, her teeth worrying her bottom lip. "And I—uh—in case you didn't notice, I take after my birth mother. I don't have a maternal bone in my body. You should be really worried that I'm going to be the mother of your child."

"I would be, except that I've seen the way you dealt with my sister and mother. If you can do that without losing your cool, a baby will be a piece of cake."

Something else flashed through her gaze, and for a moment he thought she was going to deny his statement. But then she waggled her brows and grinned. "Now that I've spilled my guts and my past, you owe me a little naughty. Or we can keep talking. Your choice."

He had her in his arms and his mouth on hers in less time that it took to draw his next breath.

Unfortunately, her cell phone buzzed.

23

The tap of Stephanie's heels echoed along the otherwise silent hallway leading to the fitting room. She smothered a yawn and wished for a nap instead of the fitting that should have been finished yesterday. Maybe she'd have a nap *during* the fitting.

Okay, so pregnancy didn't exactly agree with her...and neither did a one way trip to heartbreak hotel.

What was she going to do about Stone? Every time she thought she'd erected enough barricades to keep him at a distance, he somehow weaseled his way through. Heck, if her phone hadn't buzzed, she would have been naked in bed with the father of her child right now.

Which maybe wouldn't be such a bad thing, especially if she could have a nap afterward.

Except she knew he wasn't done with the marriage idea. He was just biding his time, trying to figure her out, but she was determined to keep him at arm's length.

Only she was doing a really horrible job of it.

As she turned the corner and entered the fitting room, she

cleared her thoughts of the troublesome male who haunted her every other waking moment, and looked around. The seamstress had her back to her and was packing up her case. Liz was nowhere in sight. "Did I miss the fitting?"

The seamstress whirled around, her face pinched and angry. "You and Liz both. My time is valuable. I refuse to stand around and wait for the prima donna bride to appear. I have another appointment in town."

Shocked by the attack, Stephanie stepped back out of reach and stared. "What do you mean Liz didn't show? Where is she?"

With a shrug, the other woman turned her back on her again and continued to pack her things. "I don't know and I don't care."

The blood red gown with the entrails sewn into the lace was nowhere in sight. Instead a gorgeous white wedding gown fit for a princess hung on the rack. "Where is Liz's gown?"

With a jut of her chin, the seamstress indicated the gown. "Liz called me last night. Said she'd changed her mind. Asked me to bring by the original dress she'd tried on."

Stephanie fingered the lace. "It's gorgeous."

"And yet, the bride didn't show up for her fitting. Well, she'll have to make do with her original choice. Ugly as it is, it won't matter that it doesn't fit properly."

"Wait." Stephanie whirled around and grabbed the seamstress's arm. "The wedding is in two days. If that's the gown Liz wants, then she needs to have it altered. Please. I'll find Liz right now and get her down here."

"You have five minutes." She glared down at the hand on her arm until Stephanie clued in and released her. Then the other woman tapped the face of her watch. "The clock is ticking."

Stephanie pulled her cell out of her pocket and made tracks for the entryway. She was thankful now that Stone had put his number into her cell. Except when he heard about Liz's absence, he was so going to gloat and point out that his younger sister was irresponsible, impulsive, and not ready to get married.

And whether or not she agreed with him—and just for the record, she totally did, which was beginning to make her feel bad for plowing full steam ahead—she had a wedding to plan and a bride to find.

A moment later, Stone's smooth voice came through the connection. "Miss me already?"

She heard the smile in his voice and ignored it along with the pleasure unfolding in her chest. "We have a problem."

"You've fallen deeply, madly in love with me, and now you regret turning down my marriage proposal."

Okay, that stopped her, because on some level, he might be right.

As panic set in, she shook away the thought. "Liz is missing."

"Missing? As in you found a letter from a kidnapper?"

"No, missing as in she didn't show up for the fitting." Before he could gloat and say *I told you so*, she rushed on. "Liz decided to go with a different gown, so it has to be fitted. The seamstress is high strung, very temperamental. She doesn't like to be kept waiting so you have to find your sister or there won't be any dress alterations. And then she'll have to wear that horrible red zombie dress."

"Okay, okay, take it easy, sweetheart." Stone's soothing voice came across the connection. "The stress is no good for you or my son."

"Son?" She straightened up, startled, and looked around to make sure no one could overhear. "What if it's a girl?"

"I don't care what our baby is, as long as both him—"

"Her."

"—and his mother are happy and healthy. Speaking of which, come back here and we'll have a nap together."

"Right, if I lie down with you, there won't be any napping." Sorely tempted, she huffed out a sigh and refocused. "So you'll find your sister?"

"Yes, because you asked so sweetly."

157

"You have five minutes. Call me the moment you find her."

Before he could say another word, she clicked off the phone and raced back into the room, nearly tripping over a loose rug in her haste to make tracks. She caught her balance at the last moment and forced herself to slow down. Way slow, because she didn't want to hurt the baby.

This was all Stone's fault. This whole pregnancy, throwing up thing. Because he was irresistible and now she had to pay for being weak.

He'd implanted the seed of motherhood in her, so that the idea of becoming a mother was slowly blossoming. In less than nine months, would she be ready for this tiny human being they'd created?

Inside, the seamstress shoved pins and needles and thread back into her bag.

"I'm so sorry for the confusion. Liz will be right along."

The seamstress turned, her thin nose held high, her nostrils quivering the slightest with restrained anger. "I've been waiting over half an hour. How much longer do you expect me to wait?"

Stephanie began to hyperventilate. "We're fetching the bride right now. It should only be another five—" She quickly calculated the time it would take Stone to get to Liz's cabin, but if she wasn't there, what would they do? "Five minutes. Ten at the most."

The seamstress returned to packing up her things. "Not soon enough. I'm a busy woman. I have other clients."

Dora walked into the room just then, and Stephanie wanted to rush over and hug her. Her mom would know how to deal with the seamstress.

Except as she sidled up to Stephanie, her gaze darting around the room, she hissed, "Where is he?"

Stephanie raised her eyebrows. "Who?"

"That nasty divorce lawyer."

Right. Her mom never forgave and never forgot, which was too bad because it would hurt Stone. "He's looking for the bride. She's late for her fitting. If you could just—"

Her mom huffed out a sigh and headed for the wedding gown. "He's probably one of those men that likes his women big boobed and dumb."

"Mom, that's not very nice."

She bent her head to examine the stitching and muttered, "He probably hates children, too."

Stephanie remembered how he'd taken Mariam's little tyke into his arms, as though handing a toddler was an every day occurrence. She clasped her hands over her abdomen. "Actually he's pretty wonderful with kids."

But her mom chose not to hear her.

"Your father was right. The moment he saw that man's hand up your top, he said, *no good can come of this*. But did I listen?" Dora tsked, then straightened her back and retraced her steps to Stephanie's side. "I was so very, very wrong. I should call your father and apologize."

She knew her mom's obsessive personality well enough to know she wasn't going to be of any help with the current situation. As Stephanie glanced down at her silent phone, she said, "Yeah, you go ahead and do that, Mom. I can take care of this on my own."

On her way out, Dora nudged her on the shoulder and lowered her voice to a stage whisper. "If the seamstress walks, she'll be doing you a huge favor. Her stitches are atrocious."

Great. Stephanie gritted her teeth, and as expected, the seamstress turned, her face a granite stone.

"That's it. I'm out of here. Tell your mother she can fix my bad stitching."

Stephanie stepped into the other woman's path. "Please, don't go. My mother thinks she has the market on wedding and party events, but she's an amateur, not a professional like you and me. She doesn't know what she's talking about. Your stitches are beautiful." Thankfully, her cell phone rang. "Wait, this will be Liz."

"It better be."

Stephanie turned her back and headed toward the door, determined to thwart any attempt the seamstress made to escape.

"Did you find her?" she hissed.

Stone's voice came clear through the connection. "No. I'm heading over to Roger's cabin to check there. And if she's not there, I'll check to see if she's with Kevin."

"Kevin? Kevin who?"

"Never mind," he said. "Leave Liz up to me. I'll find her and get her there."

The phone went dead. Stephanie met the seamstress's shrewd gaze and gave her a weak smile. "Just another five minutes, please."

With her index finger, the seamstress tapped her mouth, her gaze traveling down Stephanie's body. "You and Liz are close to the same size."

"What?" Stephanie glanced down at her too tight top and thought of the button on her jeans which she'd had to leave undone, then back up at the other woman.

The seamstress pulled the gown off the hanger and held it up in front of Stephanie. "You'll do."

It dawned on Stephanie what she was thinking. She took a step back. "No, I don't do fittings."

"If you want this dress done in time for the wedding, you'll put it on." She shook out the dress. "Come on. Climb in."

The gown was beautiful, with a fitted bodice, fitted waist and a princess style skirt. The fine bead work glittered in the light as the full skirt swished and swayed.

She reached out and touched the material and experienced a

sense of awe. It wasn't as though marriage had ever been in her plans anyway. Especially now that she was pregnant. It was better to raise her child alone rather than raise her baby with a reluctant father.

Except Stone wasn't all that reluctant. He was willing to step up and take responsibility.

With a shake of her head to clear her thoughts, Stephanie took another step back. "It's bad luck to try on someone else's wedding gown."

"That's just a rumor started by brides to keep their bridesmaids from trying on their gowns." She pulled her lips into a smile that looked more like a sneer. "Either you put on the gown or I walk."

"But we have a contract."

"A contract which clearly states you will meet my time requests. Which of course, you haven't." She huffed out a sigh. "Look, I'm giving you a break because we're in the same business. Take it or leave it."

Stephanie turned her back and in one last ditch attempt, pulled out her cell and typed. *Desperate mother-to-be here...did you find her?*

Almost at Roger's.

"Where are you, Liz?" she muttered as she reached for the top button on her shirt. Deflated, she turned back to the seamstress. "Fine, you win. Let's get this over with before anyone comes in and catches me wearing that dress. There are certain people who could get the wrong idea."

Like her mother.

And Stone.

Although, as the other woman pulled out her supplies to measure and fit, Stephanie eyed the open doorway, and wondered if maybe it was all an act to make her agree to his marriage proposal.

Maybe he'd take one look at her dressed in the gown, and turn tail and run.

How much worse could her luck get? She was already pregnant, unmarried, and planning the most unlikely-to-happen wedding ever.

24

Roger answered the door with a smile. "Hey there, almost brother-in-law. I wondered how long it would take you to track me down."

Stone stuck out his hand and noted that the other man's handshake was firm and confident. "Roger. It's a pleasure to meet you."

The other man stepped aside and waved a hand toward the seating area. "Would you like to come in?"

"Another time. I'm looking for Liz. Have you seen her?"

"She's shopping." He took a hard look at Stone and sobered. "Is it urgent?"

What had Stephanie said? Something about Liz changing dresses? Stone wondered if his self-centered sister had shared that information with the groom.

He glanced down the path, hoping to see her, shopping bags in hand. "She's late for her appointment with the seamstress. I tried calling her and texting her, but she's not answering."

"No offense, but that's because you're her older brother." Roger bent his head and started thumbing the cell in his hands.

A few moments later, he glanced up, the smile still in his eyes and on his mouth. "She always answers me right away."

The younger man glanced back at the screen, and as the silence stretched between them, he began to fidget and frown. "I don't understand. Where could she be?"

Stone backed up a step, uncomfortable. "I'll keep looking. If you hear from her—"

Roger nodded, his mouth grim. "I'll let you know as soon as I do."

"Thanks, man." Stone thought of Stephanie and how somewhere between the lust and fear, there was another emotion threatening to break free. He shook off the thought. "Usually one encounter with our mother is enough to get rid of the potential life partners."

"I love your sister. Nothing is going to scare me off." The truth of his statement was there, in the set of his jaw, the light in his eyes, the solid stance of his body. "The only way I'm leaving is if Liz tells me to go."

Stone glanced past the man where he saw the neat and tidy living room. And he thought of Liz's room, clothes lying helter skelter everywhere. And he realized this kid—this young man— might be good for his sister. "I'm glad Liz picked you."

The surprised look in the younger man's gaze was followed by relief. "One down, the rest of the family to go."

With a wave goodbye, Stone headed to Kevin's cabin and when Kevin answered the door, he stared at the man on the other side of the doorway.

The soldier stood in the center of the open doorway, his arms crossed over his chest, legs braced to take the brunt of whatever came his way. He looked like a rock, unmovable without the proper backup.

And he gave nothing away. He was the perfect soldier. A stone cold killer.

Why would Liz be with him? They were total opposites. She was vibrant and alive. Kevin was cold and lifeless.

He peered around Kevin's broad shoulders. "Is Liz here?"

Kevin's eyes hooded over. "No."

But Stone didn't believe him because it was obvious he was hiding something. He tried to look around the man into the cabin beyond. "If you see her, remind her she's late for her dress fitting."

"I will."

A noise behind Kevin brought Stone up another step. "Who's in there with you?"

Kevin's stance broadened. "No one."

Stone took another step up. "Don't lie to me, Kev. We've been friends a long time. I can tell when you're lying."

Mariam's head popped up behind Kevin and she brushed past him, careful not to touch him. "Don't get your panties in a knot," she said as she hurried past, skipped down the steps, and headed down the pathway in the direction of the house.

Stone stared after her, noting that her usually neat appearance had been...mussed. He returned his attention to his friend and raised one eyebrow.

Kevin just stared at him.

With a sigh, Stone knew he'd get nothing out of the other man. Quietly, he said, "If you hurt my sister..."

He let the words drift off, because really, what could he do?

But Kevin gave a bitter laugh. "It's not what you think. If anything, it's the other way around."

Stone didn't like the sound of that any more, and as he headed toward the house, he wondered why love couldn't be easy.

He rushed the rest of the way to the main house, bounded up the steps and through the house to the fitting room where he halted in the open doorway.

Stephanie stood in the middle of the room on the raised platform, the skirt of the wedding gown floating around her bare feet, the soft skin of her shoulders gleaming in the morning sunlight.

His body stirred, woke with something primitive, and even though he knew he should be running as fast as he could, he couldn't make his feet go anywhere because his mind and his heart were suddenly working in unison. And they both urged him toward the woman staring back at him with a mixture of exasperation and worry on her face.

"Where's your sister?"

"Shopping."

"How could she forget about this appointment?"

"Haven't a clue." He crossed the room and stared up at her, feeling poleaxed. "Wow, you look gorgeous."

She narrowed her eyes at him. "Shouldn't you be running and screaming in the opposite direction?"

He caught her hand in his and gave a tug, but she stood solid. "Come down from there."

"Why?"

"Because you look sexy in that gown and I want to explore what's underneath."

Her smile turned dour. "Flattery from the king of divorce. What do you want?"

You, he nearly said, but he forced himself to take things slow and easy with the mother of his child. He didn't want just here and now. He wanted forever. "Is this the new gown?"

Silent, she nodded, and broke eye contact when she looked down and fingered the lacy material.

"Why are you wearing it?"

"Because the seamstress is more impatient than your mother. It was put on the dress or she was out of here. And then half way through the fitting, she left anyway. Without, I might add, taking the gown with her. It's my mom's fault. She didn't like the stitches and let the seamstress know." Raising her head, she took hold of his outstretched hand, grabbed the edge of the skirt, and pulled it up to her knees so she could climb down. "Help me get this thing off."

"Oh yeah, that's high on my list of things to do," he murmured.

She stopped mid-step and stared at him, a puzzled look in her wide eyes.

He gave a tug on her hand, tipping her off balance just enough for her to fall into his arms. He caught her by the waist and held her close. "Where's the seamstress now?"

"Probably sticking pins into a Barbie doll or something." She pulled down the shoulder of the gown, revealing more of her delectable skin. "Look. She's stuck me at least a dozen times and I'm sure more than half of them were delib—"

He shut her up the easiest way possible, by laying siege to her mouth until her eyes drifted shut and she leaned into him, returning the kiss like one drugged into submission. Good, because he felt that if he had to wait one more second, he was going to go stark raving mad.

"I want to make love to you," he whispered against her mouth.

She reached around behind her back. "Give me a moment to take off this gown."

He started pulling out the stickpins and set them aside. "No, keep it on. I want to be the one to take it off you."

She paused and with a sigh, stared up at him. "Why do you do this to me?"

He kissed the side of her neck, the bared skin of her shoulder. "Do what?"

"Cloud my mind so all I can think about is you."

He nipped at her shoulder, felt her shiver in response. "Because, baby, that's exactly what you do to me."

25

Stephanie shook her head in disbelief. "A wedding dress is turning you on? Are you sick? Mental? Something you'll pass on to our baby?"

"Yes. No." He chuffed out a self-conscious laugh, his breath warm against her shoulder. "If you must know, it's not the dress, it's the woman inside it."

"Smooth talker." She placed her palms against his chest, felt the thump of his heart against her palms. "The dirt—"

"I'll get it cleaned before Friday."

Stone took her by the hand, and weak-willed woman that she was, she gave in and followed him out of the fitting room, out of the house, and down the path toward the cottages.

He held on to her hand and they moved quickly, as though he were afraid they would get stopped by someone and wouldn't make their destination.

The moment they were inside his cottage, he locked the door, pulled her into his arms, and kissed her until she forgot all about getting the dress dirty, until all she could think about was how good he felt pressed against her.

Slowly, as he backed her toward the bedroom, his mouth

fused with hers, he worked his magic on the buttons until they no longer impeded his quest to remove the gown.

Which was a really good thing, because Stephanie was losing control...but what good did control do when he was so close, so irresistible?

He pulled back and peered down at her. "I've never seen you look sexier."

"I suppose one day I'll find you ogling a bride magazine as if it were a nudie mag." He looked at her with a moment of horror and as her stomach dipped with disappointment, she forced out a laugh. "Here it comes, the real Stone Kincaid. Want to borrow my sneakers?"

The horror disappeared from his expression, replaced by one far sneakier. "Maybe I'm getting over my fear of weddings and brides."

"And wedding planners?"

"Especially wedding planners."

She reached up, unpinned the hair piece, and pulled the train down, setting it carefully across a chair so it wouldn't wrinkle. Then she turned her back to him. "Finish this, will you?"

"Not yet," he murmured as he proceeded to kiss his way across one shoulder and up her neck to her ear.

A shiver crept over her and she leaned her head back so it rested against his shoulder. His arms came around her waist and he caught her mouth in a bone melting kiss, which turned her knees weak and her brain even weaker. She forgot about everything but what it was like to be naked in his arms.

He raised his head and met her gaze. "You taste good."

She smiled back at him. "Strawberry lip gloss."

"Mmmm, tastes more like Stephanie," he murmured as he turned his attention back to the buttons.

Even through the layers of the gown, she could feel the heat of him behind her and she wanted his hands on her bare skin so bad that she ached. "This is taking too long."

"Almost done," he said, and seconds later, he caught her by the shoulders and turned her around to face him.

Stephanie let the gown slowly drift down her body. She watched as his gaze follow the material down to the floor where it landed in a pool of white lace. Everywhere his gaze touched, her body came alive.

"You're beautiful," he whispered into the quiet between them.

She stepped out of the gown and bent to gather it into her arms. "Let me just—"

He brushed it out of her arms back onto the floor. Then he swept her into his arms and carried her toward the bed, where he laid her down so gently, almost as though he were afraid she would break. "So beautiful."

With one last longing look at the gown abandoned on the floor, she pushed up on her elbows and focused on the man tugging off his tie.

Desire pulsed in the center of her body, and she came to her knees to help him with the buttons on his shirt. She pushed the material away from his hard chest, off his broad shoulders, down his strong arms, and let it fall onto the floor next to the wedding gown.

Everywhere she touched, he was hot and hard and strong. He was everything she could ever want, kind and gentle and devoted to his family.

And as he bent his head to kiss her again, her heart did another pitter-patter, and she could no longer deny the truth.

Mine.

26

The lady was an enigma. A blend of mystery and sexy delight. Despite his attempt to stay away from her, Stone found himself drawn in.

There was something permanent about her. Something that scared him more than the fact that she carried his baby. Something that had kept him away from the phone until he'd come face-to-face with her on Serendipity Island.

He could admit to himself now that he'd fallen fast and hard, for those eyes and that mouth and that body. Straight into bed where he'd kept her naked in his arms for an entire night. Until she'd snuck out the next morning and left that phony business card.

But by then it had been too late. After a single night, she'd been so embedded in his thoughts that he found himself thinking of her upon wakening, in the middle of the workday, and fantasizing about her late at night while he laid in bed wanting her so badly, he ached.

And no other woman would do.

She smiled up at him then, and his heart gave a tiny sigh.

"What are you thinking, Stone?"

"That I'm a Steph-a-holic." Feeling self-conscious, he broke eye contact, and brushed his hand down her body and touched her belly where the new life had begun. He lowered his voice. "It's hard to believe you're pregnant."

She laid her hand over top of his, her touch soft and motherly. "There's no baby bump yet, nothing to give away our secret."

Our secret.

He met her gaze, and his heart and body stirred in unison.

This woman was special, he'd known that from the beginning, and he wondered what his life would be like if he let her slip away. She'd raise their kid on her own and never ask him for anything.

And he'd miss her. Not just for a month or a year, but quite possibly forever. From the moment he'd met her eyes across the Cranberry Cove Community Hall, he'd been sunk.

He bent his head to kiss her, and she cupped his cheeks with her small hands and deepened the kiss.

Is this how Roger felt about Liz? Kevin about Mariam? Barely able to breathe in their lover's presence? Unable to tear his gaze away for fear she'd vanish in a heartbeat?

"Uh oh," she said as she broke the kiss, and he cleared his thoughts and focused on what was coming out of her delectable mouth. "Stone Kincaid, if you change your mind, I am so never doing you again."

He laughed and tugged her against him, burying his face into the sweet curve of her neck. "I promise, I'm not about to change my mind. Ever."

Against his chest, he felt the thunder of her heart. It pulsed through his own body, wakening him to the realization that he needed her. He couldn't walk away without a backward glance.

Where Stephanie was concerned, he'd discovered he was never disinterested.

And then all he could think about was the utter softness of her in his arms.

He raised his gaze.

In the sunlight streaming through the window, she stared at him, wide eyed, her solemn gaze on his face.

The old fear of commitment raised up inside of him, until he breathed deep and inhaled the scent of her, which banished the fear riding his shoulders, quieted the unexpected thought of losing her.

As her fingers tangled in his hair, wandered across his shoulders and back, and pulled him closer, he knew in that moment that she meant something more to him than just a quick romp in the sack.

But instead of running like he'd once thought of doing, he slid one hand down her belly where their child rested, and set his forehead against hers. "I don't want to hurt you."

"You won't."

And as she welcomed him home, the words popped out again before he could stop them. "Marry me, Steph. Let me take care of you and our baby."

This time the proposal felt right, like he actually meant it. Maybe he did.

Clasping him around the back, holding him tighter, she gave him the answer he expected. "No."

As he made sweet love to her, he prayed she couldn't hear the sound of his heart shattering in his chest.

Afterwards, with her eyelids getting heavier by the second, he curled around her and they spooned, and soon she was fast asleep.

He knew it because the lady snored.

For the first time in his life, he realized that he felt more for this woman than lust.

He was in love.

The prenup agreement had been a stupid idea. Asking her to

marry him while in the throes of passion hadn't been one of his most brilliant ideas either. All he knew was that he better figure out a way to convince her to marry him before she disappeared from his life again.

Because they were good together—both in bed and out.

27

Stephanie woke from her nap, feeling well loved and well rested. She stretched, but when she opened her eyes, she yelped.

Liz sat on the chair beside the bed, her gaze fixed on her. "Sorry, didn't mean to frighten you."

With a furtive glance toward the other side of the bed, which was thankfully empty, she grabbed the sheets to her chest and pushed to a sitting position. Scraping her hair back from her face, she leaned against the headboard.

Liz broke the silence. "I'm sorry I missed the dress fitting."

Stephanie followed the other woman's glance toward the other side of the room. Liz's gown was spread neatly over a chair and it was obvious Stone had gone back for her own clothes, because there they were on top of the gown. "I—that's okay. The seamstress used me for a pincushion."

"Sorry." Liz shifted her gaze and stared at Stephanie intently. "Why are you naked in my brother's bed?"

In an attempt to distract the younger woman from the obvious, she asked, "Why weren't you at the fitting?"

"I was shopping." Liz glanced down at her blouse and trousers. "What do you think? I'm going for a new look."

"You look...normal." At Liz's wry grimace, Stephanie hurried to explain. "I mean, you look really great. This outfit really fits your journalist persona far better than the other look. What does Roger think?"

Liz slumped on the chair and chewed a thumbnail. "I haven't shown him yet."

"Why not?"

With a shrug, the younger woman glanced at the bed. "So why are you naked in Stone's bed?"

Stephanie gave a tug on the sheet and inched it higher. "How do you know I'm naked under here?"

Liz gave her a rueful glance, but didn't say a word.

"I'm—uh—having a nap?" Which was the truth, something she might have to get used to, considering she was pregnant and all.

Liz leaned forward. "It looked like you just finished making love."

Oh boy, the younger woman wasn't going to give this topic up until she was satisfied she'd gotten the truth. Stephanie gritted her teeth. "It was just sex, okay? I know it's your brother. I know it's unprofessional of me. But it just happened and I promise, it won't happen again." Maybe. He could be awfully persuasive and she seemed to have a weakness for his persuasiveness. "Please don't tell your mother."

"I thought there was something going on between the two of you." Liz tilted her head. "I've never seen my brother look at anyone like he looks at you. Like he's gone all caveman." But then pity crossed the younger woman's face, ruining Stephanie's utopia. "My brother doesn't do long term. Once he gets tired of you, or if you get too clingy, he'll be gone with barely a word goodbye."

"I know." Stephanie sighed and clasped her hands together.

"We were supposed to be a one night stand. No attachments. No calling one another to say *I miss you, I need to see you*."

"And then you ran into each other here." At Stephanie's nod, Liz's pity morphed into compassion. "Whatever you do, don't fall for him. Protect your heart. It's the only way to survive a romantic encounter with my brother."

Liz refocused on the wedding gown.

As the silence in the room grew, Stephanie eyed her clothes. "If you wouldn't mind turning your back, I'd like to get dressed."

But either Liz didn't hear her or she was ignoring her.

Dragging the sheet with her, conscious of her swollen breasts and the barely discernible baby bump, she swung her legs out of bed and headed for the bathroom. After using the facilities, washing her face, combing her hair, and brushing her teeth, she went back into the bedroom, hopeful that Liz was gone along with her questions.

She wasn't. Instead, she stared into space, a pensive expression on her face.

"What's wrong, Liz?"

"I was just thinking about that first flush of desire and what a heady feeling it is." The younger woman sighed. "What happens when it's gone?"

Stephanie couldn't ever imagine losing her desire for Stone. Maybe it would one day turn into comfort, but the desire would always be there. "What do you mean?"

"Roger and me." She met Stephanie's gaze. "At the beginning, it was really hot. You know? We couldn't be in the same room without tearing each other's clothes off. But now...the heat is gone. We're like an ancient couple, too tired to get out of our rocking chairs for a little nookie."

Stephanie gentled her annoyance with the woman. "It's the pressure of the wedding preparations. Every couple goes through it."

"Do they?" She pushed to her feet and smoothed the wrinkles

out of her new trousers. When she spoke again, her voice was barely audible. "I think I'm in love with someone else."

Stephanie swallowed back a groan. Almost every couple she encountered reached this point. Sometimes she felt like a love jinx. "Liz, don't."

The younger woman's voice softened to a near whisper. "What if Stone is right? What if I don't love Roger? What if I'm too young to love someone forever?"

Next time she saw Stone, Stephanie was going to kill him. "Your brother knows nothing about love or marriage. Remember that he's a destroyer of relationships. A marriage terminator."

Liz frowned. "Wow, considering you don't seem to like him very much, the sex must be really hot."

That silenced Stephanie completely as she acknowledged the sex was really hot. But she wouldn't be with him if she didn't like him at some level. Well, maybe that first time, but now?

She sat down on the bed, and took Liz's hand and gave a gentle squeeze. "Oh honey, it's just pre-wedding jitters. Stay strong. Two more days and then you'll be Mrs. Roger Gordon. All you have to do is get through the engagement party and the wedding ceremony, and then all of the tension and doubt you're experiencing will disappear."

There was a world of hurt in the younger woman's eyes. In a whisper, she asked, "What if it doesn't?"

"It will, I promise you. All brides experience this feeling of panic."

Liz tugged her hand free, placed her hands on her knees and pushed to her feet. She looked old, ancient, like a ninety-five year old. "I'll catch up with you later. I'm going for a walk. I have some thinking to do."

"No." Stephanie jumped to her feet and stood in Liz's way. "No thinking. It's too late to think. Thinking at this point will only get you into trouble and cause you to have regrets."

"Whatever."

And then Liz was gone.

Stephanie followed her out of the cabin and watched as the younger woman raced along the path and disappeared into the trees. And she couldn't help but wonder if she should say something to Stone about his sister or if that would just make things worse.

Making her decision, knowing he only wanted his sister to be happy, she grabbed her cell, found Stone's number, and hit call.

He picked up on the first ring. "Hi babe. Did you have a good sleep?"

"Yeah, yeah, fine," she said impatiently. "I need you to do something for me."

"Anything."

"I'm putting you in charge of Liz."

He gave a gruff laugh. "That boat sailed a long time ago."

"You don't understand. She's having second thoughts."

The silence on the phone stretched out, until Stephanie thought for sure he was going to tell her *I told you so.*

And yet he surprised her once again. "I like Roger. He'll be good for Liz."

"You really think so?"

"I do." There was a moment of silence, during which time she realized that she trusted him and his judgement. And then his low voice broke through her thoughts. "How are you feeling?"

"Great. The nap was wonderful. Now I'm going to go for a walk, then get busy finalizing some of the plans."

"Do you want my help?"

She felt a smile break across her face, and everything in her lightened. "I would love it. Meet you back at my cabin in thirty minutes?"

"I'll be there."

After she hung up, she left her sandals in the cottage and went for a stroll along the beach. The white sand squished between her toes and she walked along the edge of the water, mindful not to wander in too deep for fear of the undertow dragging her out.

She truly did believe that Liz was experiencing pre-wedding jitters. But the tiny bit of her that wondered if the pre-wedding jitters were an indication of bigger problems kept poking and prodding at her until it wouldn't let her alone.

She pulled out her cell and dialed her dad's cell number. He answered on the first ring.

"Hello, kiddo. Are you taking good care of my sweater?"

"Yes, Dad, I am." Stephanie plunked down on a boulder to enjoy the heat of the mid-afternoon sun. "Please don't make me keep Mom."

His warm familiar chuckle came through the phone. "Don't worry. I miss her and I'll eventually want her back. Do you know this is the first time we've been apart since we got married?"

"Really?" Relief swept through her. Her dad wasn't mad and furious like she thought he'd be. "So what was with the argument in town?"

"Want to know the truth?"

"Of course I do."

"It's much easier to plan your mom's birthday party without her interference and input."

She laughed. "So you sent her to torture me so you could have an easy time?"

"Yeah, that pretty much sums it up."

"Dad, I didn't know you had it in you." She hesitated, then plunged ahead. "Can I ask you a personal question?"

"Sure, let me put this on speakerphone. I have a cake to pull out of the oven." A moment later, he said, "Can you still hear me?"

"Yes." She took a deep breath. "Dad, were either you or Mom nervous on your wedding day before you said your final *I do's*?"

His voice came from a long distance away. In the background, she could hear the stove timer buzz. "I don't know about your mom, but that morning, I woke up with an overwhelming urge to join the navy."

"Seriously?" Well, that shot her theory all to heck. She slid down the rock and plopped down on the warm sand.

"Why do you ask, kiddo?"

"I've always thought that when two people were perfect for each other, there would be no hesitation or fear."

Her dad picked up the phone and the speakerphone turned off. "Before every great stride in our growth, we have to battle that which we fear. Committing yourself to one person for the rest of your life is a huge step."

"No kidding." She sighed. "Mom hates Stone and it's all my fault."

"What did you do?" There was a moment of silence. "You didn't tell your mom he was a divorce lawyer, did you?"

She groaned and covered her face with her hands. "Yes. I'm an idiot."

"I still don't like him, but now I feel sorry for him." Tom cleared his throat. "Is he nice to you? Does he treat you with respect?"

Stephanie thought of all the occasions when he'd put her needs first. "Yes on both accounts."

"Doesn't change my opinion, but then no man will ever be good enough for my baby girls."

She blinked away tears. "Thanks for the talk, Dad. I love you."

"I love you too, kiddo. Talk to you later."

The connection went dead, and Stephanie sat there, the warmth of the sun on the top of her head, the crash of the waves against the shoreline soothing.

As she mulled over her dad's words, a man jogged past, his bare back tanned and smooth, the sand offering no resistance to his movements.

Then Liz ran onto the beach and skidded to a stop in front of him. "Kevin, I need to talk to you."

So this was the man Stone had mentioned. She watched him rake a hand through his hair.

"Go away, Liz."

"No, not till you hear me out."

He sighed, heavy. "What do you want?"

Liz risked a step forward. Her voice broke and she blinked back tears. "I want you. I love you, Kevin. I'm willing to do anything, to give up anything, so I can spend the rest of my life with you."

Kevin shook his head. "You don't love me, Liz. You know nothing about me."

"I know enough," she insisted. He tried to step around her, but she moved into his path. With a deep breath, she rushed on. "Tell me you'll give me a chance and I'll call off the wedding."

"I'm sorry, I can't do that. I'm in love with someone else."

He stepped around her and jogged away.

What was Liz doing going after another man?

Why wasn't she with Roger?

Roger.

Stephanie felt pity for the younger man. Did he have a clue about what was going on with his bride-to-be?

She stayed where she was, unable to watch Liz's heartbreak and unable to offer comfort. If what her dad said was true, then the young woman had to be suffering from nothing but cold feet. Her and Roger seemed so perfect for each other.

At last, Liz ventured on and Stephanie pushed to her feet and headed back to her cottage where she expected to find Stone waiting for her. Instead she found her mom puttering in the kitchen. "Hey, Mom."

"Where have you been? I hope it wasn't with that nasty divorce lawyer."

"He's not all that nasty." She sat down at the kitchen table and opened her laptop. "In answer to your question, I went for a walk. Alone."

As she scrolled through the list of items she still needed to take care of, she could feel her mom's gaze on her. At last she looked up. "What?"

"Why are you wearing that old sweater again? Go put on something nice, then toss it out with the rest of the trash. I don't know how you ended up with it anyway."

Stephanie grinned. "Actually, if you must know, Dad rescued it from the garbage and gave it to me to keep for him until he deemed it safe to bring it back into the house."

"He did what?" Dora eyed-balled her. "That man. He's intolerable. I don't know who he thinks he's been living with all of these years. When did he start to believe I was his slave in the kitchen?"

She peered back at the screen and bit back the grin threatening to break free. "Yeah, the nerve."

A frown creased lines into her forehead. "Still, I wonder how he's doing? We've never been apart like this."

"I'm sure he's doing just fine without you, Mom. He's a grown man."

A knock sounded on the door. She pushed to her feet, and when she reached the door, it was Stone, tall and strong and so undeserving of her mom's new attitude. As she let him in, she whispered, "My mother is here. Prepare to be insulted."

He followed her into the kitchen, and the moment Dora saw him, she wiped her hands on a tea towel, crossed the room, and stopped in front of him, her hands on her matronly hips. "You might be lower than pond scum, but I might need a good divorce lawyer. What are your rates?"

"Mom, you are not divorcing Dad. You'll see. He'll come around."

Dora huffed out a sigh and slid a glance her way. "Maybe. The makeup sex *is* pretty good."

She swept from the room, once again careful to ensure her skirts didn't touch Stone, and as the door closed behind her, Stephanie met Stone's gaze.

"What was that all about?"

"She doesn't know it, but Dad deliberately riled her up to get rid of her."

He raised his brows. "Why?"

"He said it was easier to plan her birthday party without her."

He laughed. "So you got stuck with her?"

"Yeah, and it's totally unfair."

His gaze dipped to her stomach, then returned to her face, and there was heat there, and something more. Affection. "So do you have a job for me?"

She decided not to worry about the future until after Liz's wedding, and closed the distance between them. Sliding her hand up his chest, she inhaled the scent of him, and the tightness in her stomach eased. "You know, we can probably take a minute or five before we need to get back to the party and wedding arrangements."

A millisecond later, she was in his arms doing the naughty.

28

Grace stared out the bedroom window at the lush greenness of the golf course. Where was Jim?

Normally he'd be on the course at this time of day, getting in one final game before supper, hitting that stupid little ball, with his friends jeering him on, and now his little golf bimbo...bimboing.

Before she ended up more depressed than she already was, she forced herself to turn away and head for the shower to get ready for tonight's party.

In the bathroom, in front of the full length mirror, she pulled off her robe and stared at her naked body.

She wasn't bad looking. A little thick around the middle, but not so much that men had stopped looking at her. Well, except for her own man.

What was the matter with him?

Or maybe she should quit asking what was the matter with him and start asking what was the matter with herself? Why was she hanging onto him, waiting for a small crumb of his affection? Why didn't she go out and find herself another man?

She needed a man.

Badly.

Here she was, in the prime of her sexual life—or at least, that's what the experts claimed—and there was no one willing to fulfill her fantasies...her desires.

She rubbed one hand down her belly and with the other hand, captured her breast, trying hard to remember the feel of Jim's hands on her body.

It had been so long.

She closed her eyes and guilty pleasure filled her.

Proper women didn't do this, did they?

Her eyes popped open and she looked back at herself in the mirror.

Well, when proper women's husbands didn't do their duty, then proper women should be entitled to find their enjoyment wherever and whenever they could.

As she rubbed one hand across her breast and bit back a moan of pure pleasure, she noticed a small puckering on the edge of her breast and stilled.

What was that?

Grace lifted her arm over her head, the dizzy pleasure gone from her head, and with one hand shifted the breast to the light and proceeded to do a breast examination.

She encountered a small painful lump and fear rocked through her as she dropped her hands to her sides and stared at her naked body in the mirror.

Maybe this is what proper women who weren't so proper in private deserved.

With shaking hands, she picked up the phone and punched in her doctor's office number.

By the time she was ready for the party—makeup on, hair swept up, perfumed and dressed in an exquisite teal gown—her nerves were on fire. She'd arranged the appointment with the local doctor and was scheduled for an overnight stay at the

Serendipity Island Hospital tomorrow. They'd assured her she'd be back in plenty of time for Liz's wedding.

As she swept into the ballroom, she refocused on the evening, her shrewd gaze taking in everything from the glittering lights to the *Congratulations Liz and Roger* sign to her family scattered among the guests.

Family.

These days, it was almost a foreign word. Liz wasn't talking to her. Mariam was always distracted. Stone was making eyes at a woman so totally inappropriate that it made Grace want to scream.

And Jim...non-existent, as usual. Caught up in his golf game and course.

No, she wouldn't think of that tonight. In fact, she wouldn't think of it ever again. Jim could do whatever he wanted and so could she. Which made her narrow her eyes as Stone's rascal friend, Kevin Donahue, walked into the room.

Sandy Strom stopped at her side, a drink in one hand, a canapé in the other. "He's positively yummy."

"Reminds me of my Andy when we first me," Leta Johnson said as she parked herself on the other side.

Grace looked over at Andy, with his bald head and distinctive paunch, and wondered about that starry eyed look in Leta's eyes.

Nancy Strom stopped beside her sister-in-law. "Mmmmm, give me a piece of that hunk of meat."

Grace had to admit that Kevin Donahue was easy on the eyes, hair shaven just short of not being there, that oh-so-popular five-o'clock shadow that gave him a hint of a dangerous bad boy. Tonight, a jean jacket covered his well muscled shoulders and broad chest. Beneath the jacket, a black t-shirt hugged his physique. Blue jeans encased long legs and cowboy boots finished the casual outfit.

"He knew we were celebrating tonight. Couldn't he have

dressed up? At least washed the mud from his boots?" Grace asked in annoyance.

"Honey, no one will notice the mud way down there, not when there's so much more to look at...higher," Nancy drawled. "Maybe you should have hired him as your assistant instead of that other one."

Liz swept into the room at that moment, her fiancee nowhere in sight, and Grace watched her daughter's face light up when she spotted Kevin.

Nothing good could come of that attraction, except that it proved she needed to stop her youngest daughter's wedding.

Then Mariam walked into the room, her little boy cradled in her arms, Roger at her side. Her gaze slid toward Kevin, and for just a moment, there was something vulnerable in her eyes, before she shuttered her emotions, and turned her back on him.

Grace watched her oldest daughter's progress across the crowded ballroom as her younger sister headed in the opposite direction.

As far as Grace knew, Mariam hadn't looked at anyone since her divorce.

"Wow, doesn't that get you wet just watching him," Nancy muttered as she pulled out a cigarette and stuffed it between her lips.

"Not in the house." Sandy pulled it out of her mouth, broke it in half, then gave it back to Nancy who responded with a, "*Hey.*"

Grace followed Nancy's gaze to where Roger had joined his fiancee. He bent Liz back and claimed her mouth with his, and Grace stopped thinking of anything but...sex.

Hard sex.

Mind blowing sex.

Sex so spectacular, it could make any woman a slave to her man.

She blinked and stared down at the champagne glass in her hand.

What was the matter with her? She should be focused on her health instead of sex.

Leta sighed wistfully, drawing everyone's attention. "No wonder Liz has her heart set on that man."

"For now," Sandy added with a narrow eyed look.

"No man is worth keeping forever." Nancy stuffed the broken cigarette into her purse and pulled out another one.

Sandy grabbed this one too, then hooked her arm through her sister-in-law's and started toward the patio. "Come on. We'll finish this discussion outside so that Nancy can kill herself slowly."

"Stuff it," Nancy muttered as she pulled her arm free and sailed ahead of them.

"I should really stay here. Be with my guests," Grace protested, but even to her own ears, the protest sounded weak.

Leta grabbed Grace and tugged her along. "We're guests."

She pulled back. "But the party—"

"Will survive without you," Nancy threw over her shoulder. As they stopped on the patio, Nancy lit her cigarette and took a huge puff, then blew it out. The smoke hung in the air between them.

Leta gave a polite *cough, cough*. Grace waved the smoke away from her face. Sandy grabbed the cigarette from her sister-in-law, dropped it on the stones underfoot, and ground the toe of her very expensive, very lovely shoes into it. "Okay, let's get down to business."

Grace didn't want to go there tonight, so she played innocent. "What business?"

"Husband business," Leta stated, her mouth firmed with determination.

Grace noticed they were all looking at her. "I did my part when I hired the assistant."

Nancy grabbed another cigarette from her purse, gave them all a dirty look, then lit it. This time, though, she made a point to blow the smoke away from them. "Well, it didn't work. We need a better plan."

Sandy nodded. "Jim doesn't seem to have noticed your boy-toy, so no way is that young man going to help our situation."

Leta hooked a thumb toward the ballroom. "Do any of you remember the last time your husband treated you like that?"

"Before golf," Sandy stated.

"Never," Nancy replied.

Three pairs of curious eyes turned toward Grace. Panic infiltrated her body, starting a chain reaction of heat that moved from her chest, to her ears, and finally infused her face. Oh, how she hated menopause.

"I really am a marriage fraud." *In more ways that one.* With a sigh, she gave in. "Before he retired and decided to build the golf course."

Leta patted her arm. "It's okay, dear. Your secret is safe with us."

Nancy dropped her cigarette on the patio and ground it out with the tip of her pointy shoe. "It's time to get dirty, ladies."

"Dirty?" Grace squeaked.

The three women exchanged glances, then grinned at Grace. "We've been taking golf lessons."

Grace stared at the women who were staring back at her with studied patience in their eyes. She frowned back at them. "And?"

With a grin, Sandy said, "It's time to disobey that *No Women Allowed* rule."

"You don't mean—" Grace shook her head and began to back away. "I'm sorry. You're more than welcome to use the golf course, but I can't be part of this plan."

No, she thought as she turned and reentered the ballroom. She couldn't commit to anything, not right now. By tomorrow, she might discover that she had months of chemo treatments in her future.

Then Jim walked into the room, freshly showered and shaved,

handsome as handsome could be. And on his arm was his golf bimbo.

The woman clung to him as though he were a prized possession, his arm pressed against her amble bosom, her dress so tight and smooth, Grace was positive she was naked beneath it.

She clenched her hands at her sides, fury robbing her of every thought but one.

When was the last time he'd treated her as though she were more important than air?

When was the last time he'd spoken to her like a true friend?

When was the last time they'd had sex just for the fun of it and not because it was all about makeup sex?

She glanced back over her shoulder at the three women with their heads huddled together.

They were talking about mosquitoes, the hot afternoon sun, and sweat. Three of Grace's least favorite things in the world.

Jim currently being the fourth.

29

Stephanie glanced around the ballroom, taking in everything from the glittering lights on the outdoor patio to the warm tropical breeze drifting in the open doors, from the *Congratulations Liz & Roger* banner to the elegant cream and pink color scheme.

Grace had overseen the decorations—rolled linen napkins draped with tiny pearls, crystal glasses fill with blush pink roses, and lights to illuminate every table.

The guests had started to arrive an hour ago, and the guests of honor were doing their part to mingle. Stephanie prayed Liz had come to her senses after Kevin's rejection on the beach.

Leaning against a decorative post near the buffet table, her thoughts drifted to Stone. Where was he? After their sexual interlude, she'd sent him to keep watch over Liz to ensure the younger woman made an appearance at this evening's party.

Although right now, she'd much prefer he was standing right beside her so she could lean into his shoulder and inhale the delicious scent of him. It would help deflect the smells of perfume, aftershave, and food all mingling together and turning her stomach.

As if her thoughts conjured him up, he walked into the room, and the beat of her heart faltered and picked up pace. As he scanned the crowd, the needy woman inside of her jumped up and down, and screamed *pick me, pick me.*

Oh yeah, she had it bad, all right. So bad, she was willing to beg for a scrap of his attention.

As his gaze connected with hers, she stopped breathing, stopped hearing, stopped thinking.

Mine.

It had to be the pregnancy hormones that were making her so territorial. She couldn't remember ever wanting anyone else the way she wanted him.

Without breaking eye contact, he headed her way, but every few feet, someone stopped him to shake his hand and talk. At this rate, it would be hours before he reached her...which was probably a good thing because every time he was nearby, she forgot about the job she'd been hired to do.

A noise to her right caught her attention. She reined in her libido and turned her head as Dora stopped at her side, a drink in one hand, a canapé in the other. "Liz's fiancee is positively yummy. He reminds me of Tom when we first met."

Stephanie resisted the urge to choke. Still, she couldn't help but wonder about that starry eyed look in her mom's eye. After forty years of marriage, her parents still showed signs of desire for one another. Maybe not all of the time, like a new relationship —like her and Stone—but often enough that she could tell there was still heat between them.

She wrinkled her nose. "Mom, that's gross. You're old enough to be his...well...*mother.*"

Dora threw her a patient glance. "Honey, just because I've aged doesn't mean I've stopped appreciating the finer things in life."

"Yes, well, it's embarrassing."

Dora sighed. "I wonder how your dad is doing and how he's

making out at Mandy's without me. I hope he's started decorating the house for my birthday party."

"I'm sure he's doing fine."

"Maybe I'll give him a call."

Dora slipped away, her cell already in her hand.

Alone again, Stephanie watched Liz with Roger.

They were both so young. What did they know about love? At their age, Stephanie had been infatuated with more than one man, sometimes at the same time.

Right now, they were locked in a lip lock that didn't look like it was going to end any time soon, ignoring the dinner bell and the guests as though none of it existed but themselves.

How could Liz claim to love one man while she married another?

She turned her attention away from the couple.

It wasn't her business or responsibility. *They* weren't her concern. All she needed to do was focus on the wedding, get through the next two days without saying a word about what she'd seen.

Then her gaze locked on Stone. He was staring at his sister and her fiancee, a frown on his face.

She knew that he was concerned about Liz's hasty decision to marry the rock star. He was worried that she was too young to handle the responsibility of marriage.

He was worried that he'd have to represent his baby sister in court one day.

Was it possible to be in love with one man but lust after another?

Should she tell him about what she'd seen on the beach?

Another glance toward the young couple and she cleared her head of the image of Liz throwing herself at Kevin. They weren't her problem. She had enough problems of her own.

Like ending up with that engagement ring back on her finger.

The last thing she wanted was a forced marriage.

Marriage was hard enough when two people started out with love in their hearts, but when they didn't? Getting married because she was pregnant just seemed wrong.

Her attention got caught by a movement on the balcony and she spotted the stranger.

Kevin.

If he wasn't here for Liz, then why was he here?

He was watching Liz kiss Roger, his body tense, his face expressionless. But then his focus changed and zeroed in on Mariam, and everything clicked into place.

He had a haunted look in his gaze, and for some reason, even though she didn't know him, it broke her heart.

This man—this stranger—was looking at Mariam as though he wanted her more than his next breath. And she knew just by looking at him that if Mariam were pregnant with his child, he would never let her go. Never, in a million, zillion years. He'd claim her and their child like an old fashioned caveman.

Is that why Stone had tried to put a ring on her finger? To lay his claim?

Stephanie dragged her attention back to Stone and ignored the fact that all she had to do was connect gazes with him and her own territorial instincts came on full force. Not a good thing when faced with a confirmed bachelor and a pregnant woman.

But she had to do what was best for her and her baby. And the best she could do right now was to stay sensible and single. So what if she melted every time he came within the sphere of her vision. So what if she couldn't control her own body.

Heck, she'd rather raise her child alone than be forced to endure the kind of marriage that Grace and Jim had.

Her stomach did a belly flop.

The kind of marriage Liz and Roger would have if Stephanie didn't step up and say something.

30

Stone circled the crowded ballroom, shaking a hand here, tossing a greeting there, and inched his way toward the mother of his child.

Her refusal to marry him still stung, although he didn't have a clue why. All he really knew was that he should be relieved...and yet, he was anything but.

Instead, he was fascinated beyond reason with her, and the desire to close the distance between them, sweep her into his arms and carry her off to bed, totally consumed him.

Someone jostled him from behind and he dragged his attention away from the woman who consumed his every thought, and came back to reality to shake another hand, smile at another familiar face.

Then he spotted Liz dance past with her fiancee.

Despite the groom's youthful looks and lack of formal attire, Roger appeared relaxed and happy, and not at all apprehensive that in two days, he would spend the rest of his life tied to one woman.

The kid was a whole lot braver than he was.

And even if they didn't make it—even if Liz one day called

him to represent her in front of a judge—they'd still be tied together. By shared memories, a child, or the possession that one spouse won in the battle with hopes of destroying the other.

It would always be there, the love they once shared, the betrayal that tore them apart.

And knowing his sister and her flighty ways, he couldn't help but wonder how much time—days, weeks, months—before she came knocking on his door, crying because she'd realized her mistake.

Liz and Roger came to a stop in front of Stephanie, and while Liz spoke to her wedding planner, Roger wandered off, his cell phone in his hands, his thumbs tapping at the screen without a single pause.

He headed their way, his progress slowed down by the exceptionally large crowd in the ballroom. Every few feet, someone else stopped him and he was forced to make small talk. When he neared them, he caught the scent of Stephanie's perfume on a drift of air and his body stirred.

No matter how much he was determined to keep his distance, his body had a totally different agenda.

While she spoke with Liz, she was busy checking the table centerpieces. He could picture her with her dress pushed off her shoulders, her head thrown back in ecstasy, her eyes smoldering with passion.

He'd never met a woman he couldn't push from his thoughts like he couldn't push her. And her laughter and smile did something strange to his insides.

But she wasn't laughing or smiling now. She'd stopped, a furrow between her brows, her hand on her stomach, appearing a little green.

His sister didn't seem to notice.

Concern for her grew, and when he reached her, he stopped beside her and quietly asked. "You okay?"

Her eyes were clouded with distress, but with a quick nod in his direction, she turned her attention back to the bride, and Liz rattled on.

The groom returned, his cell still in one hand, gave the bride-to-be a kiss on the cheek, then thrust his hand toward Stone. "Hello, brother-in-law. Sorry for the distraction." His attention returned to his phone and he began to type. "My band is about to release our fifth album and I'm determined to release it at the same time as the wedding so I can dedicate it to your sister."

He was nothing like his stage presence, Stone noted, and without the garish makeup and outlandish clothes, he was quite normal looking. "No problem."

"Ah, something interesting to tweet." And he began typing on the screen keyboard. "Wedding update. The bride's big brother hasn't killed me yet, so does that mean I've been accepted into this warm family fold?"

Stone couldn't help it, he laughed. The kid seemed genuine.

Liz turned to her fiancee. "I've been meaning to tell you that my mother invited another seventy-five of her friends. The guest list is going to be awfully one sided now. I'm so sorry."

Roger glanced up from the screen, and with an understanding smile, leaned forward and gave Liz a peck on the cheek. "No worries, babe. Whatever keeps her happy."

Liz leaned forward to kiss him on the lips and she appeared genuinely in love with this man. "That's one of the things I love about you most. You spoil me rotten. You're so understanding and flexible."

Maybe all of Stone's doubts and concerns had been for nothing. Maybe, as Liz had said, she'd just had a moment of cold feet.

A maid walked in with a tray holding an assortment of baked goods and set it on the table, and as the scent of yeast and sugar reached Stone, he heard Stephanie choke. But before he could do anything, Roger looked up from his cell phone.

"You look like you're going to be sick again. What's wrong with you anyway?"

"Food poisoning," she squeaked.

"You should see a doctor."

"Already done. Just waiting for confirmation."

Roger grabbed the tray, pity on his face. "Let me take this to the other end of the table."

And with another kiss on Liz's cheek, and a nod toward Stone and Stephanie, he wandered away, holding the tray with one hand, tapping on the cell with the other, humming a turn, and singing, "*Whatever keeps my baby happy.*"

And then he walked past the end of the table and headed out of the ballroom, the tray forgotten in his hand.

Liz swiveled her gaze past Stone and gave Stephanie a bright smile. "Well, it's settled then. The guest list is done, providing Mother doesn't keep adding to it. I better go mingle till Roger comes back."

And then she was gone in a swirl of perfume and skirt.

Stone turned his attention to the mother of his child and put his hand on the small of her back, feeling the heat of her bare skin against his palm as he bent closer to her ear so she could hear him. "Want to get out of here?"

She glanced up at him, distress in her eyes, one hand over her nose and mouth. "I can't. I need to—it's the sweet breads and the olives—"

And then she was gone, dashing out the closest doorway with him hot on her heels.

She'd obviously scoped out the nearest bathroom before the party.

Stone waited in the hallway, one shoulder against the wall, his cell in his hand as he texted Wanda that he needed her assistance. Hopefully she was back from whatever had occupied her for the afternoon because he wanted her to take over from Stephanie for the evening.

As he received confirmation that his assistant was back on the property, something in him twigged, the thought that he might be willing to wait for Stephanie for the rest of his life.

Not good. Not good at all. He might have originally asked her to marry him out of responsibility to their child, but now—

She came out of the bathroom, paler than chalk.

He took her arm. "Come on. I'm taking you back to your cottage so you can rest."

She pushed a stray lock of hair away from her forehead. "I have to check on the cooks—"

"I've already arranged for Wanda to take over and keep an eye on things. Besides, the cooks are professionals. They don't need you." Not like I do, he wanted to add, but the sheer revelation of the strength of his emotions made him swallow back the words.

He thrust his hands in his pockets, fearful that he might touch her and never be able to stop. While a part of him acknowledged the need to push her away—and do it hard and fast—another part of him wanted to hang on to her forever.

She glanced up at him, and as the frown cleared from her face, her mouth morphed into a smirk. "I'm still not marrying you."

He quirked one brow. "Just because I asked once—"

"Twice."

"—doesn't mean I plan to ask again."

"Good, because marriage sucks."

He followed her gaze down the hallway to where Liz was talking to Kevin. "For a wedding planner, you sure have some strange ideas."

She turned her gaze up to his face, and for just a moment, Stone felt sucker-punched by the tenderness and concern in her eyes. "What would you do if you saw something that didn't bode well for the married couple?"

As Kevin disappeared one way and Liz disappeared the other, Stone set his hand on the small of Stephanie's back and guided her down the hallway before she could find another excuse to go back to the party.

"I'd tell her brother." When she didn't say anything, he smiled down at her. "Marriage is hard. Liz is young. I've seen enough divorces to want to protect her from going through that."

Silent, they headed outside and Stone noticed Stephanie shiver. He tugged off his suit jacket and wrapped it around her bare shoulders.

She gave an appreciative smile, grabbed the lapels, and hugged it to her chest. "And yet you asked me to marry you."

"That's different."

"How?"

"We're older and you're carrying my baby."

She shook her head. "That's not enough, Stone."

He quirked one eyebrow and leered down at her. "How about the sex? You can't deny that it's outstanding."

She laughed and waggled her eyebrows at him. "Since apparently I've abandoned my duties, maybe we could—you know."

Oh yeah, he knew. His heart did a strange sizzle that threatened to take his breath away while desire unfurled and his lower extremities jump to attention. He stopped her in the middle of the path and gently turned her to face him. "Are you sure you're up to it?"

"We'll have to go to your cottage, though. Mom likes to pop in and out of mine." Her eyes drifted closed. He saw her touch her stomach and inhale deeply. And then she opened her eyes and he saw heat, desire, need. "This doesn't mean anything, Stone. It's just sex."

At the moment, he didn't care. He lowered his head and he took her mouth with his own, kissing her until his head was spinning and she was standing so close against him, he felt as though he could absorb her into his body. When she moaned into his mouth, he swung her into his arms and practically ran the rest of the way. He loped up the stairs, waited impatiently for the few seconds it took her to reach down and open the door.

Once inside, he kicked the door shut and released her legs, enjoying the feel of her sliding down his body as their mouths meshed and he backed her toward the bedroom.

For the last month, he'd alternated between the insane longing to call her just to hear her voice and her laughter, and the desire to bury himself deep within her body and never come out again.

He knew he should be concentrating on other things—the divorce case for that idiot, Bill Tremaine, Liz's upcoming nuptials and her fascination for Kevin, the tension between his parents—but with Stephanie in his arms, he didn't care about those things.

As he slanted his mouth across hers and tried to inhale her, he felt every inch of her body as she pressed up against him. And her breathy little moans. It made him feel like her man—

He jerked back, his hands on her shoulders, holding her within his grasp but no longer pressed against her. She blinked back up at him, her eyes unfocused and glazed with desire, her mouth swollen from his kiss.

With the pad of his thumb, he touched her cheek and felt the softness of her skin against his thumb.

She gave him a saucy grin. "What are you waiting for? Was I too subtle?"

Stone ran one hand up under her top, ran his hand up the ridge of her spine, then shifted till he'd cupped her breast in the palm of his hand. No bra and definitely fuller than he remembered. He growled deep in his throat as she tilted back her head to give him better access to everything.

"We should get naked and get this over with before one of us has a premature moment," she breathed and the already elevated temperature of Stone's body heated and engulfed him.

He felt himself drown in the slick heat of her mouth, in the soft moans of pleasure, in the way she responded so willingly to his every touch. He gave himself license to explore the soft curves and valleys of her body, felt her respond in kind as the cool air rode off his back as she tugged the shirttails out of his slacks and ran her hands up his back, around to his chest, sending more heat spiraling through his body.

He knew that he was in deep, way over his head, because being with her this time felt strangely like he'd come home. He tried to clear his head, but then his tongue got tangled up with hers, and everything blanked out but the woman in his arms.

Yet somewhere in the distance recesses of his mind, the squeak of the front door registered in his thoughts. He'd locked the door, hadn't he? Or had he been in such a rush to get his mouth on hers, his hands on her body, that he'd forgotten to be careful? Stephanie's presence always seemed to cloud his judgment and ruin his cool objectivity.

And then he heard the sound of his dad's voice calling through the darkened cabin. "Stone, are you in here?"

Stone jerked his hand out from under Stephanie's top, saw surprise on her face right before the flush of desire on her cheeks bleached from her face. She clasped her hand over her mouth, turned and ran into the bathroom, slamming the door shut behind her.

"Sorry, son, I didn't know you had someone in here with you." The older man flipped on a light switch and crossed the room to stand beside him, hands in his trouser pockets, a speculative light in his eyes as he gazed at the closed door. The sound of Stephanie puking her guts out was unmistakable. "So now that you're over thirty, you get to ignore the dragon lady's rule?"

Stone raked his fingers through his hair and willed his body under control, thankful that Steph had pulled his shirt out from his pants. Otherwise, he'd be facing the older man with a full blown erection standing at attention between them. It was embarrassing enough to see the knowing gleam in the old man's gaze.

Next time, he vowed, he wouldn't lose his head until *after* he locked the door. "You won't tell Mom, will you? You know how she gets. All weird and determined to protect me from my latest mistake."

"Are you kidding? Knock yourself out, son. Sew your wild oats. I only wish I'd done more of that when I was your age." His dad winked and glanced back at the door. "Is that the wedding planner? And can I safely assume you're responsible for her current condition?"

He kept his expression carefully neutral. "She's got the flu."

"Right."

He threw one arm over his dad's shoulders and turned the older man toward the door. "I'll be around for the entire week. We have plenty of time to catch up."

"Looks like you're not too busy now." Jim ducked under his arm and headed back toward the kitchen, where he poked his head inside the fridge and came out with a bottled water in his hand. "So, keeping busy?"

Stone leaned his hip against the counter top, folded his arms across his chest, eyed the closed bathroom door, and thought, *Not now, Dad.* "What's up?"

"Nothing. Just wondering how you're doing. How's work? With divorces on the rise, I expect you've got business coming out of your yin yang."

"I'm not hurting for clients," he responded easily. But something wasn't right. It was in the nervous movements of his dad. Casually, Stone reached into the fridge for a bottle of water. "What's up with you? Enjoying retirement?"

"Sure. What's not to love? I have the freedom to spend all day doing exactly as I please. Golf." Jim pushed away from the counter and paced to the fireplace in the corner of the room. "Morning, noon, and night. This wedding of Liz's is really interfering with the golf time."

Something wasn't right. Stone sensed it, but knew the older

man wouldn't talk about it until he was ready. Which might be never. "You know, Dad, anything you say to me will be held in the strictest confidence."

His dad shot him a disgruntled look. "I'm not one of your clients."

"No, but if you want to talk man to man, I'm way too old to tattle tale on you."

Jim gave him the eye. "Women and sex. When the chemistry is right between two people, the sex can be amazing."

Stone thought of Stephanie and the chemistry that flared between them, then thought of all the women before her where it hadn't been just so, and gave a shrug. Which would explain why he'd been unable to get her out of his mind.

Yeah, that was it.

Chemistry. Spectacular sex. It had nothing to do with *feelings*.

He refocused on his dad. "Is there someone else?"

For a split second, Jim looked startled. "No, of course not."

"Then stop beating around the bush. What's going on?"

His dad hesitated, then sighed and spilled. "What happens when the chemistry isn't right, but the sex is so hot, you can't stay away?" He gave a groan and turned away. "It's this retirement gig. It's making me nutty."

Before he could say another word, the bathroom door swung open and Stephanie stopped in the opening to turn off the light. For a moment, Stone just took in the essence of her—clean scrubbed face, shoulder length hair pulled into a ponytail, sleek sexy body. She reminded him of a girl fresh out of college, even though he knew she was closer to his age.

That first night together, after Morty and Elvira's wedding, she'd known the score. No attachment. Just a good time to be had by both parties.

But now they had the baby to consider and it changed things for them both.

He pushed away from the counter and headed toward her,

meeting her halfway. When they both stopped, the distance of one foot separating them, the other man's presence a damp cloud in the room, it felt like a chasm to Stone. "How're you feeling?"

"Better." She leaned in closer, and he could smell lavender soap on her skin and the hint of toothpaste. Her gaze darted past his shoulder to his dad. "Hello, Mr. Kincaid."

His dad moved forward. "Sounds like you have a nasty flu."

"I do." Her gaze flitted to the front door. "I should leave."

"Don't leave on my account," Jim inserted. He backed toward the door. "We can finish our discussion another time, son."

"Goodnight, Dad," Stone said taking his gaze from the woman in front of him. As soon as the door clicked shut, he put his hands on her waist and pulled her against him. "Sorry about that. You get me so insane with lust, I can't even remember to lock the door."

She gave him a wry grin and waggled her eyebrows at him. "So should we hurry up and get back to it?"

Except she looked so cute trying to squelch a yawn, the words popped out before he could stop himself. "I like to be with you for more than the sex, Steph."

She eyed him, suspicious-like. "When did this happen?"

With a self-conscious grin, he shrugged and finally admitted the truth. "I believe it happened the first day you had your head over the toilet."

"Yeah, I'll bet that was attractive." She stared at him, silent and considering. Then she walked her fingers up his shirt. "You're pretty smooth, I'll give you that. So do you think flattery will get that engagement ring back on my finger?"

Another knock sounded on the door. He stared down at her, determined to ignore whoever was out there, because this woman —these feelings—were more important than anything else in his world. "I'm serious, sweetheart. You, me, and our baby. Doesn't that tempt you to explore the possibilities?"

The knock sounded again, and as a tired smile blossomed across her mouth, she shifted back. "I'm toddling off to bed before my mom does a bed check and not finding me there, starts poking and prying into everyone's affairs. I guess I'll see you in the morning."

She skirted around him and pulled open the door.

Roger stood there, his hand raised to knock again. "I'm sorry. I didn't mean to interrupt."

"You're not. I was about to leave anyway." She sent Stone a glance over her shoulder and one of her heart-stopping grins. "Be gentle with him. He's had a full day already."

With a wave, she moved past the musician and disappeared down the path toward her cottage.

Roger whistled low. "That's one hot babe."

"Cool it, kid, you're already taken."

The musician grinned and stepped inside. "Sorry if I interrupted something."

Stone regarded his future brother-in-law. "What are you doing here instead of being at the party?"

"Liz said she needed some alone time, so she went for a short walk. I figured if she could leave, I could take a breather from the party too." Roger glanced around the room. "Your family has some nice digs."

Stone headed to the fridge. "Want a beer?"

"Sure."

As he pulled out a couple of beers, cracked them open, then passed one over to the other man, he wondered where his sister really was, and if she was alone.

Roger took a deep drink of the beer, then regarded him. "So you and the wedding planner? Is it serious between you?"

"Maybe," Stone hedged. He regarded the other man. "How did you know Liz was the one for you?"

"Because she totally gets me. She knows when I wander off in the middle of a conversation that I'm not being rude. But when inspiration strikes, I gotta go, man. I gotta record those lyrics or they're gone forever."

"Roger—" He clamped his mouth shut.

"Yeah?"

He remembered his promise to Liz, that he wouldn't tell Roger about her almost mis-step.

He raised his beer and tapped it against the bottle in Roger's hand. "Nothing. Just wanted to congratulate you, and wish you a long and happy marriage."

"Thanks, man." Roger chugged the last of his beer, then set the bottle on the countertop. "Well, I better find your sister and drag her back to the party before Grace-the-Menace notices we're gone."

Stone followed his future brother-in-law onto the front deck, then sat down in the quiet of the night and watched the other man cross the compound, heading for Liz's cottage.

And despite his original aversion to this marriage, he couldn't help but think that maybe Liz had made the right choice after all.

Now, all he had to do was convince his sister to grow up, avoid Kevin, and go through with her original plans.

31

Jim headed back to the party. An hour later, he glanced out the ballroom windows for what seemed like the thousandth time. He was impatient to get back out to the lush greens and quiet and solitude.

He pushed aside the sleeve of his tux to check the time.

Eight o'clock.

Barely enough time to get one last game in before the sun disappeared below the horizon. Now, if he could just figure out a way to get out of here.

Gisele's nasally voice interrupted his thoughts. "Isn't that cute, if you're into puppy dog eyes, that is. Liz and Roger are dancing the first dance, just like they will at their wedding."

The woman clung to his other arm as though she were a five-thousand-dollar-an-hour call girl. He forced the tension from his body and turned his attention back to the young couple at the center of the room.

Somewhere along the years, while he'd been too caught up in himself and his career, his youngest daughter had grown into a beautiful young woman. Out of all of his children, Liz took after her mother the most.

His chest puffed out with pride. "I don't think I've ever missed a single one of her newscasts."

Gisele arched one fine eyebrow at him, a disappointed pout on her glossy lips. "How do you manage to do that? I thought you spent all of your time on the golf course."

"Satellite. Portable device. Amazing what you can do with technology today."

"Jim. How can you even concentrate?"

He heard the censure in her voice and he shifted uncomfortably on his feet, wishing more than ever that he was on the course, the breeze rustling through his hair, the sunshine warming his back, a golf club in his hand, a golf ball poised on the tee. Alone and peaceful. And most important of all, no stress.

What had the doc said? Don't get excited? Which was getting exceedingly more impossible, what with all of the people currently in his life. "Don't you start in on me, Gisele."

"No wonder your concentration is off," she said, as though he hadn't said a word. "No more TV on the course."

Jim gritted his teeth and tried not to care. "No problem. I can tape the show and watch it later."

"I mean it, Jim. No more thinking about your family or what's for dinner or anything but what exists on that course. First thing tomorrow, we're going to start work on your mental attitude..."

Jim tuned her out and turned his attention to the young couple on the dance floor.

Even though he'd had his doubts about Roger, it was obvious the young man was so over the moon for Liz that Jim found it almost embarrassing.

Had he ever been that crazy about Grace? It was so long ago, they'd drifted so far apart, led two separate lives for so long, that he couldn't even remember liking her.

"*And now for the second dance of the evening, can I have the parents of the bride join the happy couple on the dance floor?*"

Jim noticed the music change. He glanced over at the dance

floor. Liz and Roger were both staring at him, and his daughter was motioning him onto the floor.

As father of the bride, he'd known this was inevitable. He glanced around the room for his wife and the minute he spotted her, he knew that she was ready to explode.

"Excuse me," he mumbled to Gisele. Then he headed across the ballroom, stopped in front of Grace, and silently held out one hand in invitation.

She was just as silent when she took his hand and moved onto the dance floor with him. As the music swelled around them, she glided into his arms, soft and warm in all the right places. The memory of their accidental meeting in the bedroom came back to him as he smoothly performed the steps of the dance and led Grace around the dance floor.

He remembered the brief glance over his shoulder, and the surprise of seeing her in only her bra and panties as she informed him that she was laying down for a nap. He'd taken that as a "get out of my room, get lost" order, but had it been an invitation? He'd been wrapped up in the unsteady beat of his heart and the constant pinch of concern that the simple act of sexual release might put him six feet under.

Although that might not be a bad way to go.

He'd been thinking with his head, but now his dick was in full control.

Through the barrier of clothes, he felt the imprint of her body against his, the unintentional—he was pretty sure it was unintentional—bumping of their body parts together. Jim felt himself swell within his pants as the memory of her half naked invitation collided with the fact that he couldn't remember the last time he'd made love to his wife.

She used to turn him on with a crook of one eyebrow. She had the sort of body that he loved. Full and lush and curvy.

Over Grace's shoulder, he caught a glimpse of Gisele and knew that she was much too skinny for him to ever be attracted to. Not that he wouldn't be flattered if she was attracted to him, but the feeling wasn't mutual.

As the song finished and the last strains of music drifted through the ballroom, Grace jerked out of his arms. Jim let his arms drop to his sides and for a moment they just stood there, staring at one another, and he saw storm clouds gather in her beautiful blue eyes.

"Next time you get a woody for your plaything," she gritted through her teeth. "Don't you dare even think about touching me or I'll pull a Bobbit."

Bobbit?

Her words sent fear racing through his body, and his erection shriveled in a millisecond. There was no doubt in his mind that the woman he'd been living with for the last thirty-five years was capable of just about anything.

From that point on, he stayed away from his golf instructor. The first chance he got, he escaped to the golf course, where the first whack to the ball sent it rolling fifteen feet down the fairway. "Fu—"

"There is no swearing in the game of golf," Gisele stated from behind, which made him jump and whirl around.

He gripped the club in his hand. "What the difference does it make whether I swear or don't? Who's here to notice?"

She slammed the palm of her hand against his chest and nose to nose, said, "The difference is, Jim, you stop swearing or I walk."

He turned his back on her, dropped another ball on the ground, wound up and swung. The ball spiked through the underbrush and rolled onto the next fairway.

Giselle threw her hands into the air.

"That's it. You're hopeless. You're never going to improve your game." She turned away, then turned back. "And you know what else? Before you make peace with your golf game, you have to make peace with your wife. She's got your head so screwed up that you can't think."

She stomped off the course.

"Bitch," Jim grumbled as he wondered how he could of ever thought this drill sergeant of a golf pro was a blessing.

He stopped pretending that he was concentrating on golf and glanced toward the house.

He could see them—Grace, Leta, Sandy, and Nancy—all clustered together around the outdoor table as the buff young man Grace had hired as her new *assistant* swaggered onto the patio and handed them each a drink.

What did Grace think she was doing? Did she think he cared whether or not she kept some young stud on the side to satisfy her sexual needs? Did she think he'd give up his dream of playing like a pro for a relationship that had been dead for longer than either of them would admit?

Jim slammed the five iron into the bag and headed for the next fairway to retrieve his ball. On his way through the bushes, he stubbed his toe on a tree root.

"I hate this stupid game!" he yelled, then sat down to nurse his wound and stare back at the house.

Where had he gone wrong?

And what was he going to do to make it right?

32

Thursday morning, in preparation for her tests, Grace threw a pair of silk pajamas into her overnight bag along with a matching robe and slippers. The entire ensemble made her eyes bluer, her skin fresher, her whole self feel younger and more playful.

Her shoulders slumped and tears burned at the back of her eyes.

Liz wouldn't care if she didn't show up at the wedding. No one would.

She felt ancient, put out to pasture like some old cow who'd outlived her purpose and appeal. She'd thought her and Jim were past that stage, where she needed to dress in something sexy to make him pay attention to her. Apparently, she'd been all wrong.

What scared her the most was that she might not be able to hold his attention ever again. If the tests came back positive, if the doctors recommended a mastectomy, she feared the man she loved—yes, *loved*—would never look at her with desire again.

Please, dear God, don't let it be cancer.

But pity wouldn't get her anywhere except back into bed, the covers pulled up over her head, where she would willingly hide for the rest of her days if it meant she didn't have to deal with life.

It seemed that everything in her life had fallen into a state of disarray. Her marriage, her relationship with her children, even the flowerbeds.

If she was going to die, then she had to straighten out a few things first.

She picked up the phone and dialed her youngest daughter's cell.

"Liz? The wedding is off. I am not allowing you to marry that man. You'll be stuck at home, barefoot and pregnant, while he traipses around the world doing who knows what with who knows who."

"And a good morning to you too, Mother."

"You listen to me, young lady. You're too young and inexperienced to understand that men like Roger Gordon were put on this earth for one thing and one thing only. Sex, that's it. I'm telling you again. Have sex with him if you want—for heavens sake, Liz, I'm doing you a favor—don't marry him or you'll regret it every day for the rest of your life."

The phone clicked in her ear.

Liz had disconnected the call.

Well, fine, she'd take care of canceling everything herself.

She started punching in numbers, making one call after the other until she'd cancelled everything...the floral arrangements, the food...everything.

When she was done, she sat there slumped in the chair, exhausted and depressed, and praying that Liz would one day forgive her.

What about her relationship with Jim?

If she could only get him to pay attention to her for a few minutes. If she could get him to make sweet love to her, like he used to do. If she could just get him to forget about that silly golf game and focus on her instead.

Would she be happy then?

The cancer wasn't something she could keep to herself. Jim deserved to know. She glanced over her shoulder toward the golf course and saw him talking to his golf bimbo.

Her eyes narrowed.

It was time to get her life—and her man—back, even if she had to play dirty.

She turned her back on the view she hated more than anything else in the world, grabbed the cordless phone, and punched in a number. On the third ring, Nancy Strom picked up.

"Strom's Insurance. How may I help you?"

"Nancy, it's Grace. Do you still want me to join you for a game of golf?"

There was a beat of silence. "You bet we do. Sandy and Leta will be thrilled."

"I'll need clubs."

"Definitely, darling. Meet me at the pro shop in town at ten and I'll help you buy a set."

Grace pressed the off button.

She forced herself to move ahead with her new plan of action, and by the time she'd returned home and headed upstairs to tuck the golf clubs into the back of her closet so no one else—and by no one else, she meant Jim—could find them, she was ready for a nap.

But as she opened the closet door, the bedroom door crashed open. She jumped and whirled around. Jim stood in the opening, his eyes a little crazed, his face flushed, his hands in fists.

And then his gaze landed on the golf bag and clubs. "What are those?"

She closed the closet door—no need to hide them now—and raised her chin a notch. "I've decided to take up a new hobby."

She could see him physically grind his teeth together.

"Your gigolo wasn't enough?"

She placed one hand over her heart with hopes of stilling the suddenly erratic beat. "He was...a mistake I won't make again."

"You know my rules. No women allowed on the course."

Now she was just pissed. "And yet your golf tramp comes and goes as she pleases."

His gaze zipped to the overnight bag, then back to her.

He strode toward her, his expression purposeful, stronger and sexier and more out of control than she'd seen in him since... forever. Without a word, he grabbed her by the shoulders, moved her aside, grabbed hold of the bag, then marched over to the open window and threw it outside.

"Now just hold on a—" She jumped again, caught off guard by the loud crash and the vehemence on his face. But when she tried to back up a step, the back of her legs came up against the bed. She raised her chin. "What do you want, Jim?"

He rounded on her, and at the ferocious look on his face, she snapped her mouth shut.

He pointed to the bed. "You. Naked. Now."

Indignation flushed her skin, along with the hot flash that always occurred whenever she got upset...or excited. "I'm not your little trollop."

"No, you're my wife, so get on the bed and do your wifely duty."

Grace ground her teeth together and wished she could grind him under her heel. "That ship sailed twenty-five years ago when you quit asking me to marry you."

Before the stupid oaf could say another word, she stormed out of the room and went after her belongings.

But a part of her—the part that wasn't wishing for a shotgun so she could put him out of *her* misery—was so turned on, she almost ignored her anger and the fact that he was a jackass so she could jump his bones.

As she clomped down the stairs to retrieve her overnight bag, she smiled to herself.

In the last twenty-four hours, nothing had changed.

Except for the fact that the man she loved had actually noticed that she was alive.

33

The sun was shining, the wind cooperating, and yet all Jim could do was sit on the bench at the first tee off area, and remember the expression on Grace's face, and her words.

Marry her? He'd quit asking years ago because she'd finally convinced him that she wanted to live without the constraints of matrimony.

Had he only heard what he'd wanted to hear?

Had her *no* really meant *yes*?

Jim was so confused that when the sound of female chatter reached his ears, he didn't pay much attention, at least not till they walked onto his golf course.

Four slow moving bodies.

Each with a golf bag slung over her shoulder.

He jackknifed to a standing position.

Grace led the pack. She was dressed in a floral blouse that hugged her ample bosom, then narrowed to her slender waist. A pair of tan slacks showed the sweet curve of her full buttocks, and spiffy white golf shoes finished off the neat look.

She set down her clubs, tugged on a golf glove. Sunglasses hid her eyes, but a smile stretched across her mouth. And it occurred to him that he hadn't seen that smile directed at him in forever.

His stomach began to burn, which started a chain reaction straight for his heart and made the defective organ squeeze with pain. As she pulled her five iron out of the pouch and strolled past him, he stepped out of the shadows and into her path. "Are you trying to kill me?"

She froze, her gaze hidden by the over-large sunglasses, the smile fading to the unemotional mask she usually reserved for strangers. "Your insurance is paid up, isn't it?"

His heart squeezed in his chest again. Did he matter so little to her? He forced a calmness he didn't feel. "The guys and I are playing in a half hour."

She tugged on her other glove and didn't bother looking at him. "We decided to walk the course. Better exercise, you know. Since we'll have a head start, I'm sure we won't get in your way." She sidestepped him, then stopped and partially turned his way. "Oh, and Jim, since you've never had to share the course before, I expect you to share nicely. After all, if I remember correctly, it was half of my hard earned dollars that built it for you."

An hour later, standing and watching the four women tee off from the second hole, Jim listened to his companions complain.

"You need to control your wife, Jim," Ned said.

"They should at least let us play through," Harry muttered.

"You need a bigger *No Women Allowed* sign." Andy jammed his club into his golf bag. "What fun is this? I'm going back home for a beer. Who's in?"

And as his three golfing buddies abandoned him, Jim felt the erratic beat of his heart flatline. He turned his back on them, climbed onto the golf cart, and drove back to the house.

This was it.

The end of his life-life.

There was nothing more to live for.

As he clutched his chest and made his way up to the master

bedroom, he thought about the early days of his relationship with Grace, and wondered if the shackles of marriage would have made a difference?

But it didn't matter now. He was ready to lie down and die. The way his heart squeezed so painfully in his chest, he was certain he wouldn't last long.

He made a side trip through Grace's office with the intention of leaving her a note. Something simple, something to cause her great guilt when he was gone, something like *I'm sorry you were so miserable with me as your partner. Love you forever, Jim.*

Except that when he opened up the drawer to grab a pen and paper, he found a note with a single word.

Cancer.

This time when his heart stuttered in his chest, it didn't slow him down.

34

That evening, as Stephanie went over her list of things to do, she stopped to gaze at her surroundings.

With the sun on its final descent of the day, the western horizon was shaded in hues of pale pink and peach and purple. The golf course in the background was a lush green, and the ocean sparkled in the sunshine.

It looked like heaven on earth—she touched her belly—the perfect place to raise her child.

With a soft sigh, she turned her attention back to the immediate area.

The entire family had descended on the grounds designated for the wedding and reception for one last inspection.

Liz walked alongside Roger, quiet and subdued. Fortunately for her, the groom-to-be talked non-stop and didn't seem to notice that she was withdrawn.

The mother-of-the-bride and Mariam stood at the edge of the chairs where the ceremony would take place. They faced Stone who appeared to be focused on whatever they were saying. But then, for one brief moment, he raised his gaze to look at Stephanie, and she stopped thinking, stopped breathing.

There was something new in his eyes, possessiveness and something more. And it was the something more that really had her concerned.

She pulled her gaze away first, unable to maintain eye contact and still keep her distance. As she looked across the lawn, past Liz and Roger, she saw her mom straightening centerpieces on the tables scattered across the lawn for the reception. It looked like she was changing place cards.

Needing something to keep her busy, she headed that way. "What are you doing, Mom?"

Dora straightened so fast, she nearly knocked over a chair. She caught it, set it back in its place, then turned to face Stephanie, her hands behind her back. "Honey, you startled me."

Stephanie tried to see around her. "From where I was standing, it looked like you were rearranging the place cards."

Her mom sighed and held up the card in her hand. "It's that divorce lawyer. Somehow his card found its way over next to yours."

Stephanie frowned. "What's it doing here? He's supposed to sit with his family."

One elegant eyebrow quirked upward and her mom's face flushed. "My question exactly. Did you move it?"

"No." Stephanie eyed her mom's flushed cheeks. "You moved it, didn't you? Before you knew he was a divorce lawyer."

"Now, honey—"

"Besides, why would I want to sit next to Stone?" she interrupted. There was something in the way her mom looked at her —really looked at her—as though she could see straight through Stephanie's denial. She reached out and snagged the card from her mom's grip—yes, Dora held on to it like she intended Stephanie to pry it out of her cold dead hands—and set it back on the table. "Fine, maybe I want to sit with him a little."

"He's nothing but heartbreak, honey. Besides, once you sign

Grace's contract, you won't be able to fall in love, get married, or have children for three years."

She stilled. "What?"

"That's right. I eavesdropped on Grace's conversation with Stone." With a sigh, she gnawed on her bottom lip while she fiddled with the cards at the table. Picking up the card with Stone's name on it, she studied it. "I know you're just fooling around with this man right now, but what if you signed that contract today, then tomorrow met the man you want to spend the rest of your life with? You'd have to put your life—and your relationship—on hold for the next three years."

She pulled the card from Dora's hand and set it back on the table. "What if I've already met him, Mom?"

"Then in good conscience, you have to tell Grace no." The older woman hummed, then reached out and nudged the cards closer together. When she glanced up, there were tears in her eyes. "You already have a wonderful career, honey. What you need at this stage of your life is a wonderful man who will love and support you no matter what path you chose in the future."

"Maybe." If those were the show's conditions, she wouldn't be able to sign the contract anyway. With a shrug, she smiled. "Grace may have changed her mind because I haven't even seen the contract yet."

Her mom blinked. "She gave it to Stone so he could go over it with you."

"She did?"

Her mom kept shuffling things at the table. "Why, the same day she had it drawn up."

"How do you know everything?"

"It's one of my special talents."

Stephanie glanced across the yard and pinpointed the man who wanted to marry her because of the child she carried with what she hoped translated to a death stare. "You know, Mom, you're totally right."

"I usually am." She blinked again. "What am I right about this time?"

"My taste in men is really bad."

Her mom just stared at her, a hint of disappointment in her eyes, before she shrugged. "Since you refuse to take my advice, I think I'll go back to assistant mode. What do you need me to do before the big day arrives?"

Thankful her mom had dropped the topic, she pulled the cell out of her pocket and studied the list. "Can you check on the wedding cake? It should be here by now, but I haven't had a chance to see if it's in the kitchen."

With a kiss on the cheek, her mom left.

Stephanie watched her go until she was out of sight, then she turned to Stone and glared. Almost as though he sensed her look, he shifted his head and met her gaze.

Oh, she was so going to tell him they were through. If he could lie to her face...

A noise beside her brought her attention around and she turned to see Mariam's little boy crawl across the grass toward her. Panic tightened her stomach and she fought the urge to throw up. But as the kid reached her and grabbed for the tablecloth, she caught his hand before he pulled the contents of the table down on top of himself.

He pulled himself to his feet, then almost in slow motion, tipped and fell back with a plop onto the padding of his diaper.

Stephanie crouched down in front of him.

"Hey there, big guy." He stared up at her and she stared back, fascinated by his chubby hand, his fat little cheeks and double chin, and the precious smile that blossomed across his mouth. "So why are you way out here when your mom is way over there?"

"Gooofplt."

She smiled back at him, aware of the tug of her heart and the desire to hold him in her arms. "You don't say? Well, I just between you and me, I feel exactly the same."

"Bftalup."

She laughed softly. "I'm inclined to believe you, but I suspect you take after your uncle. A smooth talker who knows exactly what to say to make the ladies fall in love with him."

"Tsrap."

He tugged his hand out of hers, and she felt a little sad for the lost contact, but she watched with interest as he scooted onto his knees, grabbed her leg, and pulled himself into a standing position in front of her while he gurgled and blew spit bubbles.

And in that single moment, Stephanie fell in love with motherhood, and wondered how she was going to protect herself now.

35

From a distance, Stone watched Stephanie interact with his nephew and with a flip-flop-thud of his heart, the last remnant of resistance fell away.

She was beautiful, glowing in that special way that seemed to be reserved for pregnant women. As she slowly straightened, careful to keep hold of Jim Junior's chubby little hand, she turned his way and met his gaze.

A tiny smile flirted with her lips, and one delicate eyebrow swept upward as though asking *what are you staring at, buddy?*

It was probably a good thing they weren't alone because he'd reply *I'm staring at the woman I love.* And he wasn't sure how she would react to his confession...whether admitting his true feelings would scare her off.

"Stone?"

Someone tugged at his shirt sleeve and he broke eye contact with the mother of his child to find his mom staring up at him.

"You haven't heard a word I've said, have you?"

He flushed and rubbed the back of his neck. "Sorry, Mom, I got distracted."

His mom followed his gaze. "Didn't I warn you to stay away from that one?"

He shrugged and gave her a sheepish grin. "The heart wants what it wants."

His mother bristled with suspicion. "You haven't shown her the contract yet, have you?"

He shrugged one shoulder. "No. It's really not in her best interests."

"You can't decide that for her." With a cluck of her tongue, she continued. "What happens when she discovers that she can have the *Eternally Yours* show or you, but not both? Who—or should I say what—will she pick?"

He knew exactly what she would pick, but what did it matter? She was pregnant, which made the offer null and void anyway.

Guilt burned a path from his stomach to his throat.

If he'd been given a choice, he never would have gone down this path. Forcing Stephanie into marriage wasn't something he felt terribly good about, but the choice had been taken away from both of them.

If he could go back, would he change any of it?

Knowing what he knew now, probably not.

The heart wants what it wants.

How often had he heard that same thing from Bill Tremaine, but he had to wonder whether Bill had those parts south of his belt mixed up with those parts north. Because what Stone felt for the mother of his child would never go away.

He was as certain of it as he was certain Bill Tremaine would continue the marriage-divorce cycle until the day he died. Because the man was more in love with the idea of love than with the women he married.

Stone tugged his cell out of his pocket and with a simple, "If you'll excuse me," he skirted around his mom. As he closed the distance between him and his future wife, he clicked off a couple of shots.

Mariam fell into step beside him. "So when is she due?"

He tucked the phone back into his pocket and slashed a glance her way. "I don't know what you're talking about."

"Oh, come on. Every time you look at her, I see it in your eyes."

"Still don't know what you're talking about, sis."

"Fine, I'll ask her myself."

He stopped and gave a tug on her sleeve so that she faced him, and kept his voice low so no one else would hear. "Not a word, you understand."

Her face lit up in the first real smile he'd seen on her in months, which in itself was a reason not to regret the dilemma he found himself in.

"Perfectly. It'll be our little secret." She leaned closer and slashed a glance toward Stephanie, and in a quieter voice, repeated her original question. "So when is she due?"

He scrubbed one hand across the back of his neck. "We haven't done the math yet, but closest estimate would be in about seven and a half months."

"Oh, goody, I can't wait for Jim Junior to have a playmate."

Someone jostled him from behind. He turned and came face to face with Tom Goodwin. Despite the other man's glower, Stone was pretty sure he hadn't overheard Mariam's comments. Otherwise he'd be looking for a shotgun instead of simply glaring at him.

The older man growled, "Stop looking at my daughter like that."

"Sorry, Sir." He kept his expression neutral, but inwardly he cringed. In less than a week, he'd not only fallen in love with a woman who seemed to have less interest in marriage than he originally had, but he'd managed to alienate the people he now hoped would be his future in-laws. Noting that the other man didn't have anything in his hands, he asked, "Can I get you something to drink, Sir?"

"I'm driving."

Mariam reached out with one hand, a winsome smile on her lips, and grabbed the angry man's hand. "You must be Stephanie's dad. I'm Mariam, Stone's other sister."

Tom's glower disappeared momentarily and he shook Mariam's hand. "It's a pleasure to meet you." But as soon as they broke physical contact, he turned his attention back to Stone. "Didn't I tell you to stay away from my daughter?"

No point in denying it, so he gave an easy shrug. "Yes, Sir, but it appears I can't."

The older man's brow furrowed into a displeased frown. "Can't or won't?"

Stone shoved his hands deep into the front pockets of his trousers and looked the other man square in the eyes. "Just for the record, I've already asked her to marry me—twice—and she turned me down both times."

Before Tom could reply, Mariam elbowed her way between the two men and slipped her arm through Tom's. "It seems you've been worrying for nothing, Mr. Goodwin. Despite my brother's reputation, he really is a nice guy."

The glower didn't lighten up. "I've yet to see proof."

"Here, let me tell you a few stories about Stone's past," Mariam said as, with a wink in Stone's direction, she led the other man away. "Liz and I grew up in Stone's back pocket. He didn't always like it, but he bore his responsibility without complaint."

Tom grunted, and it was unclear whether or not he approved.

"Sir," Stone called after them before they could get too far. He closed the distance between them and lowered his voice. "What would you do if one of your daughters was making a mistake?"

Just by the pained expression on the older man's face, it was clear he was thinking about that moment in town when Stone had his hand up Stephanie's top, and was kissing her in front of the entire town. "Don't beat around the bush, boy. What's your problem?"

"I'm on the verge of alienating Liz and I need your advice."

One of Mariam's eyebrows quirked up. "What's going on?"

"I'll explain later."

Tom interrupted him. "Why come to me for advice?"

"Because you're a good father. I've seen how you treat your girls and how much they love you."

A thoughtful expression crossed the other man's face. "Sometimes you have to use tough love and pray they'll one day forgive you. Other times, you need to let them make their own mistakes, and if things fall apart, be there to pick up the pieces."

"Thank you." For a moment, Stone mulled over his words. Then he recalled what Stephanie had said earlier, and now he couldn't help it, he grinned. "Brilliant plan, by the way. Stephanie told me what you did to get rid of your wife."

A flush colored Tom's cheeks. His gaze swept the grounds. "Speaking of my wife, have you seen her?"

Giving Stone a *you owe me* look, Mariam dragged Tom away. "Dora? She's a lovely woman. She was here just a few minutes ago. Let me help you find her."

Stone watched them head across the lawn. He saw Mariam reach down to swing her son into her arms and Stephanie reached out to brush the back of her fingertips against the little tyke's cheek.

The love in his heart expanded to near bursting.

Because he couldn't stay away, he headed toward her, and when she saw him coming, she excused herself and marched toward him. When she reached him, she poked him in the chest...hard.

"When were you going to tell me about the contract?"

He grabbed her arm because he knew this wasn't going to be pretty.

And then he saw her place a protective hand across her lower belly, and pain ripped the anger from her face.

36

Stone had driven Stephanie directly to the Serendipity Island Hospital, and all the while he had the phone pressed to his ear as he tried to get hold of the doctor.

From the moment the pain had ripped through her lower belly, she'd realized that the thing she'd wanted least a week ago was what she wanted most now.

Her mom had been right. She'd made her choice even without realizing that she'd done so.

She wanted them both—Stone and their baby—for the rest of her life.

Would she get either of them?

As she stared at the ceiling of the private room she'd been stuck into, alone and lonely, she wished she'd told her mom and sister about the pregnancy. They'd hold her hand and cry alongside her.

Footsteps came down the hallway. Then the doctor walked into the room. He held a chart in one hand.

"Well, you dodged a bullet, young lady. It looks like both you and the baby are fine. You'll have to be careful, of course, get lots of extra rest, but there's no indication that you won't be able to carry your baby until full term."

She stared at him, almost unable to comprehend what he was saying, but as the full import of his words sunk in, she was swamped with relief...and the realization of what she needed to do. Let Stone off the hook. She didn't want him out of obligation.

"Dr. Strom," she began and was glad that there wasn't even a waver in her voice. "If we could keep this between ourselves, I'd really appreciate it. I don't want anyone else to know that I didn't miscarry."

He frowned down at her. "There's a worried young man out there pacing a hole into the waiting room tiles."

She frowned back at him. "I understand. But if you could tell him I lost the baby—"

He shook his head, effectively cutting her off. "I won't lie, not for you, not even for myself."

"Then please just tell him I'm fine and omit the rest." She sighed. "You see, he believes that he has to marry me because I'm carrying his child, but he doesn't love me any more than I love him."

He stared at her for a long moment, then shook his head again. "You young people, always playing games with love. Do you know that I love my wife even more today than I loved her on our wedding day?" He shuffled his feet, suddenly uncomfortable, and blushed. "I recently realized I've been ignoring her and, well, I think I'll stop at the flower shop and pick up a dozen of her favorite white roses." As he turned to leave, he tossed over his shoulder, "I hope you know what you're doing."

The door shut behind him and she whispered to herself, "So do I."

What would Stone say when he came into the room? Or maybe while he'd paced and fretted out there, he'd come to his senses and decided to leave her behind. But she didn't really believe he'd do that. He was one of those nice guys who took his responsibilities seriously, and she didn't want to be just a responsibility.

Let him off the hook. Let him off the hook. Let him off the hook.

It was like a mantra that she needed to keep repeating to herself, if she wanted to survive emotionally.

A sound at the doorway alerted her to Stone's presence and she opened her eyes to see him approaching. She steeled the urge to cry and forced a smile, ignoring the fact that her bottom lip still trembled.

He pulled up a chair and sat down beside the bed, taking her cold hand into his warm one. "How are you feeling?"

"Better. Thank you."

He nodded, his mouth grim. "The doctor says you're free to go. I'll take you back to the estate and you can get some rest there." He laced his fingers with hers and stared down at their entwined hands. "What a relief, huh?"

As she stared at the top of his head, the pain in her chest swelled, and she heard her voice come out flat, emotionless. "Yes."

There was a heartbeat of silence, then he raised his head and met her gaze. His dark eyes were oblique, flat, clear of emotion. If he felt something other than relief, he hid it well.

With nothing more to say, he went to the closet, pulled out her clothes, and carried them back to the bed. Suddenly he appeared fidgety and uncomfortable. "Do you need help dressing?"

She fiddled with her clothes instead of looking up at him. "No, I'm fine by myself. I won't be long."

For a moment, he stood there, and while she twisted the bed sheet between her fingers, she felt his gaze bore into the top of her head.

But she wouldn't look at him...couldn't. Because if she did, she might be tempted to grab hold and never let go.

And that wasn't what either of them wanted.

Unless maybe it was?

No, if Stone wanted something bad enough, he went after it without reservation. Nothing would stand in his way.

And he didn't want her bad enough to fight for her...not without the baby.

He finally turned, and without a word, walked out of the room. The door swished closed behind him.

Tears welled in her eyes and overflowed down her cheeks. With the back of her hand, she scrubbed them away, determined to let him go without making a scene.

After she dressed, she found him in the waiting room. "I hear your mother gave you the contract for me to sign."

He pulled it from his pocket and handed it to her. "Understand, I can't give you any legal advice. I don't just handle divorce cases. I also handle my mother's legal issues."

"Understood." She stared down at the papers and tears pooled in her eyes, preventing her from seeing the words. And even though she knew the answer, she had a part to play. "What happened to the last wedding planner?"

"Turn to page two, section three."

She blinked back the tears obstructing her vision, and as she tried to read the blurred words, his deep soothing voice washed through her.

"The contract states that you will not fall in love, not get married, and not get pregnant for a three year period, or you must return the signing bonus and you'll be fired."

"Oh." She stared blindly at the papers in her hands and wondered what to do now. It wasn't like she could pretend to sign.

Next thing she knew, he was prying the pages from her hands and tucking them back into the inner pocket of his jacket. She looked up at his face.

His jaw was working overtime. "After we return to the estate, we'll go over the papers together. I can help you negotiate better terms."

"You just said that was a conflict of interest."

His jaw tightened. "My mother is interested only in herself. I, on the other hand, am not."

She nodded and looked away. "I'd like to go now."

"Are you sure? You're not still dizzy from the pain meds they gave you?"

Sadness crept deep into the hidden regions of her heart. "I'm fine. I just want to get out of here and go back to normal."

How had she fallen so quickly? A week ago, Stone had been nothing to her but the memory of a night that rocked her world. Now, letting him go would be like tearing out her heart.

For a minuscule moment in time, she'd had everything she'd *never* wanted, and she hadn't appreciated till now how much she'd really wanted Stone and their baby. She'd fooled herself into believing lust was the basis of their relationship.

Tucking her emotions far inside where nobody but herself would see them, she turned her thoughts away from her own sadness to Liz and Roger.

And she realized that Stone had been right all along.

Liz couldn't marry Roger...not because she was young and immature, but because she didn't truly know what was in her heart.

37

As Stone stopped the truck in front of the Hole-For-One cottage and turned off the ignition, Stephanie reached for the door handle.

"Wait," he said as he reached across the seat and caught her hand before she could disappear out the door...and maybe out of his life. He had absolutely no idea what was going on in her head. She'd been silent since they left the hospital. "We should talk."

Her big beautiful eyes turned from her hand to his face and they were void of joy, empty of sorrow.

Stone's heart cracked wide open.

"There's nothing to talk about. This is what we both wanted, remember? No commitments. Just fun while it lasted."

He remembered all right, and it was quite possibly one of his deepest regrets ever. "What about us?"

"There is no us." She tugged on her hand and her fingers slipped free of his. As she gazed at him, sadness elongated her features. "I'm sorry, Stone. This all happened so quickly, it was easy for both of us to confuse lust with those deeper emotions."

He decided it was time to jump in with both feet. "Is that what you think? That we confused lust with love? Sweetheart, we may have both started out not wanting a baby or commitment, but something changed. At least it did for me, and I think right now you're scared to admit it, but it did for you too."

Dora came out the front door, a worried frown on her forehead, ending whatever response Stephanie might have had. She slipped from the truck and as the door clicked shut behind her, she whispered, "Goodbye, Stone."

"Is everything okay?" Dora called down to them. "You two disappeared so quickly, I've been worried sick."

Stephanie headed up the steps, never looking back. "Everything is fine, Mom. We had an errand in town. It's all taken care of now."

He wanted to chase after her, but maybe now wasn't the time. Maybe she needed some space to reconcile all that had happened.

Raking both hands through his hair, he turned the key in the ignition, put the truck into gear, and drove away.

All he knew was that his heart hurt more than it had ever hurt in his life.

And he had a funny feeling that given enough time, he could get Stephanie to admit she felt exactly the same.

For the first time since meeting her at the Valentine Day wedding, then here on Serendipity Island again, he had his head on straight. He knew what he had to do.

He had to do anything he could to make it work with her, because he loved her for the rest of his life. And before either of them left the island, he intended to ensure their future was tied together.

They could make it work. They *had to* make it work.

Parking the truck in front of the Three-For-Par cottage, he saw Wanda standing on the porch, her suitcase in hand. As he climbed out of the truck, she came down the steps to meet him.

Silently, she handed him an envelope.

He frowned down at her clear, crisp writing, then raised his gaze to her face. Her expression was as void as always, and he forced a smile. "Tell me you're not breaking up with me too."

Pity formed on her face. "She booted you to the curb?"

Nodding, he felt his heart pinch in his chest. "For now."

"I'm sorry." With the barest of regret pinching at her brow, she gestured toward the envelope. "It's my resignation. I never meant to stay so long, but you were nice to me."

"Why are you leaving?"

"I have personal issues that demand my attention. I've put them off long enough."

"I'll give you the time off to take care of them. You don't have to quit." He cleared his throat. "I don't want to lose you."

"Thank you, but I've made up my mind." She placed one hand on his forearm. "I'll give you plenty of time to find someone to replace me, and I'll stick around to train them, of course. Plus you'll have my cell, in case they have any questions after I leave."

He opened the letter and scanned the contents, then glanced back up at her. "Are you sure I can't convince you otherwise?"

Tears sparkled in her eyes, and she stepped into him and gave him a quick hug, then quickly stepped back before he could hug her back. "I won't forget you. In fact, I'll be watching for an invite to the baby shower and wedding."

And then she was gone.

Stone didn't even get a chance to tell her there wasn't going to be a baby shower.

Well, not unless he could convince the woman he loved that he needed her. Not unless he could convince her that the baby neither of them had wanted was wanted indeed.

He watched Wanda until she disappeared from sight, mulling over his next move, wishing he could move the clock back a few hours so he could appreciate what he'd had.

The sound of a branch breaking behind him alerted him to another's presence. He turned and saw Kevin, his duffle bag slung over his shoulder.

After the way Stone had spoken to him, he was surprised the other man even gave him the time of day.

Stone met him half way. "I'm sorry I spoke out of turn. What goes on between you and my sister isn't my business. I spoke out of line and I apologize."

"No, it's my fault for not telling you the truth in the first place." Kevin met his gaze directly. "It's Mariam. It's always been Mariam. I figured with her divorced now, I had a chance. But I was wrong. She'll never see me as anything but a friend."

Stone grimaced. "Maybe you're wrong."

"What does it matter? I'm halfway across the world most of the time, and I never know whether or not I'm coming home. That's not fair to her." A taxi pulled up the driveway and frustration bracketed Kevin's mouth. "Look, I have a plane to catch. Please don't say anything to her. Thank your mom for the use of the cabin. Wish Liz and Roger a happy life from me."

As Kevin pushed past, Stone grabbed the other man by the shirt sleeve to prevent his escape. "That's it? You're just going to walk away?"

The cab honked again. Kevin shook off his hand. "I gotta go, man. I ship out in less than three hours."

Stone followed him toward the cab. "If it's any consolation, she hasn't looked at anyone since the divorce, not till you showed up at the estate."

"Yeah, well, it's not going to happen. I tried and she turned me down."

"She needs time, Kev. Don't let pride stand in the way of your happiness."

"Maybe you're right. Maybe love isn't enough to hold two people together for the rest of their life."

"What if I'm wrong?" He thought of Stephanie, of the way she came apart in his arms, of the way he felt when he woke up in the morning with her cuddled against him. Like he could do that every morning for the rest of his life. "What if love is enough?"

Without a word, Kevin climbed into the cab.

As Stone stood there and watched the taillights disappear around a corner, he knew he had to fight for a future with Stephanie.

Or live his life alone, always with the regret of what might have been.

38

Early Friday morning, Jim finished the ninth hole with a personal best score. Without saying a word, he left the guys behind, his teeth clenched so tight, he thought they might shatter.

By the time he reached the house, his jaw was aching, his heart was pounding double time, and he thought the delicate appendage in his chest might explode. But it didn't. Just like the doctor had said, as long as he took care of himself—ate well, exercised daily, stayed away from the booze—he could do anything he wanted.

Including sex with the only woman he'd ever wanted.

But first he needed to convince her to stay.

He found Grace in the garden and stopped at her side. "When were you going to tell me?"

"Tell you what?"

Stubborn right till the end of time. He clenched his hands at his sides and refused to be put off. "About the doctor appointments. About the tests and the results."

She shoved the garden spade into the dirt and refused to look at him. "There's no need to be concerned. Women get

242

breast cancer every day. You won't have to change your life at all."

His throat suddenly closed up and he could barely breathe. "What?"

"That's right, Jim. Like with everything else, I'll take care of this myself. You don't have to put yourself out for me. Heavens, I wouldn't hear of it." She pushed to her feet, tugged off her gloves, brushed at the grass stains on her slacks, and refused to look at him. "Now, if you'll excuse me, I have things to do."

She turned her back on him and started to walk away.

"What are you going to do?" Sweat gathered at the back of his neck, under his arms, soaking his golf shirt. When she didn't answer him, he asked, "You're not thinking about leaving me, are you, babe?"

She turned to face him, her gaze clear and unconcerned. "You left me a long time ago, Jim. Maybe not physically, but in every other way possible. Maybe Stone is right. Maybe it's time to make a clean break and find happiness elsewhere."

"Do you want a divorce?" Jim studied the face of the woman he'd known for the last thirty-five years, the woman he almost didn't recognize now, and stuffed his hands in his pockets to keep from reaching for her. "Is that what you want, honey?"

"Don't call me honey." Cool as a cucumber, she tucked a lose strand of hair under her kerchief. "You have to be married to get a divorce. Since we're not, we can just walk away from each other. Split things equally so it's fair to us both. No need to even involve a lawyer." She turned her back on him. "Now, if you'll excuse me, I have a wedding to prepare for."

And with that, she strode away from him and disappeared into the house.

Jim stared after her, part of him wanting to run away until the fear of losing her left him.

She'd always been strong and independent. So much so that he'd pretty much let her run things as she wished without any

243

interference from him. In fact, they'd laughed about it in the early days, how their relationship was different from everyone else's.

So what was he supposed to do now? He'd never imagined a life without her in it.

39

After tossing and turning all night, Stephanie decided she couldn't keep her mouth shut. She had to tell Liz and Roger the truth about their relationship, and to heck with the consequences.

And then she had to tell Grace that she couldn't take the job offer, and hope that Stone didn't figure out why she'd walked away from the job of a lifetime.

Dressed in her dad's frumpy sweater and an old pair of jeans, she headed to the main house where she found Liz and Roger and Grace in the breakfast room. As expected, there was an argument going on between Liz and her mother, which apparently didn't faze the groom at all. He sat between them, his phone in one hand, a slice of toast in the other, appearing totally oblivious to the women.

Stephanie barged into the middle of the fray. "Enough."

The room went silent for all of two-point-five seconds, then Liz and her mother both started talking at once.

"Silence." Stephanie held up one hand and glared at them both until they finally went silent. She focused on the bride and the groom first. "It's time you two faced the truth. I don't care

245

what you do when I'm gone, but you're crazy to get married to each other." Out of her peripheral vision, she saw Grace open her mouth, and without turning her way, she held up her hand for silence. "Call the wedding off."

Grace humphed. "Exactly what I've been telling them."

Thankful that someone was on her side, Stephanie forced herself to continue.

"You want to know all of the reasons you're wrong for each other?" She clasped her hands together at her waist. "Liz, you love the idea of getting married, of wearing the princess gown, of being on YouTube and the Crazy Heart album and the cover of People magazine. But you won't put in all of the hard work that a relationship requires."

Liz came to her feet. "That's not true—"

"And Roger," Stephanie continued, not caring that she'd rudely cut off the bride. "You may think you love Liz, but she thinks she's in love with someone else. Deal with it and move on. I quit. If you two go through with this marriage, that's your problem, but I wash my hands of you both."

Before either of them could say a word, she turned to Grace. "Thank you for the generous offer, but I'm afraid I'm unable to take the position on your show. There are extenuating circumstances, which I don't wish to go into now. So if you'll excuse me, I'll pack my bags and go."

Without a backward glance, she walked away, out of the house, past the pool, and down the pathway that lead to the Hole-For-One cottage. As she approached, she saw Dora spritzing a clay pot of yellow pansies with water. "Pack your bags, Mom. The wedding is off. We're going back to Mandy's."

Her mom came to her feet. "Honey, are you crying?"

Stephanie swiped at her cheeks and realized she was. "No, I just have something in my eye." She stomped up the steps and into the house where she found her sister lounging on the couch.

"What are you doing here? Aren't you wedding shopping with Dane?"

"We're taking a break." Mandy shrugged as she watched her mom disappear into the kitchen. The moment the older woman was out of sight, she turned back, her expression solemn, a worried look in her eyes. "Are you okay? What's up with the baggy sweater?"

She wanted to tell her sister about the pregnancy. They told each other everything, but now wasn't the time. But gosh, she really needed to talk to someone.

Instead, she shrugged and picked at a hangnail. "Still covering up that pre-period bloat, you know."

Her sister checked over her shoulder, then turned back and gazed at her waistline. "Nothing else you want to tell me?"

Her sister always had been very perceptive, which is probably why she was able to see Grandpa George when no one else in the family could. "Nope, that's it."

"You'd tell me if something was wrong, right?"

"Of course." Stephanie forced a smile. "Everything is hunky dory."

The doorbell rang.

In the kitchen, Dora called out, "Who's at the door, honey? It's not that nasty divorce lawyer, is it?"

Mandy raised one brow and pushed to her feet.

Stephanie backed toward her bedroom and whispered, "If it's Stone, I'm not here."

Chicken that she was, she sprinted toward the bedroom and slammed the door behind her.

A few minutes later, Mandy slipped into the room. "Okay, spill. What's up with you and Stone?"

In the middle of packing her things, she sighed. "Remember when I said I was leaving Grandma Elvira's wedding with a hot guy?"

Mandy's face blossomed with a wicked smile. "It was Stone?

247

Have you been seeing him since the wedding? Why didn't you tell me?"

"Nothing to tell. It was one night of exquisite sex, and then we went our separate ways." Silence greeted her statement. Finally, she added, "Hey, I was busy. I had a lot of spring weddings and no time for distractions."

Her sister poked her in the side, her voice soft, coaxing. "But Steph, don't you want to find out if it could lead to forever?"

"He's a divorce lawyer and I'm a wedding planner. What kind of match is that?" But even as she said the words, she knew it was no longer true. And they had their child to think about.

"You're a wedding planner who doesn't believe in love or forever. I'd say that's a pretty good match for a divorce lawyer who probably believes the same thing. Maybe you two could figure it out together. You can keep each other company under the covers at night while you both hide from the reality of life."

Stephanie thought about it, then immediately discarded the idea. Because, let's face it, the Stone's of the world ran at the first sign of impending parenthood. Although Stone hadn't. Instead he'd presented her with a pre-nup and an engagement ring.

She snapped closed her suitcase. "Come on. We're getting out of here."

"What about the wedding?"

"It's been cancelled." Her fault, but no one needed to know that.

A commotion on the other side of the door caught her attention, and Stone's smooth baritone tugged at her heart.

"Where is she?"

Dora said, "She doesn't want to see you. I don't want to see you either."

Stone lowered his voice. "I want to hear that from her lips."

"Trust me, I'm her mother. She only wanted one thing from you...sex. And if it's any inclination from how often the two of you disappeared, she got that in spades."

248

"Mrs. G. You can get out of my way or I swear I will physically move you. Either way, I am seeing your daughter."

An unwanted shiver raced up Stephanie's spine.

But before a physical fight broke out—her mom was feisty and determined, and Stone would be no match for her—Stephanie pulled open the door. Sure enough, her mom was splayed across the opening like caution tape at a murder scene, determined to protect her oldest daughter from the big bad wolf.

Stephanie couldn't help but laugh through the tears that stung at the back of her eyes. "It's okay, Mom. You might as well let him in because he won't go away until you do."

Dora lowered her arms, stepped out of the way, and as Stone stepped past, her mom hissed, "Divorce lawyer. For shame."

Stone held the door open until Mandy departed, then closed the door, shutting out the furious and overprotective woman. "If I ever want your mom to like me, I may have to change my career."

"She thought that an environmental lawyer in the family might be nice." Stephanie turned her back on him and fiddled with the suitcase latch as she tried to ignore the erratic beat of her heart. "What do you want, Stone?"

She heard his soft footsteps cross the room, felt his hand capture her upper arm to tug her around to face him. She gazed up into his eyes and felt sucker punched by her love for him.

"I love you, Steph."

As tempting as it was to jump into his arms, she was certain his declaration was just a reaction to the lie she'd told him about losing the baby. He needed time. She needed time. Shaking her arm free, she turned back to the suitcase, determined to contain her emotions until she was alone. "Thank you, but I'm sorry, I don't love you back."

The entire week had been like a train wreck about to happen.

In almost every relationship, one person always loved the other person more. And when things got rocky, they were the one who ended up with a broken heart.

249

And it wasn't going to be her. No way. No how.

She picked up the suitcase and brushed past him, out of the bedroom, out of the cottage, out of Stone's life. "Mom? Mandy? I'm ready to go."

They tagged along behind her.

Dora said, "Awww, honey, I think you hurt his feelings."

Refusing to look back, Stephanie climbed into the backseat of Mandy's car. She'd have to deal with the rental car later, but right now, she didn't want to be alone.

As Mandy put the car into gear and drove away, Stephanie said, "Mom, you and Dad have something special. Don't ruin it over a little tiff."

"Oh honey," her mom said, a hint of laughter in her voice. "Marriage is about give and take, but sometimes we need to argue before we can come to a compromise. We're only human. We all make mistakes. But your dad and I...we'll be just fine. There was never any doubt in my mind."

40

Ready for an afternoon of tests—poking, pinching, prodding—Grace pulled on one glove at a time, trying to appear calm and cool and oh-so-level-headed, when all she really wanted to do was collapse into a lump of weeping womanhood. But that had never been her style. Not as a child. Not as a young woman. Certainly not now, especially since everyone seemed to have abandoned her anyway.

The flurry of activity near the cottages caught her attention and she saw the wedding planner come out of the cottage, her mother and sister on her heels. As they reached the car, Stone came out and stopped at the top of the stairs. And before Stephanie climbed into the car, her hand went to her stomach in a protective motion, and Grace suddenly realized that there might be a completely different reason for the young woman's wanness.

Well now, that put a whole new spin on things.

Even from this distance, she could see her son was upset. So what was all that about? Did he know? And if so, why hadn't he said something?

Because they didn't have that kind of relationship.

The urge to control the outcome of the young couple's relationship washed over her, but she pushed it away. It was none of her business. They were old enough to work things out themselves. And in good time, they'd tell her about the baby.

How lovely, she thought as she turned her attention back to the gloves. Perhaps when she returned from the hospital, she should spend some time with Mariam's boy. What was his name again?

The front entrance door banged open. Jim burst into the foyer, the tie around his neck only half done up, wearing a suit that had been in the closet for so long, Grace nearly didn't recognize it. The gladness she'd been feeling vanished in a heartbeat.

He headed straight toward her. "Good, I caught you."

Grace gave a final tug on the gloves, picked up her purse, and tossed the car keys in the air. "Aren't you supposed to be on the fifth hole right now?"

As he passed her by, he let go of the tie long enough to catch the keys in midair. "Right. I can golf tomorrow. Maybe you'll even take a break from the office and join me."

"Jim, give me those keys," Grace said as she followed him across the foyer. "I'm heading to town. Take the truck if you're going somewhere."

"Honey, the only place I'm going is with you." He turned at the door, pulled it open with a flourish, and stared at her. "Well?"

"I..." Grace tucked an imaginary strand of hair behind her ear. "There's no need to come."

"What kind of husband would I be if I didn't see you through this?"

"It's not as if we're really man and wife, you know." She turned toward a sound at the door and saw Stone standing there. The shocked look on his face told her that he'd overheard. She frowned across the room at him. "What's with the face? You're old enough to finally know the truth."

And as she turned her back on her son and followed the man

she loved out of the house, determined to steal the keys back and leave him behind, he turned, dropped to one knee, and said, "Marry me, Grace. Be my friend again, my partner, the love of my life. You're the only woman I've ever wanted, the only woman I'll ever want."

Heat warmed her cheeks. "Jim, get up off your knees before you grind dirt into the material."

He stayed right where he was. "Is that finally a yes?"

It hit her then, like a heatwave before a summer storm. He wasn't going anywhere. They were in this for better or worse. So what if her viewers discovered the truth about her relationship—or lack of it—with the man who'd been her partner for nearly her entire adult life.

Perhaps it was time to come out of the common-law closet. They could get married on live TV. Her viewers did love weddings.

"Well?" he prodded her, which brought her full attention back to him. "I'm not twenty anymore. These stones are hard on my knees."

She reached out one hand to help him up. "Yes."

As he clambered to his feet and swept her into his arms, she relaxed into the solid firmness of his body.

This was the beginning of the rest of her life.

41

Stone needed a drink...except he wanted a clear head so he could figure out a way to get Stephanie back.

He'd sat on the porch of his cottage all day and stared at the golf course through the trees, mulling over his options, still in shell shock over the fact that his mom and dad had never married.

Man, he was an idiot, plain and simple. He'd based his entire perception of relationships on their stormy partnership. And yet, that elusive emotion called love had kept them together through the rough patches, even though it would have been far easier for them to walk away from each other.

A rustle on the stone path drew his attention and he saw his cousin headed his way. Dane bounded up the porch steps, dropped onto the chair across from him, and simply said, "You're an idiot."

Stone didn't even have to ask what he was talking about. "How's she doing?"

"Mandy and Dora kept her busy all day with wedding and birthday preparations. She's really good at pretending everything is fine, but when she thinks no one is watching her, she lets down her guard." He shook his head. "My soon-to-be father-in-law has taken up glaring at me just because I'm your cousin. And Mandy has threatened to shut down the activity in the bedroom until I talk some sense into your thick head."

Stone sat forward, rested his elbows on his knees, and clasped his hands together. "*I* didn't leave her. *She* left me."

Dane's brow furrowed. "What did you do?"

All of his life, he'd been so careful not to allow a woman into his heart and his life. How had he fallen so deep, so fast?

Stone raked his hands through his hair for the umpteenth time and pushed to his feet, needing action of some sort to make him forget about how badly he'd screwed up. "All I know is that she doesn't believe I love her. I need to figure out a way to prove to her that I do. How am I going to do that?"

This was the question he'd been asking himself ever since Stephanie had walked out of his life.

Dane stood and watched him pace. "What's the one thing she believes you'd never do, not even for her?"

It hit him like a brick wall to the face, and the air whooshed out of his lungs. Stone grabbed Dane in a bear hug, lifted him off his feet, and spun him around. "That's it. The perfect solution."

"What is?"

He set his cousin back on his feet and headed into the cottage. "I know what I need to do."

Dane followed him in. "Any way you can resolve this before Dora's birthday party tomorrow afternoon? It would be nice if I didn't have to sit in a corner with only myself for company."

Stone grabbed his briefcase and retraced his steps to the front door. "I swear I'll give it my all."

Abandoning his cousin, he jumped onto the golf cart, then drove toward the main house at top speed, which was unfortunately considerably slower than he would have liked.

He found his mom at her desk. She looked up in surprise when he walked into her office. "I wasn't sure if you'd be home."

"Well, here I am." She glanced at her watch, then pushed to her feet. "Can this wait till tomorrow? I have a date with your dad."

"A date?" As she compressed her lips, he studied this woman who was his mother. "Can I ask you a personal question?"

She raised one perfectly formed eyebrow in his direction. "Do I have to answer it as if I'm under oath?"

"Why did you stay with Dad if you were so miserable with him?"

She appeared startled, then she cleared her expression and cleared her throat. She shrugged and studied her perfectly sculptured nails. "We weren't always like this. For the most part, our relationship worked exactly how we needed it to. But then we drifted apart and that's when the problems began."

"So everything is good between you now?"

She lifted her gaze to his face. "We're going to work on it, something we've never really done."

He set his briefcase on the top of her desk, sprung open the latch, and pulled out the contract she'd offered Stephanie. "Remember this?"

She glanced down at the papers, then back at his face. "Of course. She turned me down, so you can shred those."

He stayed where he was, flipped to the second page, grabbed a pen, and crossed off the stipulations. "I love her and I intend to marry her, so we need to take out the clause about falling in love, getting married, and having children. Because there is definitely going to be love, marriage, and children."

Stone glanced up and saw the calculating look in his mother's eyes, the same calculating look that always made him wish he could run for cover...or never come home again.

She slid the contract over to her side of the desk, studied the notations he had made, then wrote in the margin.

Stone tugged at his tie, suddenly nervous. "What are you adding?"

With a satisfied grin, she finished writing, then turned the papers around so he could read. "I'll initial the changes you made, but only if you agree to the changes I've made."

Reading the additions, he felt his heart thud to a stop, then start thumping in his chest. "That's not nec—"

"I insist."

Without further thought or hesitation, he signed his name on the document, then handed the papers back to his mom so she could initial the changes.

Because his future with Stephanie was worth any price, even if it meant he had to hand over his soul to the devil.

42

Stephanie wiped the steam off the bathroom mirror and stood sideways so she could study the soft rounding of her belly.

A baby.

At some point before she left, she'd have to tell her parents. And even though she knew they'd be supportive, she wasn't looking forward to the conversation. They'd want to know who the father was, and why she wasn't with him.

A pang of loneliness hit her right in the heart and she pushed away all thoughts of the man she loved.

First she'd tell Mandy, then after her mom's birthday party—maybe five minutes before she left to begin the long flight back home—she'd break the news. That way they wouldn't have a lot of time to grill her about her plans.

Because all she knew at this point was that she wanted this baby, even though the thought of being responsible for something so small frightened her.

A knock sounded on the bathroom door. "You almost done in there, kiddo? I'd like to use the bathroom and hit the sack some time before the next century."

From the bedroom down the hall, Dora joined the conversation. "Tom, don't get excited. Remember your blood pressure."

Stephanie slipped on her bathrobe and opened the door. "Sorry, Dad."

Dora stepped into the hallway. "Never you mind, honey. Your dad has forgotten what it's like to share the bathroom."

As Stephanie skirted around her dad, he motioned Dora ahead of him. "You go first, babycakes."

It was quite unbelievable how quickly her parents had made up, although really, it had all been for show. Her dad had spent the evening sucking up, and her mom...well, Stephanie suspected Dora had played up the hurt feelings just so she could join her oldest daughter at the Kincaid estate.

And then it happened, that thing Mandy had warned her about—

Dora sent her husband a sultry look. "If we shower together, we could save on water."

One of Tom's eyebrows rose, and Stephanie suddenly saw a side to her dad that she'd never noticed before. The rakish, babe magnet that had obviously attracted her mom.

She cleared her throat and hooked a thumb down the hall. "I'll—uh—just—"

But they were already disappearing into the bathroom, hand in hand.

Stephanie headed toward the guest bedroom, determined not to think about what her parents did when they were alone. She'd barely closed the door when Mandy slipped into the room.

"I'm staying in here until, well, you know," she said. "My bedroom is right next to the bathroom and I can hear everything."

Stephanie made a face. "Everything?"

Her sister nodded. "When they're in the house, never—I repeat, *never*—let them into the bathroom at the same time. I swear, they make more noise than Dane and I do."

259

"So how do I keep them from going in together?"

"Sleight of hand." Mandy grinned, pushed away from the door, and sauntered toward her. "You know. *Dad, I'm out of gas and I don't have any money. Or, Mom, I want to talk to you about this guy I met. I think he could be the one.*"

A laugh escaped. "Seriously, that works?"

"Every time." Her sister sat down on the bed and crossed her legs under her. "I have news for you."

"Good new, I hope."

"Grandma Elvira and Morty are moving to the island so that Grandma can be closer to Grandpa George. They're going to be living at the Heavenly Estates Retirement Resort." She lowered her voice. "There's more. Mom and Dad figured that since everyone is moving to the tropics, they should too."

"Seriously? I thought you and Dane moved to get away from...well, them."

"We did." She sighed and fell back on the bed. "I don't know how I'm going to tell Dane. What if he decides he doesn't love me enough to put up with my annoying family for the rest of our lives?"

Stephanie smothered a yawn. "Dane's crazy about you. He's not going to leave you because you have a family that doesn't understand boundaries."

"I suppose I could help Mom and Dad find a nice condo on the opposite side of the island. Someplace far enough away that they can't just drop in whenever they feel like it."

Stephanie smothered another yawn. "Good idea."

Mandy sat up, hugged her around the shoulders, then pushed off the bed. "You've had a busy week, so I'll let you get some rest. Tomorrow is another busy day."

"Goodnight, Mandy. I love you."

"I love you too."

Alone, Stephanie climbed into bed, turned off the light, and stared at the dark ceiling.

And she wondered if Stone was somewhere out there doing the same thing...or if he'd forgotten about her already.

43

By the time Stone drove into town and located Mandy and Dane's house, the revised contract in hand, it was nearly midnight. As he sat in the truck and stared at the dark house, he debated whether or not to wait till morning, then decided this was far more important than a few hours of sleep. For all he knew, Stephanie had a plane ticket off the island first thing in the morning.

He slipped out of the truck and into the yard, careful not to make a sound, wishing now that he'd thought this through while Dane had been out at the estate.

With a shrug of his shoulders, he picked up some pebbles off the road and tossed them at the window. A few moments later, the window slid open, a head popped out, and a voice hissed through the darkness, "Who's there?"

It wasn't his cousin. "Sorry, Mrs. G. It's me, Stone."

"Heavens, dear, you do have it bad, don't you?" She lifted her wrist and glanced at her watch. "Shush now, or you'll wake Tom."

He rubbed the back of his neck and kept his voice down. "I'm looking for Stephanie. Would you mind pointing out her window?"

"Last bedroom on the far side, but she's asleep. Quit skulking around in the dark like a divorce lawyer and come back tomorrow."

The window started to slide shut, but then the one a few feet away swung open, and a furious looking man poked his head through the opening. "What's going on out here?"

Stone gulped. "Hello, Mr. G."

Silence filled the air between them until finally the older man said, "Didn't I tell you to stay away from my daughter?"

Dora's voice came from the other window. "You know that thing you like to do on Friday nights—" She glanced at Stone, a pained expression on her face, then shrugged and smiled as she turned her attention toward her husband. "Well, if you ever want to do it again, you'll start being nice to Stone."

It was obvious the older man knew where to draw the line. He snapped his mouth closed, and resorted to getting his point across with a grumble and a grunt.

Dora refocused on Stone and smiled, at once encouraging and motherly. "There's no judgment here, Stone. Whatever you have to tell us will stay between us."

"What has she told you?"

"Nothing. Just that the wedding had been canceled and that she had to be back in the city first thing Monday morning. She doesn't have to tell us anything. It's perfectly obvious that for the first time in her life, our oldest daughter fell in love and now she doesn't know what to do about it."

There was more, but Stone didn't think it was his place to tell them about the pregnancy and the loss of the baby. "I'm in love with your daughter, but she doesn't believe me."

"We can't tell you what to do," she said, her voice soothing in the dark. "You have to make that decision for yourself. But no one goes into marriage knowing whether it will be forever. In fact, there's sure to be times when you wish you'd never made that choice. But if you're willing to do the hard work, it's all worth it."

Tom stayed where he was, a silent sentinel over his family.

"Thank you, Mrs. G."

As the moon came out from behind a cloud, he saw her smile and wink his way, then turn toward her husband.

"Tom, I found a Kuma Sutra book on Mandy and Dane's bookshelf."

Tom growled, "I don't want to hear about their sex life."

"It's the ultimate guide to the secrets of erotic pleasure. If you promise to leave Stone alone, I'll light a few candles and we can —ummm—read a few pages together."

Stone saw the older man struggle between fatherly responsibilities and husbandly duties. But finally, he slammed the window shut and disappeared inside.

Dora hummed. "Works every time." She hooked a thumb toward the room on the other side of the front entrance. "Good luck, dear."

Stone waited till she shut the window before he tossed some pebbles at the other upstairs window.

This was it, the moment of truth.

44

Stephanie heard something hit the window. At the same time, a knock on the door sounded, the door swung open, and her mom popped her head through the opening.

"That nice lawyer is here to see you, honey."

She sat up in bed and pushed the hair away from her face. "What does he want?"

"Why you, of course." Her mom stepped into the room, shut the door quietly behind her, then came to sit on the edge of the bed and captured her hands. "Do you love him?"

A sob caught in her throat. "He's an idiot."

Dora smiled. "All men are idiots. It's up to us women to keep them in line."

"Dad's the exception, right?"

"No, he's right in line with all of the other men on this planet." Dora patted her hands. "Honey, what happened in the past doesn't matter. Today, right now, this is your moment to start fresh. Don't be afraid. Marriage is wonderful. Even though I sometimes want to throttle your father, most of the time I want to hug him tight."

A knock sounded on the door and Tom poked his head into

the room. "Ummm, sorry to interrupt, babycakes, but that thing you promised...?"

She gave a sultry laugh. "I'll be right there. Why don't you get things ready?"

And as he disappeared, she turned back and faced Stephanie. "Even though he's a divorce lawyer, I kind of like him." She pushed to her feet, bent at the waist, and placed a kiss on Stephanie's forehead. "You girls are growing up so fast. And I'm so proud of you both."

Then she disappeared, leaving Stephanie alone with the pebbles tinkling against the window and an uncertain future.

She climbed out of bed, grabbed a robe, and headed downstairs.

As she came around the side of the house, she spotted the man she loved and her throat closed up.

What would her future be like without him in it?

Why did she even want to find out?

She must have made a noise, because he suddenly turned and faced her.

He looked good, yummy good, and those female parts that always did the Mambo Jumbo in his presence were doing double-time right now.

"I'm sorry." He held out a bunch of papers and waited for her to take them. "It's not a prenup agreement, but it gives you everything you want."

"Everything?" She glanced down at the papers and blinked back sudden tears. All she wanted was him.

"Yes. The *Eternally Yours* show. My mother's unconditional support while you're off on maternity leave."

Startled, she glanced back up at him. "Maternity leave?"

He gave a self-deprecating grin. "Yes. We made the first baby without even trying. I'm sure that when you decide you're ready for another one, we'll make another."

She placed one hand on her abdomen and glanced back

down at the contract, squinting to read the writing in the dim light. Her breath caught. "What's this?"

And even though she held out the contract and pointed to the hand-written section, his gaze never left her face. "My mother figured that if I really loved you, I'd sign anything." He shrugged his broad shoulders. "She was right."

"But every Sunday supper with your family? What about my family?"

The tension on his face eased, and he took a step forward. "Sweetheart, if it means you in my future, then we'll live in a big enough house that all of our parents can come live with us."

She pulled her attention back to the contract and gnawed on her bottom lip. "I don't think that'll be necessary."

He dropped to one knee and captured her hand. "Make me the happiest man in the world. Marry me. Make our parents tolerate our company every Sunday night. Have a half dozen children with me. Because if you say yes, I'll spend the rest of my life proving to you that I love you."

She laughed and tugging him to his feet, threw her arms around his neck. When she heard him choke, she pulled back and looked up into his face. "What's wrong?"

He pointed to the window above them.

There stood her dad, a glare on his face.

"Go away, Dad," she yelled so he could hear her through the glass panes. Then she returned her attention to the man holding her so gently in his arms, and pulled his head down for a kiss.

Against her mouth, he murmured, "I'm going to have to make an honest woman out of you or your dad will never like me."

"Hold that thought," she murmured back and kissed him again. Finally when they came up for air, she grabbed his hand and tugged him toward the back of the house. This required a special place, someplace romantic like the beach in the moonlight.

"Where are we going?"

"I have something to tell you." With her heart singing, she sent him a smile. "And I have an idea for mom's birthday gift."

Hours later, as Stone steered the truck up in front of Mandy's house and turned off the motor, Stephanie tried to still the butterflies in her stomach.

She was nervous and excited, pregnant and unmarried. How would her parents react to her news?

A hand on her belly garnered her attention and she turned her attention from the beach house to the man leaning across the console to kiss her belly.

"It'll be okay, sweetheart," he said. "We've got it all planned out."

The nervousness nearly sucked the air from her lungs. "No it won't. You don't know my mother. She likes to control everything. She'll be arranging our baby's life before he's out of the womb."

"I can't believe you tried to get rid of me by telling me you lost the baby."

"I didn't want you to want me just because I was pregnant."

Stone laughed and did up the top buttons on her summer coat. "Your dad will probably punch me in the nose for getting his baby girl pregnant."

She turned her full attention on him and realized that he was probably even more nervous than she was. He wasn't used to family, and hers could be overbearing. She laid her palm against his cheek and stared into his beautiful eyes. "He's going to love you. Everyone is going to love you."

He grunted and sat back up to pull the keys out of the ignition. "Are you ready?"

"Uh huh." She opened the car door and stepped out into the warm tropical air, her coat buttoned up tight. Stone came around to assist her, closing the car door behind her, holding on to her elbow to steady her. She smiled up at him. "I'm okay. I'm not going to fall or anything. I'm very careful."

He grinned down at her. "I know, but I like to touch you."

A wave of longing swept through her. "I like to be touched by you."

And for just a moment, they stood there and stared at each other, love mingling with desire.

His gaze dropped to her mouth. "Come on. Let's get this over with so I can take you somewhere private and make love to you until you're sick and tired of me."

"That'll never happen, so just make sure you eat properly, get enough sleep, and keep up your stamina." They walked side-by-side up the walkway toward the front door. She tilted her head slightly to look up at him. "Have you heard anything from Liz?"

"Nothing." A troubled frown creased his brow. "I've left message after message, but she's not returning my calls. Sunday night dinners with the family won't be complete without her."

Stephanie felt a squeeze of emotion in her heart for this man who loved too much, but hadn't been loved enough...until now. "She'll be back. She loves you more than you know. You're her big brother, her family."

At the bottom of the steps, Stone turned her toward him and kissed her, long and deep, and in her shoes, her toes curled. When he broke off the kiss, he murmured, "You're my family now. And if your family will have me, they'll be my family too. Marry me, Steph. Don't make me keep asking till my hair turns gray and our son—"

"Or daughter."

"Or daughter." He smiled down at her, warm and intimate. "Don't make me keep asking until our child graduates from high school."

She frowned up at him. "Didn't I give you an answer yet?"

"No."

"Are you sure? I'm certain I did."

His jaw clenched while humor glinted in his eyes. "I'm pretty sure I'd remember if you gave me a reply."

"Then yes, yes I'll marry you."

He kissed her again and when they came up for air, she squared her shoulders and turned to the front steps. "Let's get this over with."

And before they were even up the steps, the front door swung open and her dad appeared, a glower fixed firmly on his face as he glared at Stone. "Quit giving Mandy's neighbors a show and get in the house."

"Oh, Daddy," she sighed. She stepped into the house and Stone stepped in behind her, his hands on her shoulders.

"Sorry about that, Sir. I didn't mean to embarrass you."

"Be nice to Stone. I happen to like him." She turned her head so she could smile up at her fiancee, the man she'd just agreed to marry. "A lot, actually."

Her dad grunted. "Well, get all the way inside and close the door behind yourself."

Stephanie moved forward, heard the door click shut behind her, and as she slid off her shoes, leaned forward to give her dad a peck on the cheek. She whispered into his ear, "Be nice to Stone, Daddy. He's a keeper."

When she stepped back, she looked into her dad's eyes and saw him eyeball the taller man. Then he turned to her and tried to take her coat. She brushed his hands away. "I'll just keep this on. It's a little—uh—chilly in here."

"Suit yourself."

Stephanie stepped into the living room and headed straight for her mom.

"Happy birthday, Mom." She enveloped Dora in her arms, gave her a kiss on the cheek, then released her and stepped back. Playing with the top button on her coat, she glanced over her shoulder to see Stone approach. He looked nervous, kind of nauseous, exactly how she was beginning to feel. Well, best get it over and done with, and deal with the fireworks afterward. She just hoped she wasn't about to spoil her mom's sixtieth birthday party. She turned back to Dora and started to unbutton her coat. "Stone and I have a special gift for you, Mom."

Dora's eyes teared up and she clapped her hands together. "Am I going to have a double wedding?"

Tom grumbled, "I'm not made of money, girls."

Stephanie glanced over at her sister who was near the table. "I'll have to discuss that with Mandy, but no, it's not. This is something else, Mom, something you've been wanting for a long time."

Disappointment crossed her mom's expression. The tears in her eyes dried up and her forehead scrunched. "Let me guess. Is it a gift certificate for a whole body massage?"

"No, Mom—"

"One of those new fangled devices, what are they called? An e-reader? I hear you can download thousands of books on them without ever leaving your house."

"No, Mom, although now that you mention it, you should have an e-reader. They're fantastic. You can download books with a single click of the button and you can—"

"Steph." Stone's deep baritone interrupted her and she realized she was rambling, stalling.

With a sigh, she unclasped the final button on her coat and let Stone pull it off her shoulders. The room went silent as every eye turned to the red bow wrapped around her waistline. "Happy birthday, Mom."

As Dora glanced down at the bow, the rest of the people in the room went silent. She finally lifted her gaze to Stephanie's face, and tears glistened in her eyes. "Honey, are you trying to tell me something?"

"Happy birthday, Mom. You're going to be a grandma."

And then Stephanie was enveloped in the comfort of her mom's embrace and the room erupted with congratulations. Everyone was hugging everyone, congratulating Stone on becoming a father, giving him words of wisdom.

Everyone, that is, except for her dad. She saw him wipe his

eyes, then leave the room. She knew there were times when he didn't want to let go and this was probably one of them. First Mandy, now her.

But she knew he'd be back. He loved his family more than anything else in the world.

As she hugged her grandma, she looked across the room at the father of her baby, saw him almost overwhelmed by her family, but handling it magnificently, like the man he was.

Stone would fit right in, as soon as he got used to all of the hugging.

45

Stone had seen his future father-in-law stomp out of the room and he had an inkling of how he must feel.

Protective toward his daughter, helpless in the face of her choice in men. One day, he hoped they'd look back at this time and laugh, but for now, the older man was making it clear that he wasn't quite ready to accept Stone into the family.

Which Stone figured he had coming. He swore to himself that he would never let his father-in-law regret him joining their family.

So when Tom walked back into the room and headed straight for him, a football in his hands, Stone steeled himself for a challenge of some sort.

Tom stopped right in front of Stone. "I bought this when Dora and I first tried to get pregnant. Kept it around all these years because I figured I could give it to my firstborn grandchild. I was going to give it to Mandy and Dane—" His gaze landed on his youngest daughter, travelled to his wife. Then he handed the football to Stone, who took it with surprise. "Since you two beat them, I want you to have it. Maybe you'll get a shot at using it with a son. Or maybe one of your girls will appreciate the game like I do."

"Thank you, Sir. We'll keep this in the baby's room as a gift from his or her grandfather." He glanced down at the football and lowered his voice so hopefully only his future father-in-law could hear. "Sir, I don't know anything about being a husband or a dad."

"Does this mean you're planning to make an honest woman out of my daughter?"

"Yes, definitely. Stephanie finally agreed to marry me. It's why we were—uh—kissing on the front walk."

Tom clapped him on the shoulder. "Son, you'll learn the same way I did. Along side your wife with your family to support you."

Another round of noise erupted in the living room and Dora's squeal of delight overpowered everything else. A moment later, Tom had been pushed out of the way and Dora had Stone in a mother-bear's hug.

"Is it true? Do I get to plan another wedding?"

Stone laughed and as he hugged her back, he met Stephanie's warm gaze. "It will be up to your daughter, Mrs. G., but I'm pretty sure she can be convinced without too much trouble."

Then her dad was hugging him and clapping him on the back. "Welcome to the family, son. Maybe you can convince Mandy and Dane to elope to Vegas with you."

"Oh, Tom," his future mother-in-law sighed. "You know you always cry at weddings."

Stone looked across the room, met Stephanie's gaze, and saw a sheen of tears in her eyes. He mouthed *I love you.*

I love you too, she mouthed back. Then she touched her hand to her belly and smiled.

It would be hours before he got to show her just how much he loved her. But if there was one thing he was certain of, it was that they were both in this for the long haul, so they had plenty of time.

274

EPILOGUE

even-and-a-half months later...

Stephanie sat on a rocker, her hand on her humongous belly, happy, content, and finally home.

Several months ago—immediately after Dora's birthday party—Stone and Stephanie had bought a beach house on Serendipity Island with the intention of using it for the occasional romantic getaway and family vacations. Instead, as the months passed, they'd spent more and more time here, discussing future plans, which included the best time and place for a small family wedding.

Mandy and her had discussed a double wedding, as their mom had suggested, but eventually her sister had decided against it. Not because she didn't want to share the big day with Stephanie and Stone, but because she knew the moment the wedding band was on her finger, Dora would up the pressure for another grandchild.

And Mandy and Dane weren't ready to take that step yet.

Thankfully, Stone was totally on board with the family factor. In fact, Sunday dinners with both sides of the family had become a regular routine.

Which was why, on this beautiful Sunday evening, with everyone lounging around the patio, their bellies full, enjoying the gentle lap of the waves against the shoreline, the warmth of the evening breeze, and the comradeship of each other's company, Stone and Stephanie had arranged to surprise the people they loved the most with a wedding celebration.

Tonight, they were officially joining their lives together.

Everyone of importance was here, except for Liz who, right after officially canceling the wedding and breaking up with Roger, had quit her CNN job and vanished for parts unknown. Even her cell had been disconnected, which made Stephanie sad because it made Stone sad.

Roger's new album—and the love songs he'd written for Liz —had hit number one on the charts, and remained there for all the months since.

Jim Junior toddled across the patio, a smiling Mariam close behind, and climbed up on his grandmother's lap. Grace hugged the toddler, uncaring that his sticky hands left spots on her otherwise immaculate sundress...which boded well for her relationship with her soon-to-be-born grandchild.

Beside Grace sat Stone's dad, Jim. Grace and Jim had married on live TV, and the ceremony had brought in a record number of viewers which had increased the popularity of the *Eternally Yours* talk show. And for the past few months, with her devoted husband at her side, Stephanie's almost mother-in-law had undergone treatments and was now cancer free.

Dora sat next to Grace, cooing at Jim Junior, while Tom and Mandy and Dane were in a lively discussion with Jim and Stone's former assistant, Wanda.

Yes, the moment Wanda had heard about the pregnancy and Stone's decision to spend more time on the island with his very pregnant wife, she'd returned to the law firm to make his life as easy as possible. The typically unsocial woman still had secrets, but she'd become as important to these Sunday family gatherings as everyone else in the family.

A movement near the beach house caught Stephanie's attention, and she let her gaze drift toward the man approaching her.

Stone crossed the patio, his gaze fixed on her, so full of love her heart did a hiccup. She still couldn't believe that he was hers and she was his.

Shifting on the rocker to ease the pressure in her lower back, she watched him kneel on one knee in front of her and lower his head to kiss their unborn child before pressing a light kiss on her mouth. "How are you doing, love?"

"Still very pregnant." As an uncomfortable band squeezed around her abdomen and the discomfort in her lower back increased, she leaned forward and looped her arms around his neck. "Almost ready?"

He smiled back at her. "I've been ready since the day I met you."

He straightened and gently helped her to her feet, always so solicitous and careful with her these days.

Then a sharp pain ripped through her abdomen, startling a gasp out from between the clench of her teeth.

Concern settled between his brows. "What is it, love?"

She inhaled deeply and laid one hand on her belly. "It appears we're going to get a twofer today."

He glanced down at her belly, then as he scooped her into his strong arms and against the solid strength of his chest, looked back into her eyes. "I love you forever, you know that, right?"

"I love you too." She kissed him on the mouth. "Let's get married, my love, then go have a baby."

It was the beginning of their life together.

THE END

ALSO BY SHEILA SEABROOK

Find out every time Sheila releases a FREE or new book by going to www.sheilaseabrook.com and signing up for her Newsletter!

Find Sheila Seabrook on Amazon:

www.amazon.com/Sheila-Seabrook/e/B0076ALJ2K

Rocky Mountain Series

Always Remember

Terms of Surrender

A Time to be Tender

Once a Heartbreaker (TBA)

This Time Forever (Sara's Story! TBA)

Caught Between Series

Caught Between a Lie and True Love

Caught Between an Oops and a Hard Body

Caught Between a Rock and a Hunka Man

Caught Between the Mob and a Hot Cop (TBA)

Standalone Novels & Novellas

Wedding Fever

The Valentine Grinch

Love Under Construction

ABOUT THE AUTHOR

Sheila Seabrook writes love stories with heart and humor from her home on the beautiful Canadian prairies. Her romantic books are filled with smart, sassy women, hot men who love them, and a wild assortment of family members guaranteed to try to steal the show.

When Sheila's not writing, she can usually be found in her favorite chair doing research (code for reading romance books) or devising multiple excuses to avoid cooking, laundry, housework, and shoveling the snow. She does, however, love to shop for flowers in the spring, and spends copious hours digging in the dirt to plant them...although her marriage contract clearly stipulates that the man of the house must pull the weeds.

Her mission in life is to give readers emotional romantic stories and unforgettable characters, a relaxing treat for the end of the day. And if she can help them escape the laundry pile, she's totally on board.

Make sure to join Sheila's monthly newsletter to receive exclusive updates, free short stories, and more!

Connect with Sheila at:

www.sheilaseabrook.com
sheila@sheilaseabrook.com

CAUGHT BETWEEN
an Oops and a Hard Body

Stephanie Goodwin has never met a prince who didn't turn out to be a frog, but she's never allowed her personal feelings about men and relationships to interfere with her job as a wedding planner. Instead, she focuses on giving her clients their dream wedding, a magical day to get them through the trials and tribulations of the years ahead—before everything turns to dust.

Hotshot divorce lawyer, Stone Kincaid, has an aversion to marriage. His experience has taught him that wedding vows only lead to a broken heart that never really heals and an empty bank account. But when he returns to his family's Serendipity Island estate to stop his irresponsible sister's wedding, he encounters the wedding planner straight out of his nightmares—the gorgeous, sexy woman he met and bedded a month ago.

Can a woman with a history of picking the wrong kind of guy find a forever kind of love with a man who fears commitment almost as much as she does?

This story includes a marriage-phobic wedding planner, a hunky divorce lawyer whose attitude toward wedded bliss—and family—is about to change, one really big OOPS, afternoon naughtiness, peanut butter cookies, messy family relationships, and a battle-of-the-sexes secondary romance.

ISBN 978-1-7750680-6-8